THE EDGE
of LIGHT

AT HOME IN *Beldon Grove*

THE EDGE
of LIGHT

ANN
SHOREY

Revell

a division of Baker Publishing Group
Grand Rapids, Michigan

Published by Revell
a division of Baker Publishing Group
P.O. Box 6287, Grand Rapids, MI 49516-6287
www.revellbooks.com

Second printing, February 2009

Printed in the United States of America

Library of Congress Cataloging-in-Publication Data
Shorey, Ann Kirk, 1941–
 The edge of light / Ann Shorey.
  p. cm. — (At home in Beldon Grove ; 1)
  ISBN 978-0-8007-3330-8 (pbk.)
  1. Widows—Fiction. 2. Missing children—Fiction. 3. Illinois—Fiction. I. Title.
PS3619.H666E34 2009
813'.6—dc22   2008033781

For Mary Elizabeth Matot

1944–1993

Because I promised.

St. Lawrenceville, Missouri
July 1838

Molly McGarvie struggled to stand, the weight of her pregnancy an anchor fastening her to the ground. "Maybe Samuel's back. It's been almost three weeks."

Betsy walked to her mistress and extended a hand, pulling Molly to her feet. "Don't get your hopes up. Mr. Samuel said he was fixing to be gone a month."

"I worry something might happen to him."

"You're borrowing trouble. Ain't nothing ever happened before, has it?"

Molly shook her head. "No. But I still want him home." She smiled at the sight of her three children napping on a coverlet spread over the grass. Late afternoon sun angled through the grove of redbud trees, painting shadow pictures across their faces. "Children! Time to wake up. We don't want to be out after dark."

Sleepy-eyed, they tottered to their feet.

"Wolves come in the dark, don't they, Mama?" Three-year-old Luellen's voice climbed a scale of apprehension.

Molly leaned forward and stroked the black curls that fringed her daughter's face. "Don't be afraid. We'll be home in plenty of time."

Luellen jutted her chin in the air. "I'm not afraid."

Molly shook her head. "I should've named you 'Mary, Mary, quite contrary.'"

She took Luellen's hand and started along the track toward their cabin. Betsy gathered the picnic basket and blankets and fell in behind them on the dusty trail. Like puppies, her two sons chased each other in circles at the rear of the procession.

When she crested the hill above the settlement, Molly spotted their buckboard outside the stable. "Samuel's back!" She dropped Luellen's hand and hurried down the path.

Once in front of the cabin, she looked past the buckboard and saw her husband in the stable tending to his horse. She hastened toward him. "What a wonderful surprise! You're early."

Samuel met Molly near the opening of the three-sided log structure, part of the black gelding's harness draped over one shoulder. He cupped his free hand around the back of her head and kissed the place on her forehead where her black hair grew in a widow's peak. "You're a sight for sore eyes, Wife. Soon's I finish with Captain I'll be up to the house."

"I'll wait." Molly rested against a bag of grain while her husband hung the traces over a peg. She loved watching his long-fingered, broad-palmed hands as he worked. Molly believed there was nothing he couldn't accomplish with the strength hidden inside them.

"You finished building the courthouse quicker than you thought. I'm glad."

"It's not done yet." Samuel swayed slightly when he squatted to unfasten Captain's bellyband and hip straps. "When I was on the scaffold this morning, my legs all of a sudden give out. Would of fell off, but my helper grabbed hold of me and got me down. I left him to finish the job and come on home."

Molly felt a prickle of alarm. "What's wrong?"

"Don't know. Got sick to my stomach a couple times on the way." He hung the pieces of tack on another peg.

She reached up and felt his forehead. "You have a fever! Let's get you to bed—the boys can feed the horse."

"Aw, Molly, don't—" He doubled over with a grunt of pain. Clutching his abdomen, he pushed past her and ran behind the stable.

She heard violent retching. Her sons ran across the packed earth in front of their cabin, trailed by Luellen.

Franklin raced past her, headed inside the stable. "Where's Papa?"

Molly caught the back of the younger boy's shirt and tugged him away from the log shelter. "Papa's sick. You stay here." She looked at Betsy. "Help me get Samuel inside."

"Where's he at?"

"Behind the stable."

Betsy faced James. "You watch the chil'ren for a few minutes. I'll be back directly."

James reached for Luellen's hand, but she sidled away. Her lower lip protruded. "I want to see Papa."

"Not now." Molly's expression left no room for argument.

When the two women reached Samuel, they found him on his hands and knees. Between them they managed to help him to his feet. Once he started across the barnyard, he jerked free and stumbled toward the open door of their one-room cabin.

Molly's heart raced as she followed his unsteady progress. *What's wrong?*

He stopped and rested his head against the doorframe. A sheen of sweat covered his face.

Molly wrapped an arm around his waist. "Let me help you." It took her eyes a moment to adjust to the dimness inside. The small window under the loft allowed only a thin rib of light through its thick panes. Half supporting, half pushing, Molly guided her husband around a long puncheon table toward the sleeping area under the open stairway.

She rolled the patchwork coverlet back, revealing a linen sheet wrapped over a feather tick. Samuel sat on the edge, slumped like a puppet without strings.

The younger children followed them into the cabin. "Papa?"

Molly blocked their path. "I told you Papa's sick. You go outside with Betsy." James hovered near the door, a worried expression on his face. "Son, go fetch Dr. Carson."

"No! Doc Carson's a quack." Samuel's voice sounded raspy. "Get the new doc . . ." He paused, forehead wrinkled. "Spengler, I think his name is."

"Spengler's in Fox River. James can't go that far by himself. He's only eight. Besides, Dr. Carson helped when Luellen had asthma, didn't he?"

Samuel doubled up, gasping. "Get the chamber pot, quick!"

Molly grabbed it just as he leaned over and vomited a stream of yellow bile. When James hesitated at the door, she said, "Go! Now! Get Dr. Carson and tell him to hurry."

∅

The doctor stood at the far end of the table that bisected the cabin, his leather satchel open in front of him. A florid-faced man, he had the stub of a cigar clamped between his teeth. "It's probably cholera."

The words struck like bullets. Molly stood speechless, roaring filling her ears. *Please, Lord, don't take my Samuel.*

Apparently reading the terror on her face, Dr. Carson added, "If we're lucky, it's a mild case. There's every reason to believe he'll recover."

She grasped at the hope in his statement. "But . . . I thought no one ever recovered from cholera."

"They do, more than folks think." He picked a shred of tobacco from his lower lip and wiped his fingers on his pant leg. "Just takes the right doctoring—and catching it early."

Molly looked at her husband, spent after bouts of vomiting, then glanced out the open door at her youngsters. "Are the children in danger?" She spoke in a whisper, as though she could sneak the question past whatever fates controlled their destiny.

"Not if you farm them out, Miz McGarvie. Keep them away from Samuel until he's well." He flicked the cigar stub into the open fireplace behind him. "Can you get your husband's brother to take them?"

Molly cocked her head, considering. *Would he do it?* "I suppose I could ask. But first, tell me how you'll cure my husband."

"He'll pull through if I can get enough of this calomel down him. It'll purge the sickness." He placed a brown bottle on the tabletop, then reached back into his bag and lifted out a footed glass jar, its top covered with a piece of muslin. A dozen or more five-inch-long wormlike creatures squirmed inside. "Leeches. Bleeding him ought to get rid of the fever."

She eyed the doctor's food-spotted shirt and tobacco-stained hands. "What do you think, Samuel? Tell me what to do."

He shook his head. "I don't know. We'll have to—" He hung his head over the edge of the bed and vomited again.

Molly stood frozen in the center of the room.

Betsy slipped an arm over her shoulders. "Want me to set with him whilst you take the chil'ren to Mr. Brody's?"

Dr. Carson looked up, a squirming leech pinched between his fingers. "You might as well go. Nothing you can do right now."

Molly nodded. She walked to the bed and bent to kiss Samuel's forehead, feeling the fever burn through his skin onto her lips. "I'll be back soon." She stopped to light a lantern and then gathered her children.

Luellen tugged at Molly's skirt and lifted her arms to be carried. Molly shook her head. "You're not a baby. You can walk. We're just going down the road to Uncle Brody's." She took the girl's hand and started south on the dirt track that led through St. Lawrenceville. "Come on," she called to her sons. "Auntie Patience will take care of you until Papa's well."

❧

Lantern light flickered across Patience's spiteful gaze. "I can't possibly look after your children. You know we're already crowded with our three."

Samuel's younger brother Brody pushed past his wife and stood on the porch. "It's not that we don't sympathize, you understand. Tell Bub I'll stop by tomorrow to see how he's doing."

A pulse throbbed in her temple. "After all Samuel's done for you? You can't make room for his children?" She glared at him. "He didn't worry about being crowded when you needed shelter."

Brody turned his back and stepped inside. The door creaked shut.

Molly's mind ran through the short list of possible families in the settlement who might watch her children. *Where can I take them?* She headed back in the direction of their cabin, frantically trying to think while she herded her brood through the growing darkness.

12

"How about Mr. Solomon's?" Franklin asked, as though he'd read her mind. "He has rooms over the tavern." He swung the bundle of clothing she'd packed for them from one hand to the other.

She stopped and stared at him. "And how would you know that?"

"That's what the men at Papa's brickyard say. There's a lady that lives up there."

"Franklin, don't talk to me about taverns, now or ever. Do you understand?"

"Mama?" James touched her arm. "The smithy likes us. Maybe we could stay with him."

"Of course. Why didn't I think of that?" The four of them turned north on the lane that passed their cabin. Luellen again tugged at Molly's skirt to be carried. With a sigh, she handed the lantern to James and hoisted the heavy child onto one hip.

⌒

The blacksmith's plump wife, Jewel, beamed at them. "Of course they can stay here. With our boys grown and gone, this house is too quiet." Behind her, a steaming kettle hung on the fireplace crane and scented the air with the aroma of boiling meat and onions. A stack of wooden bowls rested at the end of a table similar to the one in her own cabin.

Jewel drew Luellen close to her skirts. "It'll be a treat to have a little girl to look after."

"Thank you, Mrs. Stanton. You're a godsend." Molly turned to her sons, giving each of them a hug and kiss. "You behave now! Mind Mr. and Mrs. Stanton."

"Come over here and say 'howdy,' boys!" Cody Stanton called from a high-backed armchair at one end of the room.

When James and Franklin left her side, Molly tied her bonnet over her coiled braids and walked to the door.

"I've got supper ready," Jewel said. "Don't you want to set a bit? Have something to eat? You seem mighty tired."

Molly shook her head. "Thank you. It's late and I'm worried about Samuel."

"Well, don't worry about these here youngsters. They can stay as long as it's needful."

⟡

For the next five days, Molly assisted each time Dr. Carson came to apply fresh leeches to Samuel's increasingly wasted body, trusting that he knew what was best. But by week's end, she'd passed that point of belief.

With one hand pressed to her throat, she watched while the doctor removed the last engorged leech from Samuel's abdomen. Blood oozed from the open wounds. Bandages, some showing bright bloodstains, covered the effects of previous leeching. Constant doses of calomel had purged his body so thoroughly that his skin seemed to cling to his bones.

"That's enough. Let him be."

Dr. Carson dropped the fat creature into its jar, where it landed with a soft splat on top of its writhing companions. He closed his satchel and tightened the strap with a quick tug. "There's nothing more I can do anyways." He looked at Samuel and shook his head. "Maybe he was too far gone when I got here."

Nothing more he can do? Molly walked to the far end of the room, motioning the doctor to follow her. "He's not going to die, is he?"

When he reached the fireplace, the doctor pulled a new cigar from his coat pocket. He lit the end of a straw at the hearth and puffed until he had a cloud of blue smoke around his head. "Most likely he will, Miz McGarvie." He swept his satchel from the table and strode out the door.

Molly sank into a chair beside the bed. Dr. Carson's words echoed through her mind like a voice from the depths of a tomb. *Most likely he will.* She wanted to clap her hands over her ears to silence the pronouncement. *Maybe the doctor's wrong. Samuel's always been strong. He can do anything.*

She pushed limp strands of black hair out of his eyes. "I'm here, dearest."

His lips twitched in a weak smile. She stroked his forehead until he slept.

Betsy walked up behind her. "You need some rest. Let me set with him for a bit."

"What if he wakes up and I'm not here?"

"Then how about some hot broth? You haven't eaten nothing all day." Betsy placed a pewter mug in her hands. "You need to take care so's you don't get it. What do you suppose would happen to the chil'ren without you?"

Molly's eyes widened. "I've been so taken up with Samuel, I never thought about that." *And the baby! If I die, the baby dies.*

She set the mug on the floor, cupping her hands over her abdomen. A chill prickled her skin. If she and Samuel were both gone, the children would be orphans. Molly knew the plight of orphaned children on the frontier. Brothers and sisters were often separated and taken into homes where they were expected to earn their keep. She couldn't let that happen. She stood and faced her friend. "Oh, Betsy, I'm frightened." Tears slid down her cheeks.

Betsy gathered her in a gentle embrace, rocking back and forth the same way she'd soothe a child. "We just have to pray. God knows best."

"God's not listening." Molly stepped back so she could see Betsy's face. "I've been praying, and it seems like he hasn't heard a word!"

Behind them, Samuel groaned and attempted to turn over. The two women hurried to the bedside. They each gripped a corner of the linen sheet under him and tugged, rolling his body until he rested on his left side. His eyelids fluttered open for a moment, then closed again.

"Will you stay with us tonight?" Molly asked Betsy.

She nodded, pointing at the loft. "I'll be up there. Call if you need me." She turned down the flame in the lamp and climbed the stairs to bed.

Molly returned to her post beside Samuel, her body aching with weariness. A stray breeze from the open window stirred the sour odors hovering in the room. She wrinkled her nose. No matter how careful they were, it hadn't been possible to keep her husband's violent purging confined to slop jars.

Molly patted Samuel's face. An elongated shadow of herself moved over the wall like a ministering spirit.

His eyes opened and he slipped his hand over hers. His mouth formed the words, "I love you," but no sound emerged.

"I love you too." She blinked back tears.

A long sigh escaped his lips and his body relaxed.

"Samuel?" She felt his chest for a heartbeat.

Nothing.

Molly stared at his body, surprised she didn't feel like crying. She dragged the chair closer to the bed and lifted his hand, pressing it against her cheek. *I want him to myself one last night.*

2

The blacksmith appeared at Molly's door late the next morning. She glanced up when she saw his shadow fall across the threshold.

"Mr. Stanton?"

"I just heard—Brody stopped by the forge." He shook his head. "You know I set a real store by your Samuel. It's a hard thing."

Molly nodded her thanks, hearing his sympathy over the exhaustion ringing in her ears. She and Betsy had been cleaning since daylight. A damp resin smell arose from the freshly scrubbed pine floor and filled the single room. Samuel's body rested on the bed, washed and prepared for burial.

Cody Stanton cleared his throat. "I come to help." He entered the cabin, stepping around a washtub piled with soiled linen. "I hope you won't hold it agin me, Miz McGarvie, being so forward and all . . ." He stopped, twisting his hat in his hands.

Molly sank onto a bench next to the table and gestured for him to sit beside her. "I need your help." She dabbed at her eyes with the corner of her apron. "Please tell me what's on your mind."

His words came out in a rush, as though he wanted to put this awkward moment behind him as quickly as possible. "Me an' some of the men got a coffin ready. They'll be bringing it here directly."

Molly felt dizzy. She looked at Samuel's body on the bed. As long as he was still in the room, she could pretend he was merely sleeping. *When they put him in a coffin he'll be gone forever.*

Cody interrupted her thoughts. "Miz McGarvie?"

"Go on."

"Tomorrow would be about right for the buryin'. If you don't mind, I'd like to read a scripture or two over him."

Shoulders sagging, she replied in a voice she hardly recognized as her own. "That would be fine. Thank you."

He patted her hand. "What scriptures would you like?"

"I don't care. Anything."

Wagon wheels creaked in the yard. Cody stood and addressed Betsy. "Why don't you take her up to our place? She should be with her young'uns right now."

☙

On the day of the funeral, every detail in the small cemetery stood out with heightened clarity. By focusing on a pebble, a yellow dandelion, a blade of grass, Molly could avoid seeing the mound of fresh black earth that covered her husband's coffin. Fragments of dried foxtail heads clung to her stockings, scraping at the skin on her legs as she walked away from the gravesite. She carried Luellen, drawing comfort from the warmth of her daughter's presence. James and Franklin walked next to her. Silent. Their faces tear-streaked.

A stocky man in a well-cut black linen suit stepped up to her. "Excuse me, Mrs. McGarvie. I'm Colonel Cross." Bowing, he swept off his hat. "I admired your husband greatly. He had grit."

Molly knew who he was without introduction. "Thank you,"

she said, taken aback at the idea of the settlement's leading citizen admiring her husband.

A tall, slender woman stood at his side, her face shaded by an elegant black satin bonnet. "I am Marjolaine Cross." Her French accent floated in the air like a fragrance. "When you feel able, please come to call."

"Thank you." Molly said, surprised again. *Folks around here must be wrong about her. Mrs. Cross doesn't act high and mighty.*

Jewel Stanton hurried over and enveloped Molly and Luellen in a lavender-scented hug. "Come with me, dearie. Cody has the wagon waiting to drive you and the young'uns home."

Home. She thought of the scrubbed, silent cabin. Her husband's bulk would no longer fill the doorway when he returned from work each evening. She wouldn't hear his laughter rumble as he watched their children frolic. She'd be climbing into a cold, empty bed tonight and every night to come.

She closed her eyes against the pain that threatened to engulf her.

❧

Molly followed her children as they climbed out of Stantons' wagon. From their unnaturally quiet behavior, she knew they were as reluctant as she to open the door and go inside.

"If you need anything, we're just down the road," Jewel said. "I expect you'll have plenty to eat, judging from all the food that's been brought by today."

"Thank you. We'll manage. Betsy's here."

The wagon rolled away. Its wheels left a sprinkling of dust on Molly's newly dyed black dress. She took a deep breath and held it for a moment, steeling herself for her first step into her altered life. "Let's go, children," she said, taking Luellen's hand.

When she entered the cabin, she saw Jewel hadn't exaggerated about the amount of food left for them. An iron kettle hung from the crane in the fireplace, filling the room with the savor of beans stewed with ham. Beneath it, the toasted-corn fragrance of baking johnnycakes spiraled from a board propped in front of the hearth. Platters and bowls of food covered almost the entire surface of the table.

"It smells good in here, Mama," Franklin said. "I'm hungry."

"We'll eat soon." Over the top of his head, Molly noticed Betsy standing at the end of the table, a stack of wooden bowls in her hands. "You must have come back early to bake those." She nodded toward the johnnycakes.

"Yes'm." Sorrow etched Betsy's round face. "I come on back whilst you was visiting with the white folks." She pointed at a brown bowl covered with muslin resting next to a butter crock. "Figured the chil'ren would like some 'pone, 'specially with this honey someone brung us."

"Honey!" Franklin pulled off the cloth covering and stuck his forefinger into the golden syrup.

"Franklin, get out of there!" Betsy grabbed his wrist. "Soon's I make some room here you can have your supper." She turned to Molly. "You set. You look plumb tuckered."

Molly lowered herself onto one of the benches next to the table, lifting Luellen into her lap. Franklin snuggled next to her. She drew him close, dropping a kiss on top of his baby-fine black hair. James sat across from them. No one took Samuel's accustomed spot at the end nearest the fire. Betsy ladled beans into the wooden bowls, then set a plate of hot cornbread wedges in the center of the table.

Ignoring her food, Molly surveyed the familiar room. Samuel's work clothes were still draped on a peg near the bed. His tools lay on a bench beside the door. Above them his flintlock rifle rested on a set of deer antlers. *A week ago he was alive.* Tears welled in her eyes. *How can he be gone?* She stood and handed Luellen to Betsy. "I'll be outside. You children finish your supper."

Molly walked behind the cabin and sank onto a bench Samuel had built next to the west-facing wall. Late afternoon sun burned against her face, drying her tears as they fell. Bluebirds called to each other from the branches of a dogwood tree near the cabin, but Molly wasn't listening to their music. She remembered the day Samuel had come home excited about getting the job to supply bricks and build the new courthouse in Waterloo.

I didn't think I could last a month without him! How will I get through the rest of my life?

Lost in memories, she startled when she heard footsteps and saw Betsy coming toward her. "Where are the children?"

"Luellen's sleeping, and I told the boys to leave you be for a while." She slipped an arm around Molly's shoulders. "It was a fine burying. Sure was lots of folks there."

Molly leaned against her. "Most everyone around. Even Colonel Cross and his wife." She half smiled, remembering. "I didn't know Samuel had so many friends."

A tear slipped down Betsy's cheek. "He was the best, Miz Molly. Don't know how his brother turned out to be such a skunk."

~

That evening, Betsy held a lantern high in front of her as she walked the path to the slave cabin she shared with Brody Mc-Garvie's cook, Tildy. In spite of her grief for her mistress's husband, part of her mind circled the question of her own future. *What's going to happen to Miz Molly without Mr. Samuel?* Once the shock of his passing lessened, plans would have to be made. Would they include her?

The heavy plank door scraped open at her push. The light in the room flared brighter when she carried the lantern inside, where a low fire burned on the grate.

Tildy sat on one of the two cots. She glanced up when Betsy entered. "Well, if it ain't Miss High Falutin', home from taking care of your fancy mistress."

"Evening, Tildy," Betsy said, determined not to rise to the bait. She placed the lantern on a rickety table next to the fire and sat on her cot to remove her shoes, dropping them to the packed-earth floor.

Tildy held a needle and thread, mending a tear in her apron. "Push that light closer over here. My eyes ain't what they used to be."

Betsy complied, then turned her back and removed her home-spun apron and gray linsey-woolsey dress, hanging them from a peg in the wall. After dropping a long-sleeved gown over her linen chemise, she slid under the quilts and rolled onto her side, facing Tildy. "How'd you tear your apron?"

"Caught it on a splinter, throwing wood on the fire. Those two men what work for Mr. Brody cain't even chop wood!"

"Reuben and Jerry? They're all right."

"Huh! Lot you know. Everything at Mr. Samuel's was done to suit Miz Molly. Mr. Samuel even cut her firewood." Tildy rested the needle in the fabric and squinted at Betsy across the narrow room. "Cutting firewood!" she spat. "What kinda white master was that?"

"Watch out. You say something bad about dead people, they'll come back and haunt you." She knew better, but Brody's cook didn't.

Tildy compressed her lips into a tight line at the suggestion of ghosts, but Betsy saw the malice in her eyes. The older woman's

22

personality seemed to be part rattlesnake and part fox. What she couldn't get by direct strike, she'd sneak around until she could obtain it another way.

Betsy watched while Tildy lifted the apron to her mouth and bit off the thread she'd been using. Lantern light brought her face into sharp focus. Weary creases pinched her lips, deep lines etched her cheeks like scars. After blowing out the lantern flame, Tildy settled back on her cot and tucked a worn quilt under her chin. "You ever think what it'd be like to be free?"

The question surprised Betsy. She hesitated before replying, wondering if Tildy was trying to trap her into saying something she could later use against her. "Yes, I thinks about it." Her admission sounded loud in her ears. "You ever know anyone who was freed?"

"Mr. Brody and Miz Patience took me with them to Louisville once. A maid in the hotel was a freedwoman. She got paid for working, an' she could keep the money. Kin you imagine that!"

Betsy sighed. "The best part would be belonging to my own self."

Tildy rolled over, facing the wall. "Yes," she said, a hopeless tone in her voice, "that would be the best part." A log in the fire snapped sparks and sank farther into the bed of coals.

Long after Tildy's breathing signaled that she slept, Betsy lay staring into the dark. She couldn't see the walls around her, but she knew they were there.

❦

Molly walked south past Brody's house to accept Marjolaine Cross's invitation. Had grief affected her hearing the day of the funeral? Did the woman really invite her? What would they talk about?

When she climbed the steps to the Crosses' verandah, Marjo-laine hurried forward to greet her. "I hoped you'd come to visit!" She pointed at a cushioned wicker chair. "Sit and rest." Marjolaine slipped into the chair next to her. "How are you feeling? You look tired."

Molly's shoulders hunched, bearing pain. "I cry myself to sleep every night. I'm lost without him."

Nodding, the older woman lifted a silk fan from a table at her side. "When my Philippe died of the yellow fever, I was . . ." She waved the fan as though the word she searched for was a fly, and she could swat it down. "How do you say it? Devastated." The silvery curls piled at the back of her head bounced, emphasizing her remarks.

Molly twisted her wedding band around her finger. "And the children . . ."

Marjolaine leaned forward. "What is happening?"

"James seems to think he must take Samuel's place. He tries so hard, but he's only eight." She stood and walked to the edge of the verandah. Leaning against the railing, Molly turned and gazed into the other woman's coffee-colored eyes. "Franklin wanders around like a little shadow, following James everywhere. He wants to help at the brickyard, but he's small for six. He's not strong enough for heavy work." She blinked away tears. "Luellen is too young to understand. She keeps asking me when Papa will come back. And to know he'll never see this baby—" she cupped her hands over her rounded belly—"that's the hardest part of all."

Marjolaine fluttered her fan through the air. "I know how you are feeling." She must have noticed Molly's doubtful expression. "At least, I know as much as I can without having babies." She paused. "This will pass, you know. One day you will find someone else, like I found Hector, and you'll know the good Lord sent him to you."

"And what if the 'good Lord' lets him die too?" Molly shook her head. "No! I won't put myself through this again!"

Marjolaine reached out and tapped Molly's hand with the edge of her fan. "You'll need someone to help you. How will you feed your children?" She leaned back in her white wicker armchair, adjusting the ruffles on her yellow silk afternoon dress. Cicadas chirred in the still afternoon air.

"Feeding the children won't be a problem. We have the brick-yard." Her lips twitched in a watery smile. "McGarvie and Sons. There's no reason I can't learn to run the business and leave Brody to do the work he always pushed off on Samuel." In her mind, Molly heard again the words her father used to taunt her before she married Samuel—*You'll never get along without a husband.* She lifted her chin. *Yes I will, Papa!* Then, glancing beyond the edge of the settlement to where Samuel had planted corn that spring, she said, "There is one thing that bothers me right now, though."

"What?"

"This sounds foolish, but I worry about harvesting the corn crop. James can't do it alone, and when we're out there, Franklin spends the time playing hide-and-seek among the stalks."

"Ask your brother-in-law."

"I don't want to do that. He was hateful when I asked him and Patience to care for the children after Samuel got sick."

"I didn't know that. At the funeral he seemed such a gentle-man."

"Oh, Marjolaine, that was a sham. He hasn't come by once since that day!"

"Then when it's time to harvest, help will come. The good Lord will provide if you ask him."

25

"You sound like—" Molly bit her lip to stop herself from saying "Betsy." Few people could accept a friendship between a white woman and a black one. "—a preacher."

Marjolaine chuckled. "Nobody's ever said that to me before!"

The door to Brody's cabin stood open when Molly walked home that afternoon. She felt her sister-in-law's gaze following her up the road. Patience had made no effort to help her after the night she and her husband refused to take in Molly's children. Nor did she try to conceal her resentment at what she believed was Molly's special treatment by Colonel Cross and his wife.

When she neared home, she heard horse's hooves clopping in her direction. A stranger rode into view, his face hidden beneath a wide-brimmed hat. "Mrs. McGarvie?"

She shaded her eyes with her hand and looked up at the rider. "I'm Mrs. McGarvie."

The man slid off his horse. Holding the reins with one hand, he removed his hat and held it in front of his chest. "I . . . I'm Dr. Spengler. Karl Spengler." He sounded uneasy. "I knew your husband."

She searched for Samuel in every stranger's face. It made no sense, but she couldn't seem to help herself. The first thing Molly noticed about the doctor was his clear blue eyes. They shone from his tanned face as though lighted from within. He stood several inches below what Samuel's height had been, blond where Samuel had been dark-haired. Yet the large hands that held his hat made her heart twist. Strong and broad-fingered, they looked like her husband's.

Disconcerted, Molly forced her eyes back to his face. "It's good of you to stop by, Doctor. Will you come up to the house for a drink of water?" She pointed toward the hitching rail. "You can tie your horse there."

Betsy met her when she reached the doorway of the cabin, Luellen's small hand clasped in hers. "Who's that?" She nodded toward the stranger.

"Dr. Spengler. He's the one Samuel asked me to send for." She wiped away sudden tears. "Maybe he'd still be alive if I'd done it."

Betsy frowned at her. "Stop it! You'll mark the baby with all your worrying."

"I hope it's not marked already with everything that's happened." Molly picked up a crockery jug and had a cup of water waiting when Dr. Spengler walked to the door.

Luellen emerged from behind Betsy's skirts, dragging a rag doll behind her. She pushed herself into Molly's legs and stared up at the newcomer. "Who're you?"

He smiled at the little girl. "I'm Dr. Spengler. What's your name?"

"Luellen," she mumbled, chewing on one of her braids.

Turning to Molly, his expression became serious. "I just heard about your loss. The clerk at Colonel Cross's store told me when I stopped in there today." He rolled his hat brim back and forth between thumb and forefinger. "I'm sorry. He was a good man."

"Thank you."

"I wish I'd known he was sick—maybe I could've helped."

Why didn't I send for him? She shook her head. "What's done is done."

He passed her the empty cup. His eyes seemed to settle everywhere but on her face. "Well, if you need a doctor again, you can send someone to Fox River to fetch me or my brother."

"I'll remember that. Thank you."

He clapped his hat on. "Nice meeting you." Without waiting for her response, he stepped to the hitching rail and untied his horse. Raising his hand in salute, he cantered north.

Molly watched until he passed Stantons' blacksmith shop. Once he was out of sight, she turned to Betsy. "It hurts to look at him. What might've happened if he'd been here instead of Dr. Carson?"

3

A prickle of cold sweat broke out on Karl's forehead. *Thunderation! She looks like Caroline. Same eyes, same mouth—even her hair's the same color.* His heart felt as if it were trying to batter its way out of his chest. *How far do I have to go to be free?*

Dust swirled up from the horse's hooves, filling Karl's nostrils. He wanted to continue riding until he found a place where his memories couldn't follow. He dug his heels into the mare's sides and urged her to a faster gait. Molly McGarvie's face—or was it Caroline's?—floated in front of him. He groaned. *Exactly like Caroline.*

When he entered Fox River, his eyes swept over the abbreviated main street. A saloon, a trading post, and a tiny church, all built of logs. Several settlers' cabins fanned out along bottom land, each displaying squares of land covered with ripening corn. Even after six months, it still didn't feel like home.

A spotted mongrel dashed from under the wooden porch of the trading post, barking at the heels of Karl's horse. At the same moment the store's proprietor hurtled out the door. "Doc! I was just going to find you." He held up his arm, wrapped with a blood-stained rag. "I'm hurt bad."

Karl swung to the ground and grabbed a leather satchel from his saddlebag. "What happened, Jake?"

"Dang barrel hoop sprung loose when I was breaking open a new keg of vinegar. Like to laid my arm open." Jake spoke through clenched teeth while he pulled the makeshift bandage away with his free hand. His radius bone glistened bluish white through blood that oozed from a five-inch slice above his wrist.

Karl cupped the cloth strip back over the wound and led the storekeeper inside. When they stepped over the threshold, a sharp smell caught his nostrils. A broken barrel, surrounded by a pool of vinegar, lay sprawled near the door. Karl surveyed the dimly lit room seeking a space to work, and decided on the plank counter against one wall. "Got any whiskey?"

Jake pointed. "Under there." His fear-filled eyes widened. "What're you going to do?"

"I've got to patch you up before you bleed out. The whiskey's to clean the wound." He noted his patient's chalky skin. "You better have some too." Karl lifted the jug and placed it next to the storekeeper. Then, removing a clean cloth from his bag, he spread it over the bare wood. "Lay your arm here, and hand me that whiskey."

After taking a long swig, Jake passed him the crockery jug. Karl reached into his bag, removed a needle from a leather folder, then pulled out a spool of catgut, twisted thin.

"You're going to sew me? Like a quilt?"

"Won't take long. Just don't look. You'll be fine." Karl poured a stream of whiskey into the wound, his senses recoiling at the smell of spirits. Whiskey had its uses, but he hated it nonetheless.

Jake gripped the edge of the counter with his free hand, knuckles showing white. "Aah! Tarnation, Doc, that hurts worse'n the gash."

"Hold on. I'm not finished." He handed the jug back to his patient.

Jake flinched when the needle pierced the skin on his forearm, then shuddered when Karl thrust it through the other side of the wound, drawing the suture material tight.

The doctor tied off the stitch and guided another into the raw edges of the injury. "A few more, then we're done." He met his patient's anxious gaze. "You'll thank me when this heals."

Jake took a hefty swig from the jug. "Hope you're right."

When he'd tied the last piece of catgut, Karl wrapped the sutures with a clean bandage. "Keeping dirt out of cuts seems to help. Don't know why, but try it anyway." He strapped his satchel closed. "I'll come by next week to see how you're doing."

"Uh, Doc? I can't pay you today. Business is awful slow."

"Let my family take it out in trade goods."

"Most of the time all's I see of your family is your pa or brother. Your ma don't get out much, does she?"

Karl cringed inside and his face grew hot. The mention of his mother had provoked that reaction ever since boyhood, and he hated himself for his disloyalty. "No. She doesn't."

❧

As the days passed, the weather remained hot and clear. In spite of Marjolaine's assurance, no one came forward to help Molly with the harvest. If she waited longer, the kernels would dry on the stalk and there'd be no roasting ears.

Brody would have to do it, whether he wanted to or not.

Molly knew she'd already procrastinated too long over telling her brother-in-law of her plans to take Samuel's place at the brickyard. If she called on him now, she could settle both issues at once. She donned her sunbonnet, squared her shoulders, and left the house braced for confrontation.

Cody Stanton called to her from his forge when she passed

the blacksmith shop. "Howdy, Miz McGarvie! How you been keeping?"

"We're all well. Tired of the heat, though."

"Ain't it something? Makes winter look downright inviting."

"It does!"

She paused at the McGarvie & Sons, Brickmakers sign over the gate. Once those words had represented Samuel's dreams—now they brought tears to her eyes. *Once the baby's born, I'll be able to come here every day. As long as Brody does his part, we'll get by.*

Heat waves trembled in the air above rounded kilns at the north end of the yard. While Molly watched, James appeared from the work area, staggering under the weight of a brick mold filled with rectangles of yellow clay. When he spotted her, he straightened and walked purposefully toward the smoothing yard where he laid them out to dry.

Then Franklin saw her. Dropping the trowel he was using to smooth wet clay, he ran in her direction.

Brody's voice sounded from the shed. "Franklin! Get back to work!" He stepped into the sunshine but stopped when he saw Molly. Pasting an unctuous smile on his face, he advanced toward her. "What brings you out this afternoon?"

She tucked a stray wisp of hair under her bonnet. Lifting her chin, she met his gaze. "I'm ready to take Samuel's place here at the yard. You'll need to show me how the business is run."

Brody stared at her, openmouthed. "I don't need your help."

Molly hesitated. *He must've misunderstood me.* "I didn't say 'help.' I said take Samuel's place."

"It ain't going to work thataway, Molly. The brickyard's mine now."

She felt the blood drain from her face. "What're you talking about?"

Her sons moved to stand between them. She noticed the men in the yard had stopped working and were listening to their heated words.

Brody noticed them too. "Let's set in the shed and talk. Be out of the sun." He made a show of taking her arm and helping her to a bench next to the worktable. Her boys followed them.

"Here's the way it is, Molly," he said after she was seated. "Everything my brother had goes to me. It's in the partnership papers." He stepped over to the table, removed two folded pages from a tin box, and handed them to her.

She scanned the legal phrases wrapped in elaborate penmanship. "I don't understand."

Brody stabbed his forefinger at a line that read, "In the event of the death of one of the partners, the other partner shall inherit his property free of encumbrance."

She stared at him, astonished. "Samuel never intended such a thing! He founded this brickyard. It belongs to me and my children." Molly waved her hand toward the sign over the gate. "It says 'McGarvie & Sons, Brickmakers.' You're certainly not his son!"

Her brother-in-law pulled the pages from her limp fingers. "Nope. But I sure am a McGarvie!" Triumphantly, he pointed to the bottom of the second sheet. "He signed it." Brody seemed to swell up like a poisonous toad. "The law's on my side. You and them kids can go back to your pa's fancy farm in Kentucky. He'll take good care of y'all."

James sidled up to his mother. "Are we going to live in our old house, Mama?"

"No, we're not!" She glared at her brother-in-law. "We're staying right here."

She rose and pushed past Brody into the shimmering afternoon heat. "Boys! Come with me." James and Franklin ran after her as she hurried past men stacking bricks on pallets. One by one they stopped what they were doing. Taking off their hats, they stood silently while she left the yard.

Whatever will we do? Tears of anger and frustration trickled down her cheeks. Cody Stanton waved at her when she passed his forge, but she pounded by without responding.

"Mama, you're walking too fast!" Franklin called. She stopped and waited for him to catch up.

"I'm scared." He stood in her shadow, his shirt splotched with wet clay.

"Aw, don't be a baby!" James said. "Mama's not afraid of Uncle Brody. Are you, Mama?"

Molly pushed Franklin's braided straw hat up on his forehead so she could see his eyes. "There's nothing to be scared of. We'll be fine." She hugged his slight frame. "You boys run along home—I'll be there directly."

Franklin straightened his hat, then sprinted toward the cabin. "Race ya!" he called over his shoulder to his older brother. They ran down the road, leaving perfect footprints in the soft dust.

Molly trudged past the open rear door of the tavern and on toward home, the weight of her pregnancy pulling at her back while the weight of worry pulled at her mind. *We can't stay here, no matter what I said to Brody. Without the brickyard, we'll starve. But I'd rather die than go back to Papa.*

Ahead of her, their cabin drowsed in the afternoon sun. Molly surveyed its outline. Seen from the north, the small multi-paned window Samuel had set in the loft above her loom reflected the deep blue of the summer sky. *How long will it be before Brody decides our cabin belongs to him too?*

◠

After the children were in bed, Molly and Betsy sat outside in the purple twilight, waiting for the evening to cool.

"That Mr. Brody's a sly one," Betsy said, picking up their conversation where they'd left off earlier.

Molly clenched her fists on her lap. "It hasn't even been two months since Samuel died. Brody must've been waiting his chance for years."

"Humph! Just 'cause he clerked for that lawyer back home, he thinks he knows it all. He must've tricked Mr. Samuel into signing that paper."

Somewhere above their heads, a skylark sang his sweet evening song. Lightning bugs glimmered under the dogwood trees.

Molly took a deep breath and released it in a long sigh. "Those glowflies remind me of when we were little girls. Remember catching the bugs and peeking at the light through our fingers?"

Betsy answered with a soft laugh. "Sure was fun." After a pause, she continued, "You planning to go back to your pa's like Brody said?"

Molly shook her head. "No. I thought about it all through supper. You know how Papa treated me before I married Samuel. Likely he'd go right back to it if we had to live with him." She laid her hand on Betsy's arm. "Besides, if we went to Kentucky, you'd still be a slave. We've always dreamed about you being free someday—this is your chance." She tightened her grip. "I'm going to send word to my brother in Illinois. We'll go there—it's a free state. Something good might come of this after all."

"Revrund Matthew?"

"Yes." Molly's chair creaked as she leaned back to stretch her tense shoulder muscles.

"How you going to get word to him?"

"I don't know, but I'll find a way. First thing tomorrow I'll go to Crosses' store and get some paper so I can write him."

Several weeks later, Brody stopped in front of Molly's cabin, driving a wagon filled with bulging sacks. "I brung you a share of cornmeal from Samuel's harvest," he called when Molly appeared at the door. "Where d'you want it?"

"You had it ground? I wish you hadn't done that. Now I can't make hominy."

"Ain't nothing I can do that'll please you, is there? Patience don't like to fool with dried corn. Thought you'd feel the same, high-minded lady like you are."

"The miller keeps a share. You know that. I'd of got more corn by grating it myself." She didn't add she'd also have enjoyed roasting some of the ears if he'd harvested earlier. No need to antagonize him further.

She studied the bags of meal. "How many of these are mine?"

"Enough to keep you till you go to your pa's." He spit out the last word and jumped down from the wagon. Hoisting one of the sacks onto his shoulder, he pushed past her and deposited it in a corner near the hearth. She followed him out the door, watching while he dragged another filled sack from the rear of the wagon.

Molly took a deep breath to control her temper. *It's now or never.* "Brody, can we talk?"

"About what?" He brushed by her on his way inside.

"Let's sit over here," Molly said when he emerged. She pointed at the chairs under the elm tree. He flopped into one, mopping sweat from his red face with a grimy bandana.

She clenched her hands beneath folds of her loose smock, digging the nails into her palms to hide her agitation. "I want to know why you're doing this to us." Molly turned her head and looked directly into his eyes. "Samuel was never anything but fair to you and Patience."

"Yeah, if you call 'Brody do this' and 'Brody do that' fair!"

"You made a good living with his help, even before we left Kentucky. In fact, we wouldn't of left at all if you hadn't pushed for it with your big ideas!"

Brody's face seemed to distend with anger. "Leaving Kentucky was the best thing he could've done! Getting away from your rich pa and his fancy farm." He jumped to his feet and glowered at her. "I know how you and your ma, rest her soul, looked down on my wife and her family, and you're still doing it. Marching past the cabin on your way to visit Miz Cross, like you're too good for the rest of us." His words sprayed her with rage. "I'll be glad to see the last of you, Molly McGarvie."

He turned and stalked to the wagon. After two hops on his short legs, he hit the step, then swung into the seat. The horses jumped into action when his whip cut across their backs.

Molly sat, trembling, and watched his dust settle on her black skirt. Her mind went to the letter waiting in the cabin for someone to take it to Illinois. *If only I could talk to Matt right now. When I was little, he always knew the right thing to do.*

She heard her children's laughter coming from behind the cabin where they played while Betsy tended the wash boiler. *How wonderful to be that young again.* A tempting image of herself as a carefree child on her father's farm blinked in her mind. "No! Even if I wanted to listen to his drunken criticism, I won't give up on Betsy!" Molly trudged around back to join her family.

❧

Several days after her confrontation with Brody, Molly stood near the fireplace, absentmindedly stirring flax yarn in a brown dye solution. The bitter smell of simmering hickory nuts and potash stung her nostrils.

Luellen ran inside. "Mama! Someone's here!"

Molly dropped her long-handled wooden dye fork next to the hearth and hurried to the open doorway. A man on horseback sat silhouetted against the early morning sun.

James walked between her and the stranger, still carrying the axe he'd been using to split wood beside the cabin. He stared up at the horse and rider.

"Morning, Mrs. McGarvie."

Hands resting on the small of her back, she squinted into the brightness. "It's all right, James. This is Dr. Spengler—he's been here before."

"I'm passing through. Thought I'd stop to say good-bye." He dismounted and looked at James. "You must be the man of the house."

"Yessir," James said, inflating his chest and stretching himself tall. "I'm James."

"Glad to meet you." Dr. Spengler stuck out his hand.

Molly smiled, watching while her son shook it. *I wish Samuel could see what a hard worker the boy has become. He'd be proud.*

She broke the ensuing silence by asking the doctor, "You said you're passing through? To where?" For the first time, she noticed filled saddlebags draped across his horse.

His eyes fixed on a point somewhere between her ear and her shoulder. "I've heard they're needing doctors in Bryant County, over in Illinois. Thought I'd go see about it."

"Why can't you stay? Heaven knows we need someone besides Doc Carson."

He shook his head. "Carson has too many friends in St. Lawrenceville. Besides, I want to give my brother Joseph a chance. Not enough patients for both of us in Fox River." Dr. Spengler studied his hands, still avoiding her eyes. "I'm looking for someplace that isn't so crowded with us medicos."

Molly sensed there was something he wasn't telling her. After all, he'd come to Fox River knowing it to be a small village. She waited for him to say more.

Instead, his glance brushed her face and moved down her body. "Are you keeping well?"

She blushed, suddenly aware of her swollen belly. "Yes, everything seems fine."

"How're you managing? Colonel Cross told me about your brother-in-law taking the brickyard."

She folded her arms across her chest. *I don't need your pity!* "We have quite a bit of food put by—Samuel was a good provider."

Apparently detecting the change in her attitude, Dr. Spengler tipped his hat toward her and turned to remount. Gathering the reins in one hand, he said, "Well, so long, Mrs. McGarvie."

"Godspeed."

Betsy walked into the cabin after he'd cantered down the lane. "Who was that?"

"Dr. Spengler. He came to say good-bye—he's going to open a practice over in Illinois."

"Did you ask him to take that letter to your brother?"

Molly clapped a hand over her mouth. "No! I didn't even think of it!" She hurried to the blanket chest and opened the bottom drawer. "Here it is. Maybe James can catch him."

Betsy ran outside, waving the folded paper at the boy. "Bridle your pa's horse and ride after the doctor. See if he'll take this to your uncle."

James sprinted toward the stable.

4

Betsy watched James race away on Samuel's black gelding, Molly's letter tucked inside his shirt. The boy crouched low against the horse's neck and urged him forward, slapping the animal's rump with one hand.

Go like the wind, boy! Ever since Molly decided to go to Illinois, Betsy'd been moving through the days in a dreamlike state. To have freedom so close, just across the Mississippi, was tantalizing almost beyond endurance.

Once James passed out of sight, she turned and hurried to the rear of the cabin, where she'd been hanging dyed hanks of spun flax to dry. Luellen looked up from her game of peek-a-boo with Franklin when she saw her coming. She ran toward Betsy and hugged her legs.

Betsy swung Luellen into the air, then settled her on the ground after kissing both cheeks. "I'm getting closer to freedom ever day!" She cut loose with a few quick juba steps.

Molly walked across the yard toward her, carrying a washtub filled with dyed skeins of yarn. "You look happy, dancing around like that."

Betsy's cheeks warmed when she saw her mistress watching

40

her. To cover her embarrassment, she pointed at the tub. "Give that over. You shouldn't be carrying heavy things."

Molly handed it to her. "Do you think James can catch up to Dr. Spengler?"

"I surely hope so. I can't hardly sleep nights for thinking about Illinois."

"You didn't say anything to Tildy, did you?"

Betsy snorted. "Her? I wouldn't tell her it was morning if the sun was shining on her face." She hung the dripping skeins over the line and handed the empty container back to Molly.

Cicadas skreaked in the warm afternoon air. A gentle breeze stirred the limp cottonwood leaves, trailing a toasted grass smell in its wake. Molly tipped the washtub upside down and sat on it. "I wish things could be like they were when we were children."

Loneliness brought quick tears to Betsy's eyes. "I know I was blessed to stay with my mama and papa for my growing up time. It don't happen to many colored folks." *Lord, keep good care of them, wherever they is.* She pointed down the road toward Brody's house. "Tildy got sold off from her mama when she was twelve. She ain't never seen her since." Betsy moved to the shade near Molly's feet and pulled Luellen onto her lap. "That Reuben, his pa done got sold down the river before he was born, then his mama died of a fever. Poor soul. Brody's the only master he's ever had."

"I didn't know that." Molly jumped to her feet and picked up the washtub. "I'll be right back." She hurried around the cabin and returned a few moments later, arms wrapped around what appeared to be a mustard-colored blanket. "This is for you."

Betsy stood Luellen to one side and rose, hands outstretched. "What . . . ?" Turning one corner back, she saw a blue border framing blocks of appliquéd red sunflowers. Tiny stitches done in a wave pattern covered the surface. Then she knew. Her voice

41

trembled as she spoke. "This is the last quilt we worked with your mama before she took sick. It's yours . . . you can't give it away."

"Yes I can. I brought it from Kentucky. Now you carry it to freedom in Illinois." Molly slipped an arm around her waist and hugged her. "One way or another, we'll get there."

Shaking the coverlet free of its folds, Betsy regarded the design. "Your mama spun and wove every bit of this cloth."

"You glazed the wool. And we all sewed the blocks and quilted it, remember?"

"I surely do." Betsy traced one of the flowers with her fingertip. "You can't even see your mama's stitches on the petals, they're so tiny." She looked at her mistress. "You sure?"

"It's yours."

Betsy lifted a corner of the soft wool and cradled it against her cheek. *I never dreamed when we was sewing this that I'd be taking it to freedom one day. And that day's almost here.*

☙

Standing on the Crosses' verandah some days later, Molly scrutinized her friend's face. *Is she teasing me?* "You want to ask a favor? What can I possibly do for you?"

Marjolaine placed her cream-colored teacup in its saucer and cleared her throat. "I'd be honored if you'd sell me one of those beautiful coverlets you weave—if you have any to spare, that is."

I have one less, now. The joy on Betsy's face when she accepted the Sunflower quilt remained vivid in her memory. Molly smiled inwardly. *Such a simple thing. And it gave her so much pleasure.*

Marjolaine clasped her hands and leaned forward in her chair. "It's been over a week since Dr. Spengler took the letter to your brother." The cadences of her French accent fell on Molly's ears like music. "He's bound to come soon. Please, I want something to remember you by."

"No. I won't sell one." Seeing Marjolaine's crestfallen expression, Molly smiled and hurried on. "You've been a dear friend. I'd be happy to give you any one you choose."

The older woman bounced to her feet. "I'll get my bonnet. There's no time like the current, as Hector always says."

Molly giggled. "No time like the present, you mean."

After they entered her cabin, Molly opened the blanket chest and laid three woven coverlets on the plank table. "These are my best ones. Which would you like?"

Each was worked in variations of blue or white, but there the similarity ended. One, dyed a deep indigo, was a solid blue quilted with scrolled vines. Another, with white linen warp, had blue stripes running lengthwise. Blue and white plaid formed the pattern of the third.

Marjolaine picked up the plaid coverlet, tracing a fingertip over the crewelwork embroidery on the white squares. "These look like violets—my favorite flower." She looked at Molly. "May I have this one?"

"It's yours."

"*Merci*. It is beautiful." She studied the two left on the table. "You do extraordinary work. Why haven't you considered selling these?"

"Who'd buy them?"

"Someone might. Forgive me for speaking of this, but you will need to do something to care for your family."

Molly looked at her. "I've been thinking—maybe I could open a school. I've been teaching my own children, why not take in pupils?"

"What if there's already a school in your brother's village?"

"Then I'll think of something else. Don't worry about us."

"Soon there will be five of you—six, counting your house girl Betsy. Are you being realistic?"

Molly's defenses rose. "All the food I have put by will go with us. Surely that will be a help."

"For how long?"

"My brother will take care of us." Marjolaine's occasional tendency to look at the dark side of things grated on Molly's nerves, never more so than now.

The older woman picked up the embroidered bed covering, holding it like a shield against her chest. "I'm sure you know best," she said, closing the subject.

After Marjolaine left, Molly stood beside the table reflecting on what her friend had said. In spite of her spoken assurances about her brother, a swirl of doubt enveloped her. *Am I expecting too much of Matthew?* Throughout her life, the basic comforts had been provided by someone else. In Kentucky it was her father's responsibility until she married, then she had Samuel to lean on. She'd only needed to see to domestic matters, not provision of food and shelter.

Molly stared at the two remaining coverlets, as though she could find answers to her worries woven into the fabric. *I'll think about it after we're settled at Matt's.* She shoved the folded bedclothes back into the blanket chest.

❧

The following week, Molly put James and Franklin to work behind the cabin helping her bundle her flax crop. The stalks had been spread on the ground after pulling to allow dew to rot the tough outer shell. A fermented, grassy smell rose from the retted stacks.

"It's really too soon to be doing this," Molly worried aloud, wiping beads of perspiration from her forehead. "I'm afraid these aren't ready for braking."

Franklin unbuttoned his shirt and dropped it beside him. "I'm tired, Mama. Are we almost done?"

Molly surveyed the remaining flax plants. "Just a few more bundles." Her heart tightened at the sight of her small son sweating in the heat, his fatigue apparent in the droop of his shoulders. She cupped her hand around his chin. "You want new britches next year, don't you? I need this to weave the cloth."

James dropped the spool of twine he'd been using to wrap the bundles and straightened, turning his head toward the road. "Wagons are coming."

She heard jangling harnesses and clopping hooves. "Could it be . . .?" Molly hurried to the front of the cabin, her sons at her heels.

"Matthew?" She scrutinized the figure sitting on the wagon seat. Her brother had been clean-shaven when he left home at eighteen. Now a full brown beard covered the lower part of his face. She took a second look. Those eyes. Nothing could change the penetrating light in his deep brown eyes, although now smile lines fanned at their corners.

He jumped down from a low-sided farm wagon and waved his hat at her. "Molly! How's my baby sister?"

She ran toward him, tears sliding down her cheeks. "Matt! I'm so glad you're here!"

His arms went around her. She leaned into his wiry strength, sobbing out weeks of stored grief and fear.

"It's going to be all right." He stroked her head, the calluses on his palm catching in her hair.

She gulped and fought for control. "Oh, Matt, I'm sorry. I

just . . ." She buried her face in his shoulder. "Without Samuel . . . it's been so hard . . ." Molly couldn't stop the tears.

"Whatever happens, we'll handle it with the Lord's help." He reached into his shirt pocket, handing her a red bandana. "It's clean." Loosening his hold, he waited while she wiped her cheeks and blew her nose. "When you're ready, I want you to meet a friend of mine."

Keeping an arm around her, Matthew called to the slim man driving a stylish Dearborn passenger wagon. "Ben, get down here. Come meet my sister."

Molly looked curiously at the stranger. When he walked toward her, she saw he wasn't much taller than herself. Judging by the gray at his temples, she figured him to be close to fifty.

"This is my neighbor, Ben Wolcott," her brother said.

Molly extended a hand. Mr. Wolcott covered it with both of his. "Ma'am. Matthew told us about your loss. You've been in my prayers ever since."

She nodded, translating his Yankee accent as he spoke. "Your" sounded like "Yo-ah," "ever" came out "ev-ah."

Karl Spengler joined the group. It took Molly a moment to register his presence. "Dr. Spengler? What're you doing here?"

"Your brother thought an extra wagon might be needed and he asked me to drive it. Hope you don't mind."

She shook her head. "Thank you for taking my letter to Matthew. I'm afraid we've caused you a great deal of inconvenience."

"I'm glad to—"

James stepped between them. Looking up at Molly's brother, he asked, "You're my Uncle Matt?"

Matthew placed his hands on James's shoulders. "I am." His tanned face creased in a smile. "I've got three sons at home that need a big brother. Think you can help them out?"

"Yessir, maybe." James scuffed his big toe back and forth in the dust. "I've already got a little brother, though."

"Well then, you're just the boy for the job!"

Betsy came to the edge of the gathering and waited until Matthew noticed her. "Betsy?"

"Welcome, Rev'rund Matthew." Her round face shone with pleasure.

He turned to the other two men. "Betsy and my sister were playmates on our father's farm in Kentucky." He grinned at her. "What one of them couldn't think of to get into, the other one could."

Mr. Wolcott stepped forward and took her hand in the same way he'd grasped Molly's. "Betsy. You're coming with us to Illinois, I trust?"

"Where Miz Molly goes, I goes."

❧

That evening, when Molly descended the stairs after tucking the children into bed, Matthew called to her. "Come, sit." He waved his hand toward two chairs facing the open fireplace. "I want to hear all that's happened since I left home."

She sat, resting her feet on a corner of the fender surrounding the hearth. Ash-covered coals cast a ruddy light over her older brother, who straddled the other chair, his elbows propped on the backrest.

"I hardly know where to begin. I was only eleven when you left." Her voice dropped. "You know, Papa never forgave you. Especially after Mama died, he turned so bitter. Wouldn't even hear your name spoken."

"I couldn't stay. Slavery's wrong, and no matter what I said, Pa wouldn't see it God's way." Matthew shifted in his chair, his

47

eyes taking on the heavenward look she remembered. "When the Lord called me to preach the gospel, it couldn't be from a slave-holding farmstead. Riding circuit took me away from all that." He reached over and squeezed her hand. "But I wish Mama could've met my wife, Ellie. I know they'd have liked each other." Sadness touched his eyes. "Mama had been gone for months before word of her passing caught up with me." He shook his head, dismissing memories. "Tell me what happened."

Molly swallowed, wondering where to start and how much to say. "I'd just turned sixteen. Did you know Mama was in the family way?"

Shaking his head, her brother turned his chair around and moved it closer. "Nathaniel must've been fourteen by then."

"He was. I don't think our brothers knew about her condition, but she had to tell me so I could help her. She was so sick, and her legs and feet swelled up terrible." Molly stopped, drawing a ragged breath. "Anyway, when her time came, she just wasn't strong enough. The baby died too."

Matthew wiped nonexistent sweat from his forehead and ran his fingers over his unruly hair. "What did Pa do?"

"Ranted and raved and carried on something fierce. Blamed everyone and everything except himself for getting her in that condition." She stood, searching for something to do with her hands, remembering her helplessness at her mother's bedside. Bending toward the fire, she stirred the coals with a poker, feeling the respondent heat against her face.

"Then?" Matthew said.

"Then!" A sound between a laugh and a sob slipped out. "Then he proceeded to drink himself senseless every night."

"But what happened to the farm? Is it gone?"

"The boys were able to save it, Adam and Eli mostly, because

Nathaniel was still pretty young. Fortunately it was so well run by the slaves that they could manage things."

"And you, Molly? What about you?"

"I picked up where Mama left off. I tried so hard, but it never seemed good enough for Papa." She squeezed her eyes shut, hearing his derisive laughter in her mind. "He always said the reason it took me so long to find a husband was that I was such a loss as a housekeeper."

Her brother stood, placing a hand on her shoulder. "Judging from this cabin, I'd say you're a fine housekeeper." His voice roughened. "Pa was always harsh. I'm sorry you had to take the brunt of his cruelty."

"The years Samuel and I had together more than made up for it." Molly went on to tell him how they had met, their marriage, and the decision to come to the Missouri frontier with Brody and open a brickyard.

"Everything was going so well for us. This started out to be such a good year." She drew a deep breath and held it for a moment, watching flames sprout among the coals. "Then Samuel got cholera, and the doctor here couldn't help . . ." Molly shook her head, trying to erase the memory. "Oh, Matthew, Samuel asked me to send for Dr. Spengler, and I didn't do it." Tears slid down her cheeks. "I feel like his death was my fault."

Matthew wrapped his arms around her, soothing her as he had when she'd hurt herself as a child. "Don't torture yourself. You didn't kill him. Cholera takes anyone it wants to—no matter how good the doctor is." He hugged her and then backed away, looking into her eyes. "Will you try to remember that?"

She nodded, smoothing her hair away from her temples with the palms of her hands. "I'll try." Her voice trembled. "But it isn't easy."

49

He resumed his position in the chair facing her. "Now, tell me about Brody. Why's he being so un-Christian toward you and your children?"

Matt sees everything through a preacher's eyes. How can I explain Brody? She interlaced her fingers and tapped her thumbs together, considering her reply. In a flat voice she recited, "He told me he's always resented Samuel telling him what to do. He thinks I look down on his wife. He tricked Samuel into signing some kind of paper promising everything to him."

"But, surely—"

"There is no 'but surely'!" Molly's voice rose. "He sees this as his opportunity to feather his nest from our misfortune." She paced back and forth in front of him. "If you hadn't come, I don't know what we'd have done."

"I did come. And you're going home with me. Ellie's getting a room ready now." He paused, staring at the floor. "Um, prob'ly should start back soon's we can. Don't want your time to come somewhere out on the prairie." Cheeks flushed, he hurried on. "We'll start loading your movables in the morning. Your loom will be the heaviest, it'll go in first."

"I'll have it ready." She walked over and put her arms around him, feeling the scratchy wool of his shirt against her cheek. "Thank you. I'm glad I have you to depend on."

"It's the Lord you need to lean on, not me."

"Maybe that works for you, but I leaned on the Lord to save Samuel and he didn't do it—just like he didn't save Mama. I need someone I can touch, not a promise in the sky."

❧

Breaking daylight spread over the floor of the loft as Molly climbed the stairs to her loom the next morning. Settling herself

50

on the seat, she pushed the beater back and cut through the warp yarn, releasing the last woven piece from the loom.

Samuel was still alive when I dressed the loom for these blankets. She leaned back and looked down at the woolly roll in front of her knees. *Now the last one comes off and he's not here to see it.* Tears gathered in her eyes.

She stood and walked to the window. As long as she stayed in the house where her husband died, she still felt close to him. She could talk to him, and often did, during sleepless nights. Molly leaned her forehead against the cool glass. *Oh Samuel, I don't want to leave you!*

"Molly!"

She jumped at the sound of a male voice. For a moment she'd forgotten about her brother.

"I'm up here."

His feet clattered up the stairs. "Is this ready to go?" He pointed at the heavy barn-frame loom.

Molly straightened her shoulders as if facing down an enemy. "Yes. It is."

5

Saturday passed in a blur of activity. While Molly's possessions were being loaded onto the wagons, she and Betsy alternated chores. The children had to be kept out of the way, meals cooked, and all but last-minute necessities packed into trunks for the trip to Illinois.

After a supper of fried catfish, supplied by Betsy's friend Reuben, Matthew walked to Cody Stanton's to accept his invitation to preach at Sunday's church meeting. "We'll not labor on the Lord's Day," he told Molly when he returned.

Her lip trembled. "I'd rather stay busy. That way I don't have to think about leaving Samuel behind."

Mr. Wolcott inserted himself into their discussion. "If we're too busy to worship, we're too busy."

"Besides, you've never heard me preach," Matthew said, patting her shoulder. "You might like it."

❧

During Monday's breakfast of bacon and biscuits, Matthew looked quizzically toward Molly. "I haven't seen hide nor hair of that brother of Samuel's. Where's he live?"

"You passed his house just south of here. The one with the slave cabins in back." Molly pushed a bit of biscuit into the gravy congealing on her plate. "I'm surprised he hasn't been over before this. He's been so worried that he'll miss out on getting something of Samuel's." She shook her head. "I'm glad you're here. Now I won't have to talk to him anymore."

"Slave cabins?" Mr. Wolcott asked.

"Brody brought two men and a woman with him from Kentucky," Molly said. "They're his, but Papa deeded Betsy to Samuel before we came here."

Matthew turned to Molly and spoke in an undertone. "Ben runs the Underground Railroad that goes through Beldon Grove."

Molly looked at her children. "You all go and put your things in the trunk next to the bed," she said, wanting to distract them before they overheard too much. "James, make sure Franklin and Luellen don't leave anything." The three of them scrambled up to the loft.

Once they were out of earshot, Betsy moved from her listening post near the fire and slipped over to Mr. Wolcott, crouching beside the bench where he sat. "That man what brung the fish on Saturday? Reuben? Can you help him to freedom?"

He pivoted to look at her. "If he can get to Beldon Grove, I can help him." Mr. Wolcott kept his voice low. "Tell him to look for a house with a red North Star quilt on the washline. If he don't see the quilt, he'll need to hide and wait until he does."

Molly rested her hands on the tabletop and leaned forward. "Once these plates are washed, I'll be ready to finish packing." She paused, considering her next words. "I'd be grateful if you'd leave me alone to do it."

☙

Smoke stains on the bricks looked like bony fingers reaching toward the mugs and wooden bowls waiting on the shelf above the fireplace. With a clatter that echoed in the quiet cabin, Molly tossed them into a pouch formed by the apron she wore over her smock.

When she moved between hearth and table, her thighs touched the edge of the maple bedstead she and Samuel brought from Kentucky. She sat, fingers absently rubbing the texture inside the bowls. *Samuel carved these when we were first married.* She smiled at the memory of his large hands skillfully turning pieces of wood into useful objects.

Sunlight painted a bright rectangle across the floor of the cabin. A goldfinch scratched in the dust outside the open door, a bright yellow flash against the dull brown of the yard. Its focused energy stirred Molly back to her feet. She dropped her bundle into a trunk partially filled with linen sheets and climbed the open stairway to the loft for the children's bedding.

Blankets, bedtick, it all goes. Gripping the top step with her left hand, she jerked the pile of covers from the edge of the loft and dropped them onto the puncheon table below.

"Mrs. McGarvie! You shouldn't be doing that!"

Startled, she looked down into Dr. Spengler's wide blue eyes.

"Let me help you down." He reached for her hand.

"I'm fine. Don't fuss!"

She brushed him away, losing her balance in the process. His strong hands caught her hips as she fell backward against him, so that he settled her to the floor with his hands under her belly.

Blushing furiously, she wrenched free. "I asked to be left alone. What are you doing here?"

"I came to see if you needed anything carried out to the wagon, and it's a good thing I did. You could've injured yourself—or your baby."

Embarrassment gave way to indignation. "I'm fine, my baby's fine, and if I want help, I'll ask for it." Molly tried to apply as much dignity as she could muster to her disheveled five-foot-tall frame.

He turned and walked out, but not before she saw a flash of anger cross his face.

❧

Karl stalked toward the barn. *Blast that woman! Wish I'd never let Matt talk me into helping her.* Molly McGarvie might look like Caroline, but she certainly lacked Caroline's ability to make a man feel important. He ignored the fact that his former fiancée's charms had proved as artificial as the color he suspected her of applying to her cheeks.

Off to his left he heard the sound of hiccupping sobs. Luellen sat on the bare earth under an elm tree, her face shining with tears. She clutched a grimy rag doll to her chest and rocked back and forth.

Karl crouched and patted her back. "What is it, Luellen?"

She looked up at him, tears turning her dark eyelashes into tiny spikes. "I don't want to go away," she said between sobs. "I've lived here forever. This house will miss me."

"Why don't you go see your mama? She'll help you feel better."

"No, she won't. She tells me to be a big girl and not cry." She blinked back tears and gazed at the doctor. "But Mama cries. I hear her at night."

He hugged Luellen close, stroking her tumbled curls. "There, there," he said. "It's going to be all right. You'll like your Uncle Matthew's house."

"No, I won't."

Blast it! Why doesn't Mrs. McGarvie take care of her children? I don't know what to say to a three-year-old. He searched his mind for something that would distract the child. "Uh, where are your brothers?"

"James is helping Betsy hunt for Franklin. He's hiding." She hiccupped between sobs. "She loves them better than me."

The dark-skinned woman stepped into the shade beside him. "No such thing, child!" She reached for Luellen.

The little girl wiggled out of Karl's arms and flung herself against Betsy. Her wails increased.

"Looks like you're pitching a full-out fit, Lulie. You know we're leaving, and there's no sense making a big fuss." She softened her words with a kiss to the top of Luellen's head. "C'mon, you can help us find Franklin."

Karl stood, smiling at Betsy. "Thank you. I'm not much good at comforting little ones."

"Don't you worry none. We're beholden to you for helping us get to Illinois."

He thought of Matthew Craig's request that he help resettle Molly McGarvie, and his own reluctance to spend time around the woman. The wound Caroline had left on his heart still hadn't had time to heal. "No thanks necessary. I do what I can."

❧

Molly closed the lid on the last trunk, the finality of the metal hasp hard beneath her fingers. Pushing herself to her feet, she surveyed the near-empty room. *It's time to go.*

She stepped to the door. "Matt, I'm ready. You can take the bedstead and trunks now."

Betsy approached, Luellen clutching her hand. "Will we eat first? The chil'ren are getting hungry."

"They can wait a little longer—they ate a big breakfast." Molly squinted at the late morning sun. "We'll stop after a bit and set out the cold cornbread and beans. When we camp this evening, we'll make a hot supper."

✑

Once the men emptied the cabin, Dr. Spengler led the milk cow out of the stable and tied her to the back of his wagon. "That's it," he called to Matthew. "We'll keep her tied 'til she learns to follow."

Matthew nodded and turned to Mr. Wolcott, who waited next to the Dearborn. Molly sat rigid on the seat with Luellen next to her. Betsy stood beside Matthew.

"Let's go, then," he said. "We should be able to make four or five miles before sunset."

He climbed into his wagon and extended a hand to Betsy.

"Hold it right there!" Brody huffed into the yard, brandishing a riding crop. "Where you taking that gal?"

"We're going to Illinois, Brody." Molly jutted her chin and glared at him. "You've got the brickyard and the cabin—now leave us alone."

"You ain't taking that woman. She's my property."

6

Molly boiled off the buggy seat. "You stay right here!" she commanded Betsy. Stepping between her friend and her brother-in-law, she yelled, "Betsy's nobody's property! She's a person, not a thing."

Brody stood close enough for Molly to see beads of sweat dripping off the end of his nose. "Don't matter what you call her, your daddy deeded her to my brother, so now she belongs to me."

"Miz Molly, don't—"

"You shut up, gal!" Brody reached out as though to grab Betsy.

Molly stiffened her arms in front of her and shoved hard against his chest, knocking him off balance. Brody stumbled backward, windmilling his arms to keep from falling.

Matthew jumped off the wagon while Mr. Wolcott and Dr. Spengler ran toward the altercation. Molly picked up a rock and shouted, "If you come one step closer, I'll bash your head in! Betsy's coming with me."

Matthew snatched the rock out of her hand and dropped it. "Stop it." He took her hands in his. "Let me try to talk to him."

She rested her forehead against his chest. "Oh, Matt, please don't let him take Betsy." In spite of her efforts to keep them at bay, tears slid down her cheeks. "I've lost so much already."

He hugged her. "Ben's with him now. If anyone can get things calmed down, he can."

Molly looked around, seeing Betsy's frightened face. Behind her the children huddled together on the shaded wagon seat, wide-eyed and silent. Matthew joined Mr. Wolcott beside Brody. She tried to listen, but they spoke in such low voices she only heard occasional words.

Dr. Spengler walked over to her. "You'd best get out of the sun, Mrs. McGarvie." Cupping his hand under her elbow, he began guiding her to the Dearborn's low step.

She yanked her arm away. "But I—"

"There's nothing you can do right now. Let us menfolk work things out."

Reluctantly, Molly climbed into the wagon, lifting Luellen onto her lap. She rested her cheek on the child's soft black hair and rocked her back and forth, savoring her clean, fresh-air smell.

Luellen wiggled free. "Isn't Betsy coming?" Her voice quavered.

"Of course. Uncle Matthew will straighten things out with Brody." *He's got to!*

A quick breeze stirred the air, brushing past her face and disappearing before it had a chance to make a difference in the humid afternoon air. Molly twisted sideways on the seat, trying to see around the braces securing the canopy to the top of the wagon. Matthew and Mr. Wolcott turned away from Brody, heading toward Betsy. Molly held her breath.

Brody strutted over to the buggy. "The law's the law, Molly. You want that gal, you can buy her off of me." He smirked. "I gave your brother my terms."

59

"No." Molly exhaled the word. "No!" She jumped to her feet.

Mr. Wolcott walked Betsy to the Dearborn, his hand under her arm. "There's nothing we can do right now. She has to stay."

Molly climbed out of the wagon, sobbing. She clung to her friend. "I'll find a way. I promise. Whatever it takes, you'll be free one day."

"I'll be trusting the Lord, Miz Molly. Don't you worry none." Betsy tossed her head contemptuously in Brody's direction. "He ain't big enough to stop God Almighty."

Betsy reached into the buggy and scooped Luellen into her arms. The boys crowded near. "Y'all be good and help your mama, hear?" She turned to James. "She's gonna need you more than ever—you got to be the man of the family." Her gaze shifted to the smaller boy. "And you, Franklin, none of your tricks like hiding from your mama when she calls you." Betsy tapped his chest with her forefinger. "You mind that, now."

Tears streaked his cheeks. "I will, Betsy, I promise."

After kissing Luellen one more time, Betsy handed her to Molly. Then lifting her chin, she walked toward Brody's slave cabins with the dignity of a queen.

❧

Once the wagons were on the road, Brody ran after Betsy. "Where d'you think you're going?"

Not breaking stride, she called over her shoulder, "Taking my things back to the cabin." Betsy hefted the quilt-wrapped bundle from her right hand to her left and continued walking. Behind her she heard the sound of Brody's approaching footsteps.

"Don't turn your back on me! Stop this minute!"

Betsy turned, waiting.

Brody smacked the riding crop against the palm of his left hand.

"You're not Molly's pampered house gal no more. Take yourself over to my kitchen and help Tildy get supper on the table."

"Mr. Brody." Betsy took pains to keep her voice polite. "It'll just take me a minute to put my things away. I'll be in the kitchen directly."

Before she realized what was happening, Brody slashed across her left forearm with the crop. Betsy dropped the Sunflower quilt on the ground and flinched away, shocked. In all her twenty-six years, she'd never been struck by a white person.

"When I say 'git,' you git!" Brody snarled.

"Yessir." Betsy bent to brush dirt from her belongings.

The riding crop smacked hard against her right arm. "Leave it! You can take care of this truck after supper." He poked at the quilt and pile of clothing with the toe of his boot. "No one's going to steal nothing belonging to a colored gal, nohow."

Betsy smelled the kitchen before she reached it. Flies circled around a muddy spot next to the doorsill, from which grew a scraggly trumpet vine. *Must be where Tildy throws her dirty dishwater.* When she entered the small building behind the main house, Tildy glanced up from a kettle suspended over a heaped bed of coals.

"Well, look'ee here," she said in a mocking voice. "If it ain't pretty Betsy! What you doing in my kitchen, gal? Thought you was going off to be free."

Hungry for a sympathetic ear, Betsy poured out what had transpired between Molly and Brody. She pushed up her sleeves, showing Tildy the reddened welts on each forearm where she'd been struck.

After she finished her story, Tildy stood silent, frowning at her. "So," she said, "you're going to work in my kitchen?"

Betsy nodded.

"Well, don't think you'll be replacing me anytime soon. This house only needs one cook, and I'm it. I ain't afeared to tell Mr. Brody that, neither."

Betsy's shoulders sagged. "There must be something I can do to help you. I daren't go back outside. Mr. Brody might see me."

"Well . . ." Tildy paused, forehead wrinkled in thought. "You kin beat them biscuits." She pointed to a mallet and a crockery bowl filled with dough. "Just so's you know, if they's tough, I'll tell Miz Patience you done them." The cook reached onto a shelf beside the fire, handing Betsy a small covered crock. "That there's some goose grease. Rub it on your arms—it'll help."

Betsy felt a rush of gratitude for the small gesture. "Thank you, Tildy." She lifted the lid and rubbed the rancid-smelling grease over the welts on her arms.

◯

Mr. Wolcott's team of matched chestnut horses pulled the Dearborn east through golden prairie grass, retracing the track to St. Lawrenceville that they'd left the previous week. Matthew and Dr. Spengler followed at some distance behind. They'd taken James and Franklin with them, telling the boys they needed their help driving the loaded farm wagons.

Molly broke the silence. "I've been thinking . . . you said there's nothing we can do right now to get Betsy back."

He looked over his shoulder at her. "Aye-yuh."

"Do you mean there's something we can do later? Did Brody say how much it would cost to . . ." She choked on the words. "Buy her?"

"A hundred dollars."

Molly's hand flew to her mouth. Her emotions pushed her from grief to anger. "The selfish little toad! He didn't need Betsy—he just took her to spite me." She balled her fists in her lap. "I'll find a way to get the money."

He shifted the reins to his left hand and turned on the seat so his eyes met hers. Concern reflected in their hazel depths. "I've been praying about it since we left. You just need to wait on the Lord to open a door."

Wait. Since Samuel died, all I've done is wait. The baby rolled inside her, pushing itself with an elbow or a knee. Automatically, she placed her hand over the movement, feeling the pressure under her palm. *And I'm waiting for you too, aren't I?*

Mr. Wolcott lifted his straw hat and wiped sweat from his forehead with the sleeve of his brown hickory cloth shirt. Nodding at Luellen dozing next to Molly, he said, "She'll be ready for some supper pretty soon. We'll be stopping up yonder." He pointed into the distance.

Molly looked beyond the waves of grass in front of them. On the horizon she saw a tree line, which probably followed a creek emptying into the Mississippi.

After another hour's ride, Mr. Wolcott climbed off the buggy and wrapped the horses' reins around a spindly white oak. "I figure you'll want to stretch your legs." He held up his hand to help Molly down, and then turned to Luellen. "You stay with your ma, you hear? Your uncle and the doctor will be here directly with the big farm wagons, and they can't see you if you're running about in the tall grass."

Molly surveyed the camp area. "Is this where you stopped on the way out? Looks like someone left a firepit and some wood."

"Yep. We left as much as we could—figured this would be a good place to aim for on the first night. Can't always find water and trees out on the prairie." He raised his hat formally, as though they'd met on a city street. "If you'll excuse me now? I'll go help Matt with the teams."

That evening, after the campfire had settled into ruddy coals, Molly knelt and positioned a gridiron over the fire, shoving a baking iron next to it. She laid a row of venison sausages along the ribs of the gridiron, taking care not to crowd them. When the iron felt hot enough, she poured flannel cake batter inside, making four individual cakes. Absorbed in watching to be sure nothing burned, she forgot about Luellen.

"Mrs. McGarvie."

She jumped and turned to see the doctor holding her daughter under one arm. The boys trailed behind him. Molly pushed tendrils of hair off her forehead with the back of her hand, forgetting she was still holding the meat fork. "What's wrong?"

Dr. Spengler pointed at the fork. "Careful with that. You might poke someone's eye out."

A pop and sizzle from the fire caused her to whirl around in time to see flames licking at the bottoms of the sausages. "Drat!" She wrapped a corner of her apron around her hand and jerked the gridiron away from the flare-up.

"Can we talk later?" she asked, straightening and turning to face him. "I've got my hands full here."

"I can see that. Um, maybe you'd better turn those flannel cakes—they're smoking."

While Molly flipped the cakes, Dr. Spengler continued talking. "I brought this little one back from shinnying down to the creek. It'd be best if you kept an eye on her. The smell of this food cooking is bound to bring wolves in on us."

"Shinnying down to the creek! Lulie, you know better than that." *I should've been watching her.* Embarrassed, Molly took her daughter's hand and turned toward her oldest son. "James, you watch her while I cook supper."

"But, Mama, I'm helping Uncle Matthew with the tents."

She raised her eyebrows. "Not now you're not. You're taking care of Luellen."

The smell of burning food rose from the coals. Frantically, Molly rolled the sausages with the fork, then picked up the spatula and pushed flannel cakes to one side of the baking iron. *How did Betsy do all this?* With a feeling of despair, she realized she'd never cooked a meal without Betsy's help. She'd never done anything without someone's help—her mama, Samuel, Betsy. What if her father was right and she couldn't manage alone?

❧

Later that evening, Molly lay on her bedroll in the tent, listening to the support poles creak in the wind while the canvas walls bellied like sails. No matter how many times she turned and resettled herself on the straw tick, sleep eluded her. Behind her the children sprawled under their blankets, exhausted from the day's events. Sighing, Molly surrendered to wakefulness and lifted the tent flap to look out at the blazing fire. Across the triangle formed by the wagons, she saw Dr. Spengler, his back propped against a wagon wheel, taking his turn at guard duty. Mr. Wolcott and her brother slept in the tent next to hers.

Overhead, a new moon hung in the evening sky. Below it a single star dangled like a button on a string. Wind tore through the camp, ruffling the fire and drawing Molly's attention to what appeared to be yellow eyes reflected beyond the edge of the firelight. *Wolves?* Heart pounding, she glanced over at the doctor. *He doesn't seem worried.*

While she watched, he picked up a stick from the pile of

firewood and started to whittle. For a moment she allowed herself to pretend she was seeing Samuel again. The knife in his long-fingered hands made quick, flicking motions. Curls of wood showered the ground between his boots. Molly cocked her head, wondering what shape would appear when he finished carving. Whenever Samuel picked up a stick to whittle, his skillful hands turned it into a useful object or a toy for the children.

Abruptly Dr. Spengler stood and tossed the piece of wood into the fire. The spell broken, grief again overwhelmed Molly. *He's not Samuel. Samuel is gone.* She drew her head inside and dropped the tent flap.

⌒

The next morning, after Molly packed the cooking utensils, Matthew helped her and Luellen into his wagon. The procession rolled out. Molly ducked her head to keep the rising sun out of her eyes. "I've been thinking about what you said when you preached on Sunday. About how we need to live trusting the Lord. Do you really believe that?"

"Course I do. Wouldn't say it if I didn't."

Molly shook her head in disbelief. "It's probably easy for you. Nothing bad has ever happened in your life."

He snorted. "And how do you know that, little sister?"

"You have your wife, your family, a home . . ." Her voice challenged. "My Samuel's dead, his brother took my livelihood, and now he's taken Betsy! How am I supposed to trust the Lord? He's brought me nothing but grief."

Matthew laid his hand over hers. "I trust God because of who he is, not because of what he does or doesn't do." He squeezed her hand.

She turned in the seat, ready to argue, when she noticed a

column of riders coming toward them from the north. Her breath caught in her throat. "Indians!" As the riders drew closer, Molly recognized the man in the lead. "It's the Sauk chief, Keokuk."

Matthew looked at her, a surprised expression on his face. "How do you know?"

"Samuel traded with them all the time. They liked him." Then she caught her breath, remembering. "Keokuk's wife wanted to swap her girl child for Franklin when we first came to St. Lawrenceville." Her heart pounded. "Now he's back! Is he going to take my son?" She pivoted on the seat to make sure Franklin was safe in Dr. Spengler's wagon. "Hurry! Let's outrun them!"

Instead, he drew the reins toward him, stopping the team.

"What are you doing?"

"We can't outrun riders on horseback with these slow wagons. I've heard Keokuk is a reasonable man—I'll talk to him."

"Have you gone mad? At least take a rifle." She reached under the wagon seat and pulled out the flintlock.

Matthew closed his eyes and took a deep breath. Exhaling, he looked at his sister. "I can't say I trust God and then cave in at the first sign of danger. Besides, they don't appear to be armed. Let's just see what they want."

The riders stopped about twenty feet away. Two of the horses behind Chief Keokuk dragged travois piled high with bulging tow sacks. The fourth rider was a woman. Molly remembered her as part of the band who had visited their cabin when Franklin was a toddler. The woman had hung back that day, watching, just as she did now. *Who is she?*

Matthew walked toward the chief. Dr. Spengler and Mr. Wolcott stopped their wagons and watched. Keokuk swung off his horse and extended his arm toward Matthew. The two men exchanged a grip of friendship.

Keokuk tipped his head toward Molly, who crouched behind the wagon seat, her arms encircling her youngest child. "You have McGarvie's woman with you."

Molly heard her brother's reply, as strong and vigorous as though he stood in a pulpit. "She's my sister. I'm taking her to our people."

"McGarvie was our friend. At planting time, he gave us seed corn."

Matthew nodded without replying.

"We bring his woman McGarvie's share of our harvest. He was a good man. We honor him." Keokuk waved a hand at the two riders with the travois. They moved forward slowly, the heavy sacks leaving deep furrows in the soft bottom land.

When they came near, Molly grasped the side of the wagon, pulling herself to her feet. She climbed back onto the seat, sitting with her shoulders thrown back and chin lifted. Turning to Matthew, she said, "Tell the chief how grateful I am for this food. Tell him . . ." She swallowed. "Tell him McGarvie's woman will never forget his kindness."

After the corn had been transferred to the wagons, the chief and his followers headed north. Molly watched dust curl into the air behind them, seeing another link to her life with Samuel broken. *I was so afraid of Keokuk.* Shame burned through her. *He never intended me harm.*

She glanced back to where Matthew stood talking with Mr. Wolcott and Dr. Spengler. The row of filled grain sacks stood in the rear of the doctor's wagon, expanding her food supply. *Matthew would call it a blessing from God.* A bit of the hardness around her heart softened. *Maybe it is.*

Her brother strode over to her. "Ready to go?"

Molly nodded and slid over on the seat.

Matthew climbed in. "We'll reach the Mississippi soon. It'll take pretty near all day to get these wagons ferried across." He shook the reins over the horses' backs.

Standing behind the seat, Luellen said, "James says we're going on a boat."

"James remembers when we came here," Molly said. "I had a terrible time keeping him away from the edge of the flatboat." She turned and tilted Luellen's chin so she could look into her eyes. "You're to stay right in this wagon, you hear me?"

The girl's bonneted head nodded solemnly.

Molly faced forward, again feeling the pain of all she'd lost. "We had such bright dreams," she said to her brother in a low voice. "Samuel couldn't wait to get across the Mississippi and settle on the frontier."

The team plodded steadily onward. "Your life isn't over, Molly." Matthew wiped a tear from her cheek with his forefinger. "It's taking a new direction."

7

Mid-September 1838

Near the river, scrubby grassland gave way to low willows, cottonwoods, and crabapple trees. Molly jumped when a pair of mallards burst from the edge of the brush next to them and shot upward, squawking. A flock of geese passed overhead, low enough for her to hear the *wuf wuf* of their wings beating against the still, autumn air.

"Wish we had time to stop, Matt," the doctor called from the wagon behind her. "Looks like a good place to do some shotgunning."

Matthew turned his head and grinned at him. "Maybe we'll come back in a few weeks, if you're still in the neighborhood."

A narrow road had been cut through the trees, angling down to the edge of the sluggish brown river. Molly studied the tiny settlement huddled under a broad sandstone bluff on the opposite side. "Waring looks the same as it did when we crossed two years ago."

"Not much reason for it to grow," Matthew said. "I think Otto's ferry is the only thing going on there." He pulled on the reins, stopping the team several yards short of a plank road leading to the waiting flatboat. "We'll go over first. Do you want your boys up here with us?"

James and Franklin jumped out of the doctor's wagon and ran toward Molly. "Mama, can we pick crabapples?" James looked up at her, his expression eager. "We saw some back there and they're mostly ripe."

Molly's mouth watered, remembering the tart flavor of the compact fruit. "Do you think Ellie'd like to make some jelly?" she said to Matthew. "We could do it together."

An unreadable expression flitted across Matthew's face. "Hmm. Sure, if you don't mind showing her how to do it. Ellie's not much for fancy stuff in the kitchen—but she's learning."

Molly looked at the boys. "It'll be a couple of hours before the ferry comes back. Stay near the doctor's wagon. When it's his turn to cross, don't make him hunt for you."

"We won't," James called over his shoulder. He sprinted up the road, Franklin close behind.

Matthew helped Molly off the wagon. Reaching over the side, he lifted Luellen down beside her. "Be a good time to let her stretch her legs. I'm going to talk to Otto about the fare."

He strode toward the stocky man watching them from the deck of the flatboat. Mr. Wolcott and Dr. Spengler followed him.

"Let's go see where Franklin and James went." Molly led her youngest child away from the river's edge.

❧

Molly watched the gap widen between the shore and the side of the ferry. Otto pushed against the shallow river bottom with a stout pole, moving them against the current. His muscular arms bulged against rolled-up shirtsleeves. Dried mud covered his bare feet, splotched his short trousers, and stained his tan shirt. Once the boat cleared the shallows, he tipped his battered felt hat to her and grinned. "Nice day to be on the river, ma'am."

She smiled back, drawn by the kindness in his eyes. "It is."

"You and the young'un will be safe on the other side before you know it." He turned the rudder, quartering the broad craft north until the sluggish current took hold and turned them toward Illinois.

Luellen knelt behind the seat, fingers gripped over the side rails of the wagon. Each time the flatboat tilted to one side or the other, she whimpered.

"C'mere, little one!" Matthew said, lifting the sturdy child onto his knee. "You can help me hold the reins in case the horses get scared."

Once into the main portion of the river, Otto continued to work the rudder to avoid the floating branches and snags that protruded from the water. The riverman's efforts reminded Molly of trying to hurry a mule. Their craft could move no faster than the Mississippi's lazy flow.

She tilted her head in Matthew's direction. "Tell me more about Ellie. Where'd you meet her?"

"In Missouri, down in Cape Girardeau County. Six years ago now. The church conference sent me to preach in one of the little settlements. Some folks walked out to guide me there, and Ellie was one of the guides." He shifted Luellen to his other knee and gave Molly a sheepish grin. "She was fourteen."

"But you're thirty-six." She ticked the years on her fingers. "So Ellie's only twenty? And you have four children?"

"Yes." Matthew clipped off the monosyllable.

"You don't need to get all prickly. I'm just—"

The boat lurched, then shuddered as something scraped across

72

the bottom of the hull. Molly grabbed the edge of the wagon seat and scanned the surface of the water. In their wake, a tree trunk circled, roots reaching into the air like talons.

"Mama?" Luellen scrambled off her uncle's lap and wrapped her arms around Molly's neck.

Otto must have seen her checking the surface of the deck for leaks. He chuckled. "Happens all the time, ma'am. This river's good at hiding danger."

His words didn't offer the comfort Molly hoped for. She'd never lived near rivers and saw no reason to trust them. At that moment the boat swung sideways and swirled partway around before rotating back toward the Illinois shore.

The riverman turned his head toward her, both hands gripping the rudder. This time he didn't smile. "Hit an eddy."

Molly leaned back on the seat and fanned the nervous perspiration from her forehead. "I don't remember the crossing being this wild when Samuel and I came to Missouri."

"It rained last week," Matthew told her. "Water's more treacherous right now."

Glancing back, Molly noted that they'd come more than halfway across. Ahead of them, the buildings in Waring began to assume distinct outlines. "We're almost there," she whispered to Luellen. "Just a little while more."

❧

The flatboat grated against the shore, startling the horses. Tied to the back of the wagon, Samuel's horse, Captain, shied, tossing his head and jerking the rope. "Well, we made it!" Otto called over the sound of whinnying. He poled the boat until it stood even with a corduroy roadbed leading away from the riverbank. "You can tie the horses under those trees," he said, pointing to a stand of white oak. "If you want to refresh yourself whilst you wait, ma'am, my wife's in that first cabin over there. I'll have the next wagon over in a couple hours."

Molly peered in the direction Otto indicated. The cabin appeared to have been built of wood that had washed ashore during one of the Mississippi's many floods and might return to the river during the next one.

"Obliged." Matthew answered for her, flicking the reins over the horses' backs and turning them toward the trees. Addressing Molly, he said, "Be good for you and the young'un to be out of the sun while we wait. I'll stay here with the wagon." He patted her hand. "You'd best ride with Ben when we get going again—it'll be cooler for you inside his carriage, what with the curtains and all."

Molly nodded assent, at the same time scanning the far side of the river for a glimpse of James and Franklin. "I don't see the boys." Fear sharpened her words.

"The brush is pretty thick over there. I can't see them either, but I'm sure Ben and Karl are keeping a sharp lookout." Her brother helped her off the wagon, setting Luellen down beside her. Nodding at the cabin, Matthew said, "Appears you're expected."

Otto's wife stood in the open doorway. Molly glanced at her, then took a second look. She'd expected a female version of Otto. The slender woman waiting for them had milk-smooth skin, shining blonde hair done up in a fashionable style, and one of the most beautiful faces Molly had ever seen. Serenity surrounded her like an invisible cloak.

"Please do come in," she said. Her words carried the softness of summer in the South.

Molly shepherded Luellen ahead of her into the cabin. "Are you Mrs. Otto?" she asked, trying to keep astonishment out of her voice.

The woman smiled. "Otto is my husband's first name. I'm Helen Cooper." She pointed to several split-bottom chairs arranged around a shining mahogany table. "Would you care to sit? I have some cool water if you and your daughter would like some."

Molly sat, wonderingly rubbing her fingers over the table's glossy surface. "I'd appreciate a cup of water, thank you." Aside from the handsome table, the interior of the cabin resembled the one Molly left behind in St. Lawrenceville: fireplace at one end, table in the middle, bed in a curtained alcove at the back. A set of open stairs leading to a loft angled up behind the sleeping area. Molly examined the shining tabletop. She wondered how such an elegant piece of furniture had ended up in a crude frontier cabin, but she'd been taught not to ask personal questions.

Helen poured water from a heavy crockery jug like the ones Molly used, but she poured it into a crystal goblet. She handed the filled glass to Molly, drew a chair away from the table, and sat facing her. "Is that your husband outside with the horses?"

"My brother. My husband died two months ago."

"Oh, dear, I am sorry! I worry about Mr. Cooper in the rainy season. The Mississippi has claimed many a man."

Molly helped Luellen drink, then carefully placed the goblet on the table. "Such beautiful glassware. And this fine table." Curiosity won over etiquette. "Where did you . . . ?" She felt her cheeks flush at her boldness.

Apparently noticing her discomfort, Helen replied, "My mother gave me these things when I left home to marry Mr. Cooper." She leaned forward, lowering her voice. "The family thought he wasn't good enough for me. I'm a Townsend, from James River in Virginia. Papa cut me off without a penny and told me never to come back." She raised her finely chiseled chin defiantly, but her lower lip trembled. "So here I am." Helen Cooper rose and moved toward the open doorway. "And here I'll stay."

Sudden awareness jolted Molly as she considered the elegant woman living in a pieced-together cabin. *She can't go back to her old home, and I won't go back to mine. I wonder if she feels as lost as I do.*

Later, during a lull in their conversation, Molly stole a glance at the clock that ticked on a shelf above the table. Startled, she noticed that more than two hours had passed. Shouldn't the ferry have returned by now?

A gust of wind blew dust and dried leaves over the threshold. Helen grabbed the broom leaning in a corner near the door. "No matter how hard I try, I can't keep this place clean!" She chased the debris out onto the steps, pausing to look toward the wide river. "My husband just brought your carriage over," she said, shading her eyes with her hand. "What beautiful horses!"

"Yes, they are. But they belong to Mr. Wolcott, my brother's neighbor." Molly stood, shaking out the front of her dress where Luellen's weight had crushed it against her thighs. "My sons are with him. I believe I'll walk down and see how many crabapples they brought me." She smiled at Helen. "Thank you for the hospitality. We've taken up enough of your day."

The blonde woman turned to Molly, a puzzled expression on her face. "Did you say 'sons'? There's only one boy in that carriage."

"What?" Molly hastened through the doorway. She hurried across the hard-packed ground toward the Dearborn. By the time she reached Mr. Wolcott, he had unhitched his team and was chocking the wheels of the carriage. James eyed her from the seat, his face pale.

"Mr. Wolcott, where's Franklin?"

"Doc Spengler's looking for him right now. I come over to get Matthew to help us."

"'Looking for him'? He's missing?" Cold fear clutched at her stomach. She turned her head, seeking her brother.

Matthew came up behind her and put an arm around her shoulders. "We'll leave the wagons here and ride back with Otto. Don't worry, Franklin'll turn up. Likely he just wandered too far from the road to hear Ben calling."

"My son . . . ," Molly said in a faint voice. She gripped Matthew's forearm. "You've got to find him!"

Mr. Wolcott slipped bridles over the horses' heads. Using a cottonwood stump for a mounting block, he swung onto the back of one of the chestnuts. The other horse stood beside him, reins dangling. "Can you ride without a saddle, Matthew?"

"I'll have to. There's no time to get fancy."

James ran to his mother. "I shinnied up a tree to get some big ones, and when I got down, Franklin was gone." Tears slid over his dusty cheeks. "I called and called, but he wouldn't answer."

Matthew squeezed his shoulder. "Likely he thinks he's playing a game. We'll find him."

Her son lifted pleading eyes. "Can I go back with them? I can help."

Molly looked from James to Matthew. In an instant, she made a decision. "You stay with your sister. I'm going."

Mr. Wolcott stared down at her from the chestnut's back. "You can't! Not in your—"

"I can and I will. He's my son." She faced James. "Take Luellen and wait at the Coopers' cabin. We'll be back soon."

"Let's move," Otto called from the deck of the flatboat. "We're burning daylight."

During the crossing, Molly planted her hands on her hips and eyed Mr. Wolcott. "How did this happen? I don't understand."

He shook his head. "I thought Doc had them in sight, so I waited down at the landing for Otto. Had some things to talk to him about." His voice cracked. "I should've been watching."

Matthew slid off his horse's back and stood next to his sister. "Let's pray. The Lord will help us."

Molly stood with bowed head, her hand in Matthew's, paying slight attention to his words. Prayers were all well and good, but she trusted more in her own ability to locate her son. Once they were off the boat, she'd walk along the bank and call his name. Franklin had his naughty moments, but he never failed to respond when she called. He might be teasing the doctor, who was a stranger after all, but he wouldn't disobey his mother.

When the boat scratched onto the bank, Dr. Spengler stood waiting for them, his hands held up in a helpless gesture. "I'm glad you're back. I've about hollered myself hoarse and that scamp isn't answering me."

Molly glared at him. "Was it asking too much for you to keep an eye on my sons?"

Matthew walked his horse in her direction. "Now, Molly, you know how quick young'uns can get out of sight. Let's get to looking and not waste time arguing."

She blew air out of her nostrils. Her side ached from the effort of maintaining her balance on the rocking flatboat. "You're right." Molly turned and headed north along the marshy riverbank. She glanced back once and saw the men conferring. When she checked again, they'd spread out on horseback in separate directions.

"Franklin! Come here this minute!" Her boots squished in the black mud. Barely acknowledging the unthinkable, she scanned the river's edge for a child's footprints. Franklin had been barefoot—perhaps the temptation to wade had brought him down here. But she saw no sign that anything but waterfowl had walked over the ground in front of her.

By moving carefully, she could step on tufts of grass that stood like islands in the muck. It was slow going. What appeared to be a tussock could turn out to be bristled vegetation swamped by river water. The sun hovered on the western horizon, marking her progress like an uncaring deity.

Echoes of the men's voices drifted through the thickets. Molly strained to hear Franklin's response. Nothing. Her heart raced. *He's got to be here somewhere. Why doesn't he answer?* Farther and farther she walked, fanning clouds of mosquitoes and midges away from her face. "Franklin!" Her back ached. When she glanced over her shoulder, Molly noticed the boat landing was no longer in sight. *Surely he didn't come this far.* She peered into the dense underbrush that marked the river's high water line. Was that a flash of white? Franklin's shirt?

Molly staggered up the riverbank and pushed through low-growing willows to get a closer look. A great white bird lifted skyward, its bright yellow feet extended behind it. *Only an egret.* Crushed, Molly slid onto a space of dry ground and pushed her fingertips into her temples. The pain in her back intensified.

"Franklin." This time her voice was no more than a whimper.

8

Molly jumped to her feet when she heard horse's hooves splash over the marshy ground. *They found him!* She dashed from the cover of the willows and saw Matthew riding toward her from the direction of the boat mooring. Alone. In her haste she slipped, landing with a jolt in the mud.

Her brother vaulted off the horse's back and pulled her to her feet. "Be careful! You'll harm the baby."

She dismissed his caution with a wave of her hand. "Franklin. Where is he?"

Matthew shook his head. "No sign. We'll get more men together and start searching at first light."

Molly stiffened. "We can't leave him out here overnight! Wolves . . ."

"There's been no trace of them on this trip." He drew her to him so tightly she heard the thump of his heart against her ear. His voice sounded like it came from miles away. "We've got no choice but to go. It'll be full dark soon. We have to cross the river while Otto can still see to land the boat."

The enormity of his words crashed down on her. "No! I won't leave."

"You can't stay here all night—not in your condition." He pointed at the road leading west. "Ben's back there making camp. He'll build a signal fire big enough so Franklin can see it from wherever he is."

"Dear God. This is more than I can bear." Her words were a cry, not a prayer.

Tears glittered in her brother's eyes. Holding the horse's reins in his free hand, he put an arm around her shoulder and guided her steps toward the landing.

Beside them, the broad, muddy river rippled past, making almost no sound. Molly stared at the murky water, hating its inscrutability. It could have been a foot deep, or twenty feet deep. Nothing showed beneath the surface save rolling particles of soil illuminated by the last rays of the sun. Pain rode low in her back and wrapped around her heart, like hooks digging into her flesh.

Otto's boat bobbed in the darkening water. Dr. Spengler had already driven his wagon aboard. Once she stepped onto the ferry, he walked to her, his arm extended. "I'll help you onto the seat. You need rest."

She pushed his hand away. "Leave me alone! If it wasn't for you, this nightmare wouldn't be happening."

His face flushed. He opened his mouth to reply but no words emerged.

Matthew stepped between them. "Molly. Karl's spent the afternoon hunting for Franklin. No one could've done more."

"No? If he'd paid attention to my son in the first place, he wouldn't be missing now."

Back rigid, Dr. Spengler climbed into the wagon and stared straight ahead.

Molly leaned on her brother, one hand pressed against the small of her back to ease a flash of pain that seared below her

81

waist. After three pregnancies, she knew what it represented. *Not now! I've got to find Franklin.* By sheer willpower, she tried to end the contractions. A new baby required time and energy that she didn't want to give. Another spasm squeezed upward across her abdomen. Pressing her hands against her belly, she clenched her teeth and concentrated on stopping it.

Matthew's eyes met hers. "What's wrong?"

Drawing a deep breath, she leaned against him. "A little pain. It's probably nothing." For the first time that afternoon, she thought of Betsy. The slave woman had been present when each of her children were born. *I'd give anything to have her with me right now.*

The flatboat lurched when it stopped next to the corduroy road leading to Waring. Still ignoring the squeezing sensation in her groin, Molly took Otto's hand and allowed him to guide her off the boat. She moved to the edge of the road and faced across the river. A glowing column of smoke rose from Mr. Wolcott's signal fire. If she focused hard enough, maybe she would see Franklin running toward the landing.

Matthew walked up to her. "I'll go get the children from the Coopers', then we'll put up the tents. You look worn out."

The spasms returned. This time Molly bowed to the inescapable. Looking down the road, she measured the distance between camp and the few visible cabins. *There's bound to be a midwife hereabouts. Helen Cooper will know.* "I need to go with you to Mrs. Cooper's house."

"Why?"

"The baby's coming. She must know someone who can help."

"We have a doctor right here." Her brother pointed to Karl Spengler.

"I don't want him near me. This wouldn't be happening now if he hadn't lost Franklin."

Matthew pressed his lips together with his fingers and drew a deep breath. Molly assumed he intended to argue the point, but decided against it. Instead, he tucked his hand under her arm and supported her during the walk to the Coopers' cabin.

James ran to the door when Helen answered their knock. "Where's Franklin?"

Molly's heart shrank. For some reason, she couldn't get her voice to work.

Matthew pulled James to him and hugged him. "Still lost."

"Oh my dear!" Helen held out her arms.

Molly stumbled forward and collapsed against her. Shuddering, she waited for a pain to pass.

Helen's eyes widened. "Is it your time?"

"Yes. It's early—I figured we'd be at my brother's house before the baby came." She stepped back, her hands splayed over her abdomen. "Is there a midwife in this village?"

"Indeed there is." Helen raised her eyes to her husband, who stood in the doorway. "Would you go get Mrs. Brewster?"

"She's only about half a mile east of here." Otto addressed Molly as he slipped a jacket over his linen shirt. "I should be back within the hour." He slipped an arm around Helen's waist and kissed her cheek. "You'll be all right?"

Helen tilted her head. "I'm fine. It's Mrs. McGarvie you need to worry about just now."

Otto took a lantern from a shelf, lit it, and hurried out the door.

Luellen pattered over to her mother and wrapped her arms around one of Molly's legs. "Mama, I'm scared for Franklin."

Twisting flame from an oil lamp hanging over the table sent

83

highlights across the child's dark curls. Molly pressed Luellen's head against her thigh, holding her tightly. "I'm afraid too, Lulie." She turned to Matthew. "Can you get her settled in bed?"

"You forget I have four of my own." Her brother grinned. "I think I can manage." The grin disappeared and he studied her, a worried expression on his features. "I'll come back once she's asleep. James can stay with her for a few minutes."

She nodded, gasping when another pain crossed her lower back. "Please bring clean sheets when you come—they're in the blue trunk."

When the door closed behind them, Helen took her hand. "Do you want to rest?"

"It feels better to walk."

While Molly paced the room, Helen opened the curtains that surrounded the bed. "You'll like Mrs. Brewster. She delivered my babies."

Surprised, Molly glanced around the cabin for evidence of children. The Coopers didn't appear old enough to have a family grown and gone.

Helen caught her glance, a brief expression of anguish crossing her face. "I had three. They died in a smallpox epidemic five years ago."

"Oh, I'm so sorry!" Molly thought of Franklin, alone and frightened somewhere while the night closed around him. She couldn't imagine him gone permanently, let alone losing all three of her children at once.

Another pain tore across her back and groin, and she felt wetness on her legs that told her the baby wouldn't wait much longer. Grabbing the back of a chair, she hung on until the spasm passed.

The blonde woman met her eyes. "Come. Let's get you settled. Otto should be back very soon."

Molly lay on the bed, her damp hair spread over the pillow. She held her breath and waited while another contraction ripped across her back and abdomen. Helen had closed the curtains around them, and sat next to the bed, wiping sweat from Molly's forehead with a soft cloth. The door to the cabin banged open, causing the curtain to billow over her face like linen fog.

"It's Mrs. Brewster!" Jumping to her feet, Helen pushed the curtain to one side. Otto stood there alone.

"She's not coming. Her husband said she'd been called out on another delivery. She won't be back 'til tomorrow."

The curtain blocked her view of the Coopers, but Molly overheard their voices. "Is there anyone else you want me to fetch?" Otto asked.

"There's no one else in the settlement with her experience." There was a long pause, during which a chair scraped against the floor and one of them sat down. "Perhaps you could try Mrs. Cony. She's pretty young, but I know she's helped Mrs. Brewster a time or two."

Molly bit her lip to keep from crying out as another pain hit. Evidently she wasn't successful, because the chair pushed back immediately and she heard Otto's voice. "I'll go get her." The door banged shut, and Helen reappeared at the bedside.

"You heard?"

"Yes." Molly attempted a smile. "If she doesn't hurry, it will be all over."

"Water's heating. I'll put the sheets your brother brought next to the fire to warm them." Helen walked to the fireplace, leaving the bed curtains open.

The contractions came steadily. Molly pushed against them, but nothing happened. The pain in her back grew worse. Grabbing a corner of the quilt, she bit down hard to keep from screaming.

"Something's wrong, Helen! The baby's not coming." Tears ran down her cheeks. "Oh God, get this over with!"

An eternity later, Otto returned with Mrs. Cony, who hastened to Molly's bedside. As Helen had said, she appeared to be young, barely in her twenties. She removed her cloak and smiled tentatively at Molly. "How long have you been having bearing pains, Mrs. McGarvie?"

"I don't know." Molly gasped for breath. "A long time. The baby's not coming! Will you help me?"

The girl lifted Molly's shift and slipped her hand between her legs. "I don't feel the head." She turned and looked at Helen Cooper. "She's been attacked with severe obstructions." Her voice changed to a whine. "I've never helped at a birth like this—I don't know what to do." Stepping back from the bed, she wiped her hand on her apron.

Molly strained through another contraction. The baby didn't budge.

"Didn't your brother say there's a doctor with you?" Helen asked. "I think we should call him."

Weakly, Molly nodded agreement. She had no choice.

❧

As though from a great distance, Molly heard male voices. "Bring me a basin and some soap," one of them said. The curtain around the bed parted and Dr. Spengler stood beside her, drying his hands on a piece of toweling. Through her pain, Molly stared at the man who had allowed her son to wander off. She had no words for him. Instead, she turned her head away and waited to see what he would do.

86

He laid one hand on her forehead. It felt blessedly cool. "Try to relax as much as possible. I'm going to have to touch you." His fingers probed the birth canal while his reassuring voice kept up a gentle flow of words to distract her from the examination. "The baby seems to be face down." He pressed her belly, feeling for the position of the child. "I'm going to have to turn it over."

"How . . ."

"With an instrument called a forceps. I learned its use when I practiced medicine in Philadelphia." He placed a hand on her shoulder. "I'm afraid you'll lose this baby if I don't do it."

He left her side and she heard water splash in the basin. When he returned, the doctor held the two pieces of a gleaming, tong-like tool in the air. He laid a hand on her thigh, and with the other guided one blade of the forceps toward the baby. Molly screamed when he slid the second piece into place, the pressure inside almost too great to bear. More seconds of agony followed while he turned the infant. "When you feel the next contraction, push hard as you can."

She pushed, the doctor pulled, and the baby slipped free of her body, its head held by the surgical tool. When Dr. Spengler unfastened the clamp that held the forceps, the newborn sent up a tiny wail.

"A girl." He laid the baby on Molly's abdomen. "She's small, but perfect."

Molly covered her daughter with both hands, swept by waves of exhaustion. She felt the doctor deliver the afterbirth and place warm cloths over her loins. After draping her with a fresh sheet, he left the bedside.

"Thank you," Molly whispered after him.

She heard him talking to Helen Cooper, followed by the closing of the door to the cabin. After he left, Helen appeared at the bedside and gently took the baby from Molly's hands. "I'll bathe her for you. You rest."

∽

Lamplight formed a patch of yellow on the quilt covering Molly. She nursed her infant daughter, but after a brief time, the baby stopped suckling and slept. Molly turned her head on the pillow and saw Helen watching her.

In spite of having been up much of the night, Helen looked rested. Her hair appeared to have been freshly braided and was pinned in a coil at the back of her head. She wore a clean apron over her linsey-woolsey dress. "Doctor said you're not to worry about her not eating much at a time. Just be sure you feed her often until she can hold more—even if you have to wake her to do it."

Molly's gaze dropped to her newborn daughter. Her heart twisted in sorrow as she studied the purplish-red stains that marred the sides of her infant's delicate face. "She's marked, Helen." Molly blinked away tears. "It must be because of everything that's happened—Samuel dying, Franklin lost."

Helen moved closer to the bed and cupped her hands over the discoloration. "She's perfect in every other way. Perhaps it won't be so noticeable when she's bigger."

Molly looked up when she heard sounds outside the cabin, young voices mingling with the bass tones of grown men. Foggy gray dawn touched the thick window pane. The door opened and Matthew entered, followed by James and Luellen. Almost shyly, her visitors approached the bed. "I brought your young'uns to see their new sister," Matthew said. "They've been pestering me since before daybreak."

"Shouldn't you be out looking for Franklin?"

"I'm praying Ben's already found him." He glanced out the

window. "They're probably waiting at the landing for the ferry. But just in case, Otto's getting some men together. One of the fellows has a dog he swears can track anything. We should have Franklin back before suppertime tonight."

James ducked his head and sidled over to her. "Mama, I'm sorry I didn't watch Franklin better. Did I make you get sick?"

"No, Son." She slid her fingers through his thick hair, so like his father's. "You're not to blame." A cold fist closed around her heart at the thought of her youngest boy chilled and hungry, hunting for his family. *Please, God . . .*

She made an effort to smile and held the sleeping baby toward James. "What do you think of our Lily?"

Luellen pushed next to her brother. "She's awful little." She cocked her head and studied the infant closely. "And her face is smudgy."

"I think she's just fine," James said.

Matthew joined their comments. "Doc said she'd be some bruised by the forceps, but they should be gone in a few days."

"That's all it is? Bruises?" Relief surged through her. "Thank goodness! I thought I'd marked her with my worrying."

"Naw. Guess bruising's normal." Matthew dragged a chair to the bed and perched on the edge of the seat. "Doc says you need at least a week's lying in. Otto has two families willing to take the young'uns while you stay here."

"A week!" Molly struggled to push herself up on one elbow. "I can't lay here for a week. I want to go find my son."

"We'll find him for you. You need rest."

She pushed her aching body to a sitting position against the headboard. Men wouldn't know how to care for a frightened little boy. "Take food and blankets with you, and some dry clothes.

And when you find him, please tell him why I couldn't be there. I don't want him to think . . ."

Her brother loomed over the bed, pressing gently against her shoulder to urge her back onto the pillow. "I'll tell him all about his new sister. Don't you worry."

When her family left, Molly laid Lily beside her on the bed and then rolled over and faced the wall. She'd never tell anyone, but right now Molly didn't want this baby. She felt betrayed by her body. Trapped in bed while others searched for her son.

9

Molly rolled onto her side, glancing into the cradle at the sleeping face of her tiny daughter. Lily lay swaddled in the faded red bearing blanket that Molly had used for each of her children. Her eyelids were purple half-moons above a spot of a nose. Feathery swirls of black hair covered the top of her head.

Her eyes slid away from the infant and looked toward the fire where Helen stirred a pot hanging over the coals. "How late is it?"

Helen looked at the clock. "Going on toward suppertime. They should be back any minute now."

Outside the window, the sunset faded from vermillion to jaundiced yellow. Icy prickles coursed over Molly's body. "I thought sure they'd have Franklin back long before this. How far can a small boy run?"

Helen pulled a chair next to the cradle and sat. Her features softened as she studied the sleeping baby. "They probably took time to clean him up a bit before bringing him home. I'll bet he was dirty as anything."

Molly smiled, thinking of the many times she or Betsy had scrubbed Franklin clean after he'd spent a day playing in the mud.

"He can get dirty, all right. But Matthew should know I wouldn't care. I just want him back."

Before the men returned, the outside light had faded to black. When the door opened, Molly jerked upright, trying to see around Otto's stocky frame. "Franklin?"

Matthew strode to the bed.

One glance at his face told her they hadn't found her son. "Oh, Lord. No!" She rocked back and forth, keening. The sound of her wails awakened Lily. The baby's cries joined with Molly's until Helen lifted Lily from the cradle and put her in her mother's arms. Woodenly, tears streaming down her face, Molly placed the infant against her breast.

Matthew's hand stroked Molly's forehead, smoothing her tangled hair away from her temples. "We went back to where he disappeared, but guess his tracks got too trampled over yesterday. Couldn't find his trail."

Molly fought for control. "What about that dog? Didn't he find the scent?"

Matthew seemed to crumple. "We gave him one of Franklin's shirts to sniff, and for a few minutes it looked like he picked up a trail. Appears the boy went farther north than we figured he would."

"And?"

"Tracked him to the base of a big cottonwood, then lost the scent. It's like Franklin sprouted wings and flew." Her brother combed his fingers through his hair and then scrubbed his face with the palms of his hands. "We'll go out again tomorrow. It's possible he'll backtrack from wherever he's gone and be standing there waiting for us."

Beyond words, Molly studied her brother's stricken face. Would Franklin backtrack or keep running? She wished she knew. Of one thing she was certain: her son was alive and they had to find him.

⟋

Searchers went out each morning of Molly's confinement and each night returned with ever more discouraging reports. On the evening of the sixth day, Matthew came into the cabin alone. He perched on the edge of the bed and took her hand. "We're through searching." He closed his eyes briefly, as if in prayer. "You need to accept that Franklin's dead. No child could survive out there for this long." His voice caught. "We've done all we can."

Rain drizzled down the windowpane, while in the background a fire crackled on the open hearth. Molly knew she would remember this moment always. *This is how it feels to lose a child.* She'd used the word "brokenhearted" before, but never realized there could be actual physical pain. She pressed her hands against her chest and tried to breathe.

Matthew stirred, ready to rise.

She caught his hand. "Thank everyone. And bring James and Luellen to me. I need to have them here."

He nodded. "We'll leave for Beldon Grove when you feel up to traveling."

"Tomorrow. We'll go tomorrow."

That night, Molly lay awake listening to the breathing of her three children. The Coopers had pulled the trundle from under the bed, and James and Luellen slept on it. Lily lay bundled next to Molly, her tiny body radiating warmth. Molly remembered when Franklin was that small. Other memories flashed through her mind, scenes frozen in time. One minute he was a baby, and the next he was chasing Luellen around their cabin, teasing her. Then there was the day he'd come running when he lost his first tooth, proudly showing her the gap in his lower jaw. Every morning promised new adventure for Franklin.

Tears rolled from her eyes. The ache in her chest threatened to shut off her air. Gasping, she filled her lungs. Not to see him grow up—it was unbearable.

Her heart pounded, roaring filled her ears. Sound became words: "Franklin is not dead."

Startled, Molly glanced down at the trundle bed to see whether James had spoken in his sleep, but he lay with his face buried in his pillow. He couldn't have said the words, yet she'd heard them clearly. Moreover, she believed them. Molly knew she would see her son again. Sighing, she drifted into sleep.

As soon as light showed behind the glass pane, Molly swung her feet to the floor. After feeding Lily and supervising James and Luellen while they dressed, she slipped her black linen smock over her head and fumbled under the bed for her boots.

Otto descended the ladder from the loft, nodding a greeting at them before poking kindling into last night's coals to stir up the fire. Helen followed him down and hurried over to assist Molly. "Are you sure you're up to traveling today? We'd be glad for you to stay longer."

Molly shook her head. "We're not going to travel after all. We have to find Franklin first."

Otto swung around and gazed at her, his eyes wide. "Mrs. McGarvie . . ."

Helen slipped a cool hand across Molly's forehead.

She turned her head away. "I'm not feverish, I assure you. Franklin is alive. We must get him before we leave."

The Coopers exchanged glances. "At least wait until you've had breakfast." Helen used a voice suitable for soothing an irrational child. "Your brother will be here soon." She looked at Otto again.

"He'll know what to do." The last statement was directed at her husband.

Molly took a deep breath and surveyed the room. Everyone's eyes were fixed on her, alarm written across each face. *Even the children think I've lost my senses. How can I make them understand?*

Headed for the door, Otto sent her an artificial smile. "I'll go see what's keeping your party." He shrugged into his jacket and hurried out.

The iron skillet clanked on the hearthstones as Helen pushed it toward the fire to warm. "Cornmeal mush and salt pork ought to give us a good start to the day. Coffee'll be ready before you know it." Her words tumbled over themselves. "James, would you fetch a bucket of water?"

With a backward glance at his mother, James hurried to obey. Luellen wiggled up to sit next to Molly on the edge of the bed. "Mama, Uncle Matt told us Franklin is in heaven, like Papa. How can we find him? Heaven's too far away."

"Uncle Matt just thinks Franklin is in heaven. He's mistaken. Franklin is still here." The fragrance of boiling coffee and fried cornmeal made her mouth water. "Will you cook some extra?" she called to Helen. "We'll need it for Franklin."

Helen stared at her. "But—"

Matthew walked through the door and headed straight for Molly. He lifted Luellen from the spot beside her mother and sat down. His brown eyes searched hers. "We talked about this last night. You have to let him go. Don't torment yourself." Wrapping an arm around her, he cuddled her close. "I know what a blow this is, coming on top of everything that's happened to you. But you're not alone. You have me and my family to help you through it."

Molly felt his warm breath on the top of her head. She shrugged

95

free of his embrace so she could meet his gaze. "I know you mean well, but I heard a voice last night telling me that Franklin is alive."

Doubt, mingled with something like fear, crossed his face.

She hurried on. "It was a real voice, I know it was. He's out there waiting for us to find him."

Her brother heaved a deep sigh. "We've done all we could. There's no tracks, no scent, no evidence he's anywhere around. He's gone, Molly." Matthew stood. "Of course, Otto and the others around here will keep trying to find his . . . remains."

Molly flinched at his words and clapped her hands over her ears. She wanted to tell him they'd never find remains—Franklin was alive. But she knew Matthew wouldn't listen.

He wrapped his fingers around her wrist and gently pulled her to her feet. "The wagons are loaded. We're leaving today."

Mr. Wolcott and Dr. Spengler had come in and stood near the fire. On the table, platters of fried mush and salt pork steamed next to a stack of plates and forks. James and Luellen sat on a bench eyeing the food. Movement seemed suspended. Matthew's voice spoke in her ear. "Come and eat. You'll feel better."

Molly allowed herself to be guided to a seat. She hadn't given up— she'd wait until it was time to go and refuse to leave without Franklin. Then they'd be forced to resume the search.

After a silent meal, the men brought the wagons around to the front of the cabin. She bundled Lily against the chill air and followed James and Luellen out the door. Fog crouched over the river, obscuring the Missouri side where Franklin waited. Matthew approached her. "I'll take those two with me. You and the baby will be better off in the Dearborn."

She nodded, biding her time.

Matthew walked over to the covered carriage. "Let me help you." He held out his hand.

Molly folded her arms around Lily and stood her ground. "I'm not leaving without Franklin."

"I hate to do this, but you are." Her brother's hands closed around her waist. He picked her off her feet and set her on the carriage step. "Up you go."

She jerked backward and would have fallen had not Matthew pressed his hand against her back to hold her. Deliberately, she placed the baby on the seat, then swung around and faced her brother. "I'm not going. You can't force me."

Dr. Spengler joined them, holding his hat in his left hand. He exchanged a meaningful glance with Matthew.

"You!" Molly spat. "First, you let Franklin run off, now you refuse to let me wait for him."

He shook his head. His fingers clenched and unclenched around the brim of his hat. "I'm more sorry than you'll ever know, but we have to leave. There's nothing to be gained by spending more time here." His blue eyes were pools of regret.

Molly jumped from the carriage step and ran toward the river's edge, peering vainly through the white mist that rode over the water. Footsteps sounded behind her. Before she could go farther, Matthew's arms encircled her waist. "Stop it, Molly! You're not yourself."

She twisted in his grip, trying to break free. Otto pounded down the muddy riverbank toward them. In one hand he clutched a crockery jug. "Give her a drink of this—it'll calm her down."

Dr. Spengler blocked the man's approach. "No! Not whiskey!" He hurried to his wagon and fumbled in his medical bag while Matthew half walked, half carried his struggling sister to Mr. Wolcott's carriage. Dr. Spengler turned, holding a tin cup containing a dark liquid. With Matthew pinning Molly's arms to her sides, the doctor held the cup to her lips. "Drink this, Mrs. McGarvie."

Molly clamped her mouth shut and shook her head, but he pressed the cup against her lips until she opened them and swallowed. It tasted bitter.

"Just a little more."

Too tired to fight, she drank the remainder of the liquid. Within moments, warm lassitude flowed through her limbs, and she relaxed against her brother. Together, Matthew and the doctor lifted her into Ben's carriage and settled her on the backseat. Drowsily, she glanced down and saw Lily wrapped snugly in a rectangular box wedged between the seats.

"Let's go," Matthew said to Mr. Wolcott. "Doc says she'll sleep for several hours."

At the rear of the procession, Karl watched the wagons roll in front of him. As they left the river behind, the scenery changed from oaks and hickory to hackberry and briars, then to bluestem grass in autumn shades of tawny red. An endless sky stretched over the prairie, not broken by so much as a wisp of smoke. They were traveling in the same formation they'd used the day Franklin disappeared.

Alone, he had nothing but bitter thoughts to keep him company. *How could I have let this happen?* His mind circled around to the afternoon when the boys had gone off to pick crabapples.

Waiting his turn on the ferry, he'd leaned back on the wagon seat and pushed his hat over his eyes. Sun beat down on his shoulders. Before long, he'd slipped into a half doze. The boys' happy chatter came from somewhere on his left and he knew as long as he could hear them they were fine.

When he jolted awake, Karl realized it had been some time since he'd heard their boyish voices. He pushed his hat back on and jumped from the wagon seat. Looking through the brush toward the crabapple tree, he couldn't see Molly's sons. His first reaction was impatience. Disobedient children were high on his list of things to avoid.

He'd started into the brush after the boys when James ran up. "I can't find my brother!" His face looked pale in spite of the warm afternoon. The two of them searched until Ben Wolcott came up the road, calling that the ferry was back and waiting to take the next wagon over.

Now, seeing James and Luellen on the wagon seat next to Matthew, he cringed to think of their mother's hysteria at leaving her son behind. "Oh God, forgive me." Tears slid over his cheeks. As a doctor, he had pledged to do no harm. And he'd cost a mother her child.

A sound caught his attention. What was it? Karl tried to listen over the creak and rattle of the wagon and clop of horses' hooves. He heard it again—the tiny wail of a baby. Alarmed, he took his watch from his pocket and snapped the case open. They'd only been traveling for a couple of hours. Considering the amount of laudanum he'd given Mrs. McGarvie, she'd probably remain unconscious until noon. During the intensity of the moment, he'd forgotten that an early infant like Lily needed to eat often. He'd have to do something.

Karl closed his eyes and thought. The cow had been milked before they left Waring, and the milk left with Coopers. He studied the black and white animal plodding along behind his wagon. He'd only need a little bit, if she'd cooperate. Fingers between his lips, he whistled to Matthew and signaled him to stop.

After a tussle with the cow, who evidently sensed Karl's

inexperience at milking, he climbed onto the wagon seat with Lily in the crook of his arm. Wrapping a clean cloth strip from his satchel around his index finger, he held it in a bowl of milk until it was saturated. "Come on, little one," he coaxed, pushing the dripping cloth into her open, howling mouth. Her lips fastened around his finger and he felt a slight tugging. "Good." He hugged the infant to him, again and again dipping into the warm milk and transferring it to her waiting mouth.

Lily protested each time he had to pull away to re-saturate the cloth. James jumped from Matthew's wagon and came to watch him. "That's not how Mama does it."

Karl grinned. "No, I expect it isn't. But your mama's asleep and we don't want to disturb her."

James moved closer and climbed onto the wagon step, so that he stood near Karl's side. He spoke in a voice low enough not to be overheard. "Mama said Franklin is alive."

Nodding, Karl waited to hear what the boy would say next.

James leaned forward. "Do you think that's true?"

Do I give him hope or tell the truth? The doctor took a long moment to let the cloth absorb extra milk from the bowl. Once Lily's mouth fastened around his finger, he turned to meet James's earnest eyes. "Your mama is upset right now. When she's had time, she'll understand that your brother cannot possibly still be living."

The boy dropped his head and sobbed. Karl yearned to comfort him, but with the baby in his arms and her mouth clamped to his finger, he could do nothing but make soothing noises.

10

Molly stirred when she felt the Dearborn jolt through a mudhole. Thoughts jumbled in her head. She knew she was in a moving carriage, but where was she going, and why? Fragments of memory returned, floating like black feathers into her consciousness. Samuel's death. Betsy's absence. Suddenly she came wide awake. Franklin!

She bolted upright, fighting dizziness. Prairie grass swished against the side of the moving buggy. Mr. Wolcott glanced over his shoulder, concern showing on his face. "How are you feeling, Mrs. McGarvie?"

Molly ignored his question. "We left Franklin. How will he find us?"

Mr. Wolcott cleared his throat. "Your boy's gone, ma'am." He fixed his gaze on the trail ahead. "You rest yourself now. We'll stop and make camp soon."

Molly gripped the side of the buggy for support and dragged herself to her feet. She opened her mouth to demand that he let her out so she could go back to Waring. Then she remembered the scene with Matthew and Dr. Spengler. *No one believes me.* The expression on Mr. Wolcott's face told her that her presence made him uneasy. *They all think I'm out of my head.*

She dropped back onto the seat, wishing Betsy had been allowed to come with her. Betsy loved Franklin as much as she did. Together, the two of them would have been able to convince Matthew to turn back. She swallowed bitter regret. If she hadn't sent for Matthew in the first place, none of this would be happening.

When the wagons stopped for the night, Molly settled farther back into the shelter of the covered carriage, Lily in her arms. For now, she'd go along with their plans to travel to Beldon Grove.

The Dearborn swayed as Matthew swung Luellen up beside her. Molly kissed her daughter. "How's my big girl this afternoon?"

"Fine." Luellen's lower lip trembled.

Matthew scrutinized Molly's face. She knew he looked for signs of madness, so she straightened and tried to appear clear-eyed and rational. Apparently reassured, he relaxed and smiled. "This little gal missed her mama something fierce today. Do you think you'd feel up to riding with me and your young'uns tomorrow? We should be in Beldon Grove by early afternoon." As an afterthought, he added, "I've already stowed the cradle in the back of the wagon."

Molly looked at the rectangular box wedged between the seats. Lily would probably like the rocking motion of a cradle better than being jostled on the floor of the Dearborn. "Of course. It would be best for all of us to be together."

Her brother nodded. "Good." He turned toward the center of camp, where Mr. Wolcott piled wood on a snapping blaze. "Mrs. Cooper sent some venison stew for our supper. I'll warm it when the coals are ready."

"I'll take care of it. I'm fine, really," she lied.

He patted her hand. "That's my girl. You can leave James to watch Lily. I'll put the cradle in your tent."

Luellen hovered near while Molly transferred the stew to a large Dutch oven. She used both hands to place it in the coals, stepping back quickly to avoid flying sparks. In the process she nearly fell over Luellen, who stood directly behind her.

"Come, you can help me mix johnnycake." She led the clingy child to a makeshift kitchen at the back of Matthew's wagon. Helping her daughter stir the cornmeal, lard, and salt together with water was a familiar task and a comfortable one. She hoped by staying busy she'd be able to keep thoughts of her missing son at bay.

✐

Once the children were asleep, Molly stood, intending to slip out of the tent to get a cup of water. She paused a moment to study their faces in the dim light that penetrated the canvas walls. James, so earnest in all he did. She prayed he wouldn't suffer over Franklin's disappearance. It wasn't his fault. If only the doctor had been paying proper attention . . . Her eyes settled on Luellen, whose curls framed her face in sleep. Molly saw herself reflected in much of what Lulie did and said. In a flash of insight, she knew her daughter would be a little mother to the new baby.

And Lily. What would she grow up to be? Would Franklin be found while she was still small, so she'd know both of her brothers?

Her heart ached with love for her children. She was aware they'd been frightened of her that morning before they left Waring. *I can't let that happen again.* Molly tipped her head upward. "Lord, help me do right by these children. And bring Franklin back soon. Amen."

When she stepped outside, the chill evening air carried the acrid odor of wood smoke to her nostrils, while from the grass beyond camp a racket of crickets filled the air with discordant chirping. She glanced around the area lit by the blazing campfire. If possible, she wanted to avoid Dr. Spengler. Not seeing him, she headed for the water barrel attached to the side of Matthew's wagon. She'd just lifted the filled dipper to her lips when she heard a voice behind her. Startled, she jerked around and saw the doctor standing a few feet away.

"You frightened me, creeping up like that!" She stepped past him, holding her skirts close around her ankles as though avoiding a pile of horse droppings.

He reached out and placed a hand on her arm. "Mrs. McGarvie." Was that a pleading tone in his voice? "I can't say it enough. I'm sorry your son is gone, even more so since it was my responsibility to watch him. I hope one day you'll be able to forgive me."

Molly said nothing.

His shoulders sagged. "All right then." He turned, moved past the fire, and disappeared into the tent he shared with Matthew and Mr. Wolcott.

True to Matthew's prediction, by midafternoon the next day they passed cultivated farmland, rattled across a plank bridge spanning a creek, and stopped at the rear of a new-looking, two-story frame house. "Well, this is it," he said.

Molly studied his home. "My goodness. This is nearly as big as Colonel Cross's place in St. Lawrenceville."

"Figured since I was building I might as well make room for plenty of young'uns. We just moved in a few months back."

He pointed down the lane in the direction of a whitewashed log home they'd passed on the way. "Back there's the place I bought when we first came here in 'thirty-six. Ellie's Aunt Ruby and Uncle Arthur live there now."

Molly sensed he was talking too much to try to lift her out of her melancholy. "It's very nice."

The back door of the house opened, and a young woman stepped onto the covered porch. She jiggled a squalling baby in her arms. Raising her voice over the child's howls, she called to Matthew. "Praise God! I couldn't imagine what happened to you."

"A tragic occurrence." He set the wagon brake and walked to her side.

Even though he kept his voice low while he related the events of the past week, Molly heard bits of his version of Franklin's disappearance. *I wish he'd stop saying Franklin's dead. He's not.*

The woman hurried down the steps toward the wagon, shifting her infant to one shoulder. She looked up at Molly. "I'm Ellie." Her eyes filled with tears. "There are no words. You're welcome here for as long as you need to stay."

"Thank you. I'm grateful." She surveyed the farmhouse with its three sets of double-hung windows lining the second floor. While she wondered where she and the children would sleep, the door to what she presumed to be the kitchen flew open again, and identical twin boys hurtled out. When they saw Matthew, they raced off the porch and grabbed his legs.

"Papa! Papa!" Their father dropped to one knee and hugged them, calling an introduction over his shoulder to Molly. "Jimmy and Johnny." Turning to his wife, Matthew asked, "Where's Harrison?"

"Asleep upstairs." Ellie patted the fussy infant. "I can't get Maria to settle down. Aunt Ruby's supposed to come over later and help me."

Matthew held his hand out to Molly. "C'mon in—you need

to rest." Carrying Lily, she followed him up the steps. Her two older children trailed silently at her heels, apparently overcome by shyness.

Numb with heartache, Molly's brain registered the details of Ellie's kitchen through a fog of grief. One wall held a tall blue-painted cupboard, the cabinet under the window contained an oiled wooden sink, and to her left stretched a long plank table lined on both sides with an assortment of slat-backed chairs. A shiny black cookstove sat in the rear corner of the room.

Her mother had trained her to show courtesy regardless of circumstance, so Molly turned to her sister-in-law and forced a smile. "Papa always said Matthew would starve to death on a preacher's pay. It looks like he was wrong."

"He doesn't earn a great deal from our little church, certainly, but we won't starve as long as we have good farmland." A hint of pride inched into Ellie's voice. "Matthew made most of our furniture himself."

Molly blinked away sudden tears. "Samuel made ours too."

Ellie's expression softened. She slipped her free arm around Molly's waist. "Come upstairs with me. Let's get you settled."

⟋

After supper Matthew and Dr. Spengler went to the barn to unload the farm wagons. Molly remained in the kitchen, sitting across the table from Ellie and Ellie's Aunt Ruby. Through the open door she watched the sunset push through broken rain clouds, making the sky look like a bed of hot coals.

Ruby's voice brought her attention back inside. "Ellie's still not strong, you know." She had a habit of smiling and nodding while she spoke, giving the impression that what she said should be agreeable to everyone who heard her.

Molly had already lost count of the smiles and nods. She tried to seem interested, but all she wanted to do was go to bed and pull the quilts over her head. If she could sleep, she could stop thinking about Franklin for a few hours.

"Oh, Aunt, Maria's almost five months old. I'm fine!" Ellie's pale skin and tired eyes belied her statement.

Molly leaned back in her chair, studying the two women. They both had hair the color of the golden tow fiber she spun to weave toweling and grain sacks. When they smiled, their blue eyes crinkled at the corners in an identical fashion, but where Ellie's smile seemed open and trusting, Ruby's expression held a hint of smugness. As they sat side by side, Molly could almost see the invisible cord that bound Ellie to her aunt.

They haven't been apart since Ellie was three years old. Seventeen years. Her mind jumped back to her own childhood. *Betsy and I were together longer than that.* The image of Betsy walking toward Brody's slave cabins filled her mind. *If only she could be here with me.*

She stiffened when Dr. Spengler entered the kitchen with her brother. Matthew rested a hand on Molly's shoulder. "We've got your movables stored in the barn. Do you need anything more brought in for tonight?"

"No. The children are already tucked in bed. I'll worry about the rest in the morning."

Matthew shifted his gaze to Ellie. "Doc's going to stay the night. We're going out early tomorrow to go goose-hunting. Be good for him."

Molly closed her eyes at his insensitivity. Didn't he realize that the sight of the doctor added to her pain?

Karl's trousers were wet to the waist from tramping through tall grass. He and Matthew had left the farm before daylight to make their way to a nearby pond. A trace of wood smoke drifted through the damp morning air. As its fragrance washed over him, Karl felt the heavy depression he carried start to evaporate.

Matthew stopped walking near a patch of low-growing willows. "Here's where I usually take cover. They'll be along soon, I'd say."

A spot had been cleared behind the brush. Karl noticed that someone, probably Matthew, had dragged a short log into the clearing for a bench. "Looks like you come here a fair bit."

"Yep." Matthew settled himself on the log and patted a space beside him. "Get down where they can't see you when they fly over."

Karl sat, resting his shotgun across his lap. "It's good to get away from your sister's stricken face." Pulling off his hat, he combed his fingers through his hair. "How could I have let it happen?"

Matthew's eyes shone with compassion. "Losing the boy could have happened to any of us. Even Molly. One minute children are underfoot and the next they're heaven knows where. Franklin's not the first child to be swallowed up by the frontier." He squeezed Karl's shoulder. "I wish the Lord had spared Molly this, though."

"Do you think she'll be all right?"

"I pray she will. Her insistence that the boy's alive worries me."

A flock of geese honked into hearing range. They flew low overhead, their feet out for a landing on the misty water of the pond, their outstretched wings braking their descent. Karl lifted his shotgun and followed the trajectory of a descending bird. He aimed his shot slightly in front of its head. Matthew's shotgun blast echoed after his. The sound of gunfire caused the remainder of the flock to veer up and away from the clearing.

They ran to the pond's edge, carrying their smoking weapons, and discovered two birds floating in the shallows.

"Good shooting." Matthew clapped Karl on the back. "Now let's get them out of the water before they drift too far away." Once they had the geese cleaned, the men returned to the blind.

Karl remained standing, stretching stiffness out of his shoulders. "Tomorrow I'm headed north. I'll stop when I find a village that doesn't have a medico—and wants one."

"You could stay on at Beldon Grove. We haven't had a doctor here since Doc Beavers froze to death in a blizzard."

"I'm set on going. It'd be best if I put some distance between me and your poor sister." He picked up his shotgun. "I'll miss your friendship, though."

Matthew clasped the doctor's arm. "You'll not lose that."

Although grateful for his reassurance, what Karl most longed for Matthew couldn't provide: Molly's forgiveness.

11

October 1838

Several days after Dr. Spengler's departure, Ruby's husband, Arthur, pushed open the back door of Craigs' farmhouse, his arms piled with firewood. Small bits of sawdust and bark clung to his boots, leaving a trail on the floor.

Ruby's voice cut across the room. "You're making a mess!"

Without acknowledging his wife, he dropped the wood next to the stove and walked out.

Molly looked after him, puzzled. Matthew's family did all they could to make her feel a part of things, but she still felt lost. Each morning she had to will herself to rise and care for her children. Franklin's absence tore at her heart, and not a day went by that she didn't wish Betsy were with them.

She dragged her thoughts back to the kitchen. "Is Arthur deaf? He doesn't always answer you when you speak to him."

Ruby snorted. "He can hear me, all right. The old cuss just won't talk!"

Ellie spoke from a rocking chair next to the stairs. "Once you get to know him, he's the sweetest man you'll ever meet. But for some reason, it takes him forever to answer when you ask him a question."

Matthew and Ellie's five-year-old twin sons clattered down the stairs into the kitchen. "Aunt Molly, where's James?" one of them asked. "We want to play with him."

"Which one are you again? I still can't tell you apart."

"I'm Johnny. It's easy to tell the difference—see Jimmy's ear? It's wrinkled."

Molly studied the red-haired boy's right ear. Instead of a smooth curve, the outside of his ear bent downward, as though large fingers had folded it under. "Sure enough. I see it now." She smiled at both of them. "James went to the barn with your papa."

The boys sprinted out, banging the door behind them.

Molly turned to Ellie. "Such bright youngsters." She swallowed the ache that rose in her throat. "Franklin's just a year older than they are."

"He was six?"

"He is six."

Ruby leaned against the blue cupboard next to the stove. "He can't possibly be alive after all this time."

Anger flashed through Molly. "He can and he is!"

Folding her arms across her chest in a gesture that said "prove it," Ellie's aunt raised an eyebrow. "How do you figure?"

The three women had the kitchen to themselves. If she explained her reasons, surely they'd understand. "Wagons travel along the Missouri side of the Mississippi from time to time. I believe someone found him and rescued him."

Ruby bore in, apparently determined to convince Molly of Franklin's untimely end. "You poor thing. If someone found him on the trail—and mind you, that's a mighty big if—wouldn't he tell them where he belonged?"

Molly fought to keep her temper under control. "What could

he say? 'I'm going to my Uncle Matthew's'? He's a little boy! How would he know where Matthew lives?"

"There's no need to snap at me. I'm just pointing out facts."

"A family has taken him in and one day I'll find him. Those are the facts."

The back door clicked open, breaking the uncomfortable silence that filled the room. Arthur entered again, carrying one of the trunks Molly had brought from Missouri. "You'll be needing this, I reckon. You want it upstairs?" His gaze lingered on her face.

Molly's heart pounded and she knew her cheeks must be flushed with anger. She drew a calming breath. "Yes. Please."

Arthur glanced at his wife's set expression, then back at Molly, a look of understanding crossing his features. He placed the trunk on the floor and rested one hand lightly on her shoulder. "Which bedroom, my dear?"

"The one that faces east." She felt kindness in his touch and sensed she'd found an ally.

He hoisted his burden, heading for the stairs. "Give me a holler if there's anything else you need. I'm glad to help."

After he clomped up the steps, Ruby stared hard at Molly and shook her head. Ellie had smiled at Arthur when he came in, but now she dropped her gaze, fiddling with the hem of her apron. Molly wanted to scream. *Why won't they believe me?*

Ruby crossed the room and drew the curtains, shutting out the sight of drizzling rain. She turned toward Molly, not quite meeting her eyes. "Don't you need to go up and feed Lily? Not that I'm an expert, but I think it's time you woke her to nurse."

❧

Molly's mind turned over her options while she fed her infant. She couldn't remain at Matthew's, that's all there was to it. She

112

needed to find a cabin where she and her children could live. Then she'd be free to work on the means to bring Betsy to Illinois. Once Betsy arrived, Molly could leave the children with her and travel back across the river to search for the family that had Franklin. True, it would take time to earn money to purchase the Negro woman, but without Betsy she had no way to go find her son. Matthew already believed Molly to be unhinged. There'd be no help from that quarter. Maybe Uncle Arthur? He seemed sympathetic.

Lily's eyelids drooped shut, so Molly patted and tickled her cheeks to awaken her. Startled, the infant jerked in her mother's embrace, flailing her arms. Her high-pitched cry sounded feeble in contrast to Luellen's lusty wails when she was a baby. "Just eat a little more," Molly whispered. "You have lots of growing to do." She kissed the silky hair on top of the baby's head, her heart humming with love. *How could I have ever felt I didn't want you?* Lily was a final legacy from Samuel that Brody had no power to take away.

Once the infant resumed nursing, Molly leaned back on the pillow, again considering plans for the future. One thing she knew— she'd have to go along with everyone's opinion that Franklin had died somewhere on the banks of the Mississippi. Otherwise, Matthew would never permit her to take the children and live away from his protection.

The bedroom door swung silently inward. Luellen stood on the threshold, clutching a rag doll in her chubby fist. "Mama? I came to see Lily."

Molly smoothed the coverlet beside her. "Come up here. I've missed you this afternoon."

"I played in the barn with the boys, but now I'm tired of them."

113

Suppressing a smile, Molly stroked the curls that escaped her daughter's braids. She suspected the boys were tired of Luellen tagging after them too. "You can hold Lily's hand when she's through nursing."

The child snuggled close. Before long, the three of them fell asleep.

◯

The aroma of fried ham roused Molly. Her stomach rumbled. *I meant to go down and help with supper. I need to mend fences with Ruby.* She lifted the sleeping infant and settled her in the cradle, making sure the blanket was snug around Lily's shoulders.

Luellen stirred and sat up, rubbing her eyes. "Where are you going?"

"To help Aunt Ruby with supper."

"Me too." Luellen jumped to the floor.

When they descended the stairs into the kitchen, Molly saw Ruby poking something on the stove with a long-handled fork. Ellie sat in her rocking chair holding Maria. "You should've called me to help, Aunt Ruby," Molly said when she reached the foot of the stairs.

"No need. I have everything in hand."

"Have the boys come in from the barn?"

Ellie's foot tapped against the wooden floor, keeping the chair in motion. "They're still out back. Harrison's in a pout because Matt let James help with the milking."

"It's good of him to make James feel useful. That boy thrives on responsibility." Molly walked to the stove and raised the lid on a heavy iron pot. "Butter beans! My favorite." She sent Ruby an ingratiating smile. "Please let me help. I feel useless without something to do."

The older woman's reply was edged in ice. "You need to get your strength back. Sit."

Molly sighed. Ruby wasn't one to forgive quickly.

When James ran into the room, Molly opened her arms to hug him. His face felt damp and cool from being out in the moist autumn air. "I hear you've been helping your uncle. Your papa would be proud—I know I am."

Her son managed to look pleased and embarrassed at the same time. "Aw, Mama, I milked Flossie for you and Betsy all the time."

Matthew entered with Jimmy and Johnny. Uncle Arthur trailed behind, carrying Harrison piggyback. After everyone squeezed around the table, Ruby set the pot of beans in the center and plopped a platter of browned ham slices down next to it.

While Matthew asked a blessing on the food, Molly bowed her head and offered a silent prayer that the Lord would provide a vacant cabin—and show her a way to get Betsy to Illinois—soon.

⌒

Wrapped in a thick shawl and wearing heavy woolen gloves, Betsy trudged through the pre-dawn grayness toward Brody McGarvie's barn. She studied the ragged hem of her dress with disgust. "Shoveling stalls! Feeding horses! If Miz Molly could see me now, she'd probably faint."

Reuben met her at the door with a lantern in his hand. "Morning, Betsy. You look about half froze."

"More'n half!" She looked up at his friendly face. "No matter how early I start, you're here before me." She laughed. "D'you ever sleep?"

Reuben's deep chuckle rumbled toward her. "Sure I does. But

knowing you'll be here first thing pulls these eyes open before daylight."

He opened the barn doors, hanging the lantern on a nail above bagged grain. Brody's horses whickered and stirred in their stalls at the sound of voices.

Betsy crouched in the pool of light and struggled to move one of the filled tow sacks. Reuben reached over and took it from her as easily as if it had been filled with goose down rather than fifty pounds of oats.

She stepped to one side. "Mr. Brody said I'm supposed to do the feeding. If he sees you doing it, we'll both suffer."

"When was the last time he was down here at this hour of the morning?" He selected a froe from its hook on the wall. "These is good for more'n splitting shingles." Reuben used the wedge-shaped blade to slit open the top of the sack. After measuring a portion of grain for each horse, he returned to a stall containing a handsome chestnut stallion. "Mr. Brody surely sets a store by this one." Reuben patted the animal's neck. "He's gwine race him again come Saturday—if it don't rain, that is."

"He takes better care of his horses than he does us colored folks."

Reuben frowned. "Now, Betsy. Don't get yourself riled. We do best if we just try to get along."

"Easy for you, maybe. You've always been Mr. Brody's boy."

He stood the opened sack on the floor and walked over to Betsy. Placing one of his broad hands on her shoulder, Reuben pinned her with a stony glare. "It ain't easy! Never has been. But you'll make less trouble for yourself and the rest of us if you just keep quiet and do what you're told." His tone changed. "I'm afraid for you. Wouldn't take much for Mr. Brody to decide you're a troublemaker and up and sell you. I seen him do it before." He squeezed her shoulder and softened his voice. "I don't want to lose you."

Betsy placed a hand over his. "I'm sorry. I'll try and remember what you said."

His eyes held hers a moment longer, then he picked up the grain scoop and continued feeding the horses.

As he moved down the line of stalls, Betsy lifted a shovel and opened the first stall door. Its occupant, a roan gelding, chewed a mouthful of oats as she scooped piles of manure out to the center of the barn. While she worked, the animal moved its legs backward and shot a hot stream of urine onto the stable floor, splattering her cracked leather boots. *Not today!* She backed out and scrubbed at her footwear with an empty grain sack. Most of the soil came away, but telltale dampness against her toes told her some of the horse's waste had seeped inside the boots. Disgusted, she tossed the sack aside. *Daylight's coming on. I best get back to shoveling.*

When she finished cleaning stalls, Betsy climbed to the loft and forked down fresh hay. Below, she saw Reuben transferring piled manure into a cart to be taken out and dumped behind the barn. "I'm going to work for Miz Marjolaine today," she called to him.

"Good." Reuben grunted between scoops. "She'll have a filling dinner for you."

"I'll bring you back something if I can."

He flashed her a smile. "Just bring yourself back. That be enough for me."

She felt herself flush. For such a big man, Reuben had the softest heart she'd ever known. *He treats me like Mr. Samuel treated Miz Molly.*

❧

117

Betsy hurried up the steps and let herself in Marjolaine Cross's back door, hoping she'd cleaned her boots thoroughly enough. She removed a folded apron from a shelf in the storage room and slipped it over her shoulders.

Miz Marjolaine looked up from an open silverware chest and sniffed the air when Betsy entered the warm kitchen. Her nose wrinkled. "Smells like you just came from a stable."

Cheeks burning, Betsy ducked her head in apology. "I did, ma'am. Sorry. I got no other shoes."

"Then leave them by the back door. I'll bring you a pair of Mr. Cross's old slippers to wear while you're here."

"Thank you." Betsy hurried to remove the offending boots.

Miz Marjolaine stepped to the stove and lifted a steaming kettle. "I was just about to make the tea." She poured hot water into a cream-colored teapot, its handle shaped like the letter *D*. "Did Mr. McGarvie give you difficulty about coming here today?"

"No, ma'am. Long as he gets his share of what you pay me, he's happy to let me go." Betsy pulled two cups and saucers from a cupboard, placing them on the worktable. As was their custom, she poured tea for both of them. "Truth is, he don't have that much for me to do. I suspect the only reason he claimed me was to spite Miz Molly."

Rubbing the frown line between her eyebrows, Miz Marjolaine replied, "Of course that's why he did it. Why else would he take a good house girl and put her to work in his stables?"

House girl! For the second time that morning, Betsy felt the sting of reality. Miz Molly had called her a friend. She placed her cup back in its saucer. "I'd best get to polishing that silver."

"Thank you, Betsy." Miz Marjolaine carried her tea to the kitchen door. "Call me when you've finished. I'll want to count everything before I lock the chest."

118

Betsy buffed the fleur-de-lys design stamped into the back of a curved soup ladle. Miz Marjolaine had a sharp eye for spotting stains, so Betsy rubbed each piece until it gleamed. Polished silverware rested on a bleached linen towel nearby. She'd reached for a serving fork when a knock at the front door summoned her to the foyer.

"Dr. Spengler! What're you doing here?"

He stepped inside. "I might ask you the same thing. Are you part of the Cross household now?"

Betsy reached up and helped him remove his coat. "No sir. Mr. Brody hires me out when Miz Marjolaine needs someone." She hooked his coat on a peg next to the door and hung his hat over it. "Tell me, how's Miz Molly? I miss her something fierce! And the chil'ren? My little Franklin? The new baby, is it born yet?"

Dr. Spengler held up a hand to stop the outpouring. "Mrs. McGarvie is well. But I have terrible news about Franklin."

Miz Marjolaine hurried into the room. "I thought I heard a knock. Dr. Spengler! Welcome! What brings you back to St. Lawrenceville?"

"I came to see my family. I'm concerned about my mother . . . my mother's health." He bit off the words, his tone discouraging further questions.

"Well . . ." She seemed taken aback by his abrupt manner. "I hope you've brought news of Molly?"

"I have. Not all good, I'm afraid."

"Oh, no! Come, tell me about it." She held open the door to the parlor. "Betsy will bring us some tea."

He glanced at the Negro woman before answering. "I'll be along in a moment. Betsy wants to hear this too."

"Well, both of you come in then. Betsy, the silver can wait—it isn't going anywhere."

"Thank you, ma'am. I'll fix a tray and be right back."

When Betsy entered the parlor, she carried the tea service to a tripod table on Miz Marjolaine's right. As she handed Dr. Spengler his filled cup, she noticed him studying her.

"Are you getting enough food at McGarvie's? You seem a mite twiggy."

Betsy stepped away from his chair and stood near the fireplace, wondering how to reply. Reuben's admonition echoed in her mind. *Wouldn't take much for Mr. Brody to decide you're a troublemaker and up and sell you.* "Things is fine. Just haven't been too hungry lately."

Miz Marjolaine interjected, "Why, that's not true. When you're here you eat everything—" She stopped abruptly. Comprehension crossed her features, followed by an appraising look. "Hmm. Well, Doctor, please tell us what's happened to Molly."

"When we crossed the Mississippi, Franklin got lost in the brush along the bank." He swallowed hard. "It was my fault."

Betsy remembered crossing the river on the journey from Kentucky. The Missouri side was a tangle of brambles and scrubby trees. It wouldn't take long for a child to disappear. "How bad was he hurt?"

A flush climbed Dr. Spengler's cheeks. "We never found him."

Miz Marjolaine's teacup clattered to the saucer. "What! Her husband, and now one of her children?" She fixed a penetrating gaze on the doctor. "How exactly was it your fault?"

He told them of the circumstances of the crossing, and of the days spent afterward searching for the boy. "Eventually, we had to give up. No one ever found a trace of him."

Betsy wiped a tear from her cheek. Her lively little Franklin, gone. At the same time, she recognized the misery on Dr. Spengler's face. "You oughtn't take all the blame. Franklin was always one to run off and hide. He thought it was funny, scaring folks." She swept her hands over her cheeks to remove the tears that continued to fall. "Can't tell you how many times I done paddled him for it."

Her employer took charge of the conversation. "How is dear Molly holding up? Has her child been born?"

"Yes, she had a girl. Right after the boy disappeared. The baby was born early, but seemed to be doing well." He cleared his throat. "I haven't seen Mrs. McGarvie since I left her brother's house last month. She was still . . . recuperating at the time."

Miz Marjolaine spread her fingers over her heart. "I would imagine so."

Betsy's thoughts spun. Miz Molly needed her and she wasn't there. The two of them had shared every heartache and joy since they were girls. *There's got to be a way.* "When the Lord closes a door, he opens a window."

She didn't realize she'd spoken aloud until Miz Marjolaine looked at her sharply. "What window would that be?"

"No special window, ma'am. I'm just talking." Betsy lowered her eyes. *I need to send word to Miz Molly. Can I trust him to do it?* She clenched her fists inside her apron pockets, trying to devise a way to talk to the doctor without arousing her employer's curiosity.

Miz Marjolaine turned back to her guest. "Do tell me more about the baby. And the others, James and Luellen."

Betsy listened to their conversation, glad to hear news of the children but at the same time wishing he'd get to the end of his visit so she could find a moment to speak to him alone. *I got to be back at Mr. Brody's before sundown, and the silver still ain't done.*

As though reading her thoughts, Miz Marjolaine glanced her way. "Perhaps you'd better get back to your work, Betsy. You'll have to leave soon."

Betsy felt like a candle whose glow had been snuffed. No chance now to get a message to Miz Molly. "Yes'm."

Dr. Spengler checked the time on his pocket watch. "I'd no idea it was so late. I've got quite a bit of riding to do yet today." He stood and bowed over his hostess's lifted hand. "Thank you for the tea."

"It is I who must thank you. How good of you to bring me news of dear Molly, sorrowful as it is."

Returning to the foyer, Betsy held the doctor's coat while he pushed his arms into it. After polite good-byes Dr. Spengler left the house, striding down the brick path toward the hitching post.

Cold, damp air oozed into the entryway through the open door. Betsy shivered, wishing she hadn't left her shawl draped over a kitchen chair. "I'll stay your horse whilst you mount," she called after him.

Miz Marjolaine moved forward. "I'm sure he can manage his own horse."

Betsy ducked around her and scurried after the doctor. Taking the reins from his hand, she held the horse's head while the doctor put one foot in the stirrup and swung into the saddle. She shot a quick glance over her shoulder. *Good. Miz Marjolaine shut the door.*

Dr. Spengler's eyes met hers. "What is it, Betsy? Is there something you want to say?"

She studied his face for a moment. One part of her mind argued that since he was a white man she'd be a fool to trust him. *But he's a friend to Rev'rund Matthew. If he trusts him, I'll have to take the chance.*

Her words tumbled out. "If you please, tell Miz Molly I'm saving everything what Miz Marjolaine pays me so I can buy my freedom. But it's taking such a long time. I need to be with her right now." Betsy moved closer to the saddle. The horse snuffled her shoulder, its breath warming her chilled flesh. Lowering her voice, she said, "When Mr. Wolcott was here, he told me how to get away on the Railroad. I can always do that."

Dr. Spengler shook his head. "No. Don't. From all I've heard, the Railroad's much too dangerous. Brody McGarvie could send slave hunters after you with dogs, then have you whipped when you're caught."

"*If* I'm caught. Me and Reuben talk about it sometimes when we're cleaning the stable. He knows lots of places to hide along the river, on account of him fishing all the time."

"Betsy, no. Forget running away."

Cold penetrated the coarse weave of her dress. Lead-colored clouds rolled overhead, promising a storm by nightfall. "You don't understand. If I was to forget running away, I'd have no hope at all."

12

Late October 1838

Molly stopped in front of the bedroom window and stared out at the frosted landscape. Thin sunshine sliced between gathering clouds. From her vantage point, she saw Matthew's fields spreading to the east, covered with scabs of frozen puddles. *I've waited long enough. I need a place of my own.*

She turned and reached for the latch. Uncle Arthur had gone to the barn after dinner. She'd go right now and ask him to search out an abandoned cabin where she could settle with her children. He'd proved himself a trusted friend over the weeks she'd been at Matthew's. If anyone could help her, it would be Arthur.

Ruby looked up in surprise when she hurried into the kitchen. Molly stopped next to Luellen, who stood on a chair near the worktable. "Come on. Let's take a walk."

"I want to stay here." Luellen pointed to a crockery bowl. "I'm helping Aunt Ruby make pie."

The older woman placed flour-dusted hands on her hips and shot a disapproving glance at Molly. "Where do you think you're going in this cold? You'll catch your death."

"Out to the barn." Molly grabbed her shawl from a peg beside the back door.

Once on the porch, she noticed that one of the double doors on the barn stood ajar. A whap-whapping sound echoed from within. When she entered, she saw Uncle Arthur and Matthew standing to her left, rhythmically beating the flax stalks she'd brought from her cabin in Missouri. The floor at their feet was covered with dried husks and short, tan-colored tow fibers. She walked over to where they worked, loose strands of flax swirling in front of her skirt like feathers.

Molly's eyes filled with grateful tears. "When did you start the swingling? I didn't even know you'd broken the stalks!" She bit her lip. "How can I thank you?"

Arthur glanced up and grinned at her, not missing a beat in his steady rhythm. Matthew rested his paddle on the workbench and brushed lint from his beard. "No need for thanks. It had to be done—you'll want to start spinning soon, I expect."

"You're a wonder! How do you know so much about linen?"

"Same way you do. Watching Mama. Except I didn't ever learn to spin or weave." He chuckled. "Not that I want to know. That's woman's work."

Arthur leaned his paddle against one leg and rubbed the back of his neck. "What brings you out here, Molly? Ruby chase you out of her kitchen?" His eyes twinkled at her.

"No. I came to talk to you." Molly darted a glance at Matthew. She'd hoped to talk to Arthur alone, but both men looked at her expectantly. "I want you find a cabin for me and the children. I know there are places that were abandoned during the troubles with Black Hawk—you told me about them, Matthew. If it's sound, I don't care how dirty it is. A little hard work could put it right."

Arthur removed his hat and scratched the top of his head. "I

125

believe there's one just the other side of town, isn't there, Matt? The old Barker place?"

Matthew frowned at him and then turned to Molly. "I don't think you should do that. Not yet, anyways. It's too soon."

Irritation rose in Molly's throat. She narrowed her eyes and looked at her brother. "We were on our own in St. Lawrenceville after Samuel died. I managed."

"I'm not talking about how you'd live." He paused, evidently searching for the right words. "Ellie said you told her—"

"That was just wishful thinking." *God forgive the lie.* "The children and I need to make our own way. The sooner the better."

❧

Molly sat in a straight-backed chair in the chilly sitting room, combing strands of flax through the sharp teeth of an iron hetchel to smooth and prepare it for spinning. Since her conversation with her brother and Arthur the previous week, she'd been unable to concentrate on much other than moving herself and her children into their own cabin.

Aunt Ruby leaned in the open doorway. "I've said it before and I'll say it again. It's dangerous to have these bundles in the house—one spark and we'll go up in flames."

Molly rubbed her cold hands together to warm them. "What spark, Aunt?" She pointed at the empty fireplace. "This has to be hetcheled before I can spin it, and it's too damp in the barn. There'll be no fire in here until I start the spinning."

Arthur appeared in the doorway behind his wife. "Smells like something on the stove's a-burning."

"The potatoes!" Ruby hurried down the hall into the kitchen.

Molly smiled at Arthur gratefully. "You're a dear."

He grinned, rubbing his bald head. "Want some company?"

Without waiting for her answer, he settled himself in a worn armchair next to the north-facing window.

"Sometimes Ruby forgets this isn't her house. Ellie was a sickly little thing when we took her in after her parents died. Ruby's doted on her every moment since." He leaned forward, resting his hands on his knees. Lowering his voice, he continued, "I think it's time she backed off. Ellie needs to learn to manage her own household. Ruby and me won't be around forever."

Surprised at what was a long speech for Arthur, Molly stopped working and gazed at him, golden tan fibers draped over her hand.

His eyes held a merry glint. "Want to go for a ride in the buggy?"

"In this weather?"

"It's not raining that hard, and I've got something to show you."

Molly felt a prickle of excitement. She laid the combed flax on her lap and dropped a wooden cover over the wicked teeth of the hetchel. "I'll have to bring Luellen and the baby."

"Bundle them up good. They'll be fine."

"Does Ruby know about this?"

"Not yet. We'll slip out the front door before she misses us. Run upstairs and get your young'uns."

☙

Molly looked around as they passed the town square, checking cabins for signs of smoke coming from chimneys. If it didn't have a fire, most likely no one lived there. Ahead on her right she noticed a blacksmith's shop, reminding her with a pang of Cody and Jewel Stanton in St. Lawrenceville. When the buggy rolled past, she glimpsed the smithy bent over his forge inside. She wondered if he and his wife were as kindly as the Stantons.

Molly blinked when Arthur pointed to a building fifty yards or so farther up the road and on the opposite side from the blacksmith's. It was a dogtrot cabin with stone chimneys at both ends, obviously deserted.

"Here it is. This is the one I told you about."

She raised her eyebrows. *I know I told him I didn't care how dirty it was, but this place looks like a rat's nest!*

In the covered area between the two square log rooms, piles of drifted leaves had mounded in the open doorways. A lone shutter hung like forgotten laundry from one side of a blank hole cut in the logs to form a window. She glanced at Uncle Arthur, fighting to keep dismay from showing on her face.

"Want to go inside, see if it'll do?" Arthur asked, oblivious to her distress. He reached up to help her out of the buggy, still talking. "I can make new doors 'n' shutters real quick—we'll have it looking like home in no time."

She followed him through sticky mud into the shelter of the dogtrot. Arthur bent and hoisted Luellen into his arms. "We'll just wait here while you look around. I checked it over yesterday. The roof is sound and the chimneys should draw good once they're swept clean."

Gingerly, Molly stepped into the room to her right. A square of damp lay under the window where rain had blown in. A large kitchen hearth, with its crane and lug pole still attached, filled part of the far wall. The packed earth floor had been covered by seasons of leaves and wind-scattered debris, giving it a spongy feel underfoot. In her memory she saw her parents' large farm in Kentucky, then the comfortable cabin she'd left in Missouri.

Samuel had worked so hard to give them a good life. What would he think to see her in a place like this?

Searing anger at Brody McGarvie choked her. If not for him, she'd still be in St. Lawrenceville with all of her children and Betsy. Molly took a deep breath. It did no good to agonize over what might have been. *That was then. This is now.* She turned toward the doorway and crossed the dogtrot, entering the other half of the dwelling.

This side had a smaller fireplace and a window opening in the west-facing wall with a similar patch of damp beneath it. By hanging a lantern, she could work at her loom in here. She closed her eyes and tried to visualize the cabin with the floors swept clean, doors and shutters installed, and a fire burning on the hearth.

Arthur's voice followed her into the semidarkness. "Folks that built this place got scared off in 'thirty-two. It's been empty ever since. Guess you could move in as soon's it's ready if you want it."

Molly tucked her cheek against the top of Lily's head. *At least we'll have a place of our own.* Maybe down the road sometime Matthew and Arthur would put a plank floor in for her. She looked out the doorway.

Arthur stood waiting, holding Luellen. "I'll do all I can to help you, Molly. It'll be good. You'll see."

She stepped next to him and squeezed his hand. "I'm sure it will be. Thank you."

On the trip back to Matthew's farm, Molly's thoughts alternated between anticipation and dread. The bleak prairie offered no solace. Grasses blackened by cold and heavy with rain drooped on both sides of the wagon track. She turned back once for another glimpse at her new home. Its twin chimneys marked the sky like sentinels guarding the gates of an empty city.

Molly hugged Lily closer and put her free arm around Luellen. *A cabin is just the beginning. Now I need a way to earn money.* She recalled Marjolaine asking if she'd considered selling her woven coverlets. If Colonel Cross's wife, with her fine home, thought they were worth money, perhaps Mr. Wolcott would think so too.

Arthur studied her. "You're awful quiet. You change your mind about the cabin?"

"No. I want it." She hesitated. "Do you think the general store would be interested in buying any of my coverlets? I have blankets too. I brought a chest full from Missouri."

Arthur shrugged. "I'll take one to Ben tomorrow, see what he thinks. Don't know why not, myself. Everyone around here barters for goods."

"I don't mean barter. I mean sell."

"It's up to Ben."

She looked into his pale blue eyes. "Let's not mention this to Matthew until I know what Mr. Wolcott says. If I can't provide for us, there's no sense in me moving."

"Bet you could find some feller around here who'd be happy to take care of you."

Irritated, Molly bit her lip. She'd been wondering how long it would take her family to start matchmaking. "I want to do it myself, Uncle, or not at all. Samuel wouldn't expect me to go running to the first man who showed his face."

"Lots of women do. Without a husband, do you really believe you can feed three children—and yourself?"

"I don't know, but I have to try. In Matthew's sermon last Sunday he said the Bible promises God will take care of us as each day comes along."

Arthur's caterpillar eyebrows raised toward his bald scalp. "Did you ever think maybe a new husband might be God's way of doing it?" He transferred the reins to one hand and tapped her cheek with his forefinger. "You're a mighty stubborn gal, Molly."

She smiled a secret smile. Arthur didn't know the half of it.

Several days after Arthur delivered one of Molly's coverlets to Wolcott's Mercantile, Mr. Wolcott rode up to the Craig farmhouse. Molly watched his arrival from her vantage point next to the clothesline, where she stood in gusting wind, pegging wet diapers.

"Morning, Mrs. McGarvie." He dismounted, tying his horse to a hitching post. "Cold out here." He pointed to the laundry. "Better pin them down good. Otherwise, next thing you know they'll be in Springfield."

Molly tucked her reddened hands under her armpits, chuckling. "I hope not!" She dropped the diaper she held into the clothes basket and hurried toward the short, sandy-haired man. "It's good to see you, Mr. Wolcott! Did Arthur talk to you about buying my woven goods?"

He nodded. "Aye-yuh. That's why I rode out here to see you." *Oh dear, he wants to let me down easy.* She bit her lip. "Yes?"

"You think we might go inside? It's bitter cold."

"I'm sorry! Of course." She started toward the steps, then hesitated. "Could you just tell me yes or no? I haven't talked to Matthew yet."

Matthew pushed his way between the wet clothes hanging on the line and walked up next to her. "Talked to me about what?" Without waiting for an answer, he looked at the visitor. "Ben! What brings you here? Who's minding the store?"

"Charity's keeping an eye on things."

Hoping to distract her brother, Molly said, "And how is your wife? At church on Sunday she had a bad cough."

131

"Thankfully, she's well. I'll tell her you asked after her."

"We can't keep Ben standing in this wind." Matthew turned toward their visitor. "Come on in. There's probably coffee on the back of the stove."

The trio started toward the house. "What's this about, Molly?" Matthew's hat shaded his face, hiding his expression.

Feeling trapped, she glanced between the two men. If she told Matthew about her plans and Mr. Wolcott wasn't interested in the coverlets, she'd upset her brother unnecessarily. She wanted to present him with an accomplished fact—one he couldn't argue with. But if the storekeeper told her yes, then she'd have to tell Matthew anyway.

"There's an empty cabin north of here." Molly spoke quickly, leaving no opportunity for interruption. "Uncle Arthur said he'd help me ready it to live in. I wanted to know if Mr. Wolcott would buy my coverlets, so I'd be able to get . . . supplies." She stopped abruptly, her heart beating in her throat. *What's Matt going to say?*

Mr. Wolcott turned to Molly as her brother opened the kitchen door. "You do fine work. I'll be happy sell them in my store. How many can you spare?"

Molly let her breath out with a whoosh. "I have four more. Thank you!"

Aunt Ruby looked up from the kneading trough when they entered. "Sell what? To who?"

Matthew helped Molly remove her shawl and hung it on a peg next to his and Ben's coats. Then he tucked his thumb under her chin and turned her head to face him. "Don't look so scared. You know you can talk to me about everything."

Not everything. She leaned into his chest and slid her arms around his waist, relishing as always the scratchiness of his shirt under her fingers. "I just didn't want to talk about it until I knew I could manage things."

"Right now I'm puzzled. Sit down and tell me what you and Arthur have been up to." He faced Ruby. "How about some coffee for our guest? We don't often get Ben out to the farm on a weekday."

Ruby brought a mug of coffee, her eyes bright with curiosity. "Well?" she asked, sliding into a chair next to Arthur. "Is something happening I should know about?"

Annoyed, Molly ignored her and focused on Matthew. "You knew I wanted a place of my own for the children and me. I told you that almost two weeks ago."

He opened his mouth to say something, but she held up a hand to stop him. "You've been wonderful to let us stay here, but I'm sure it's a hardship to support both our families."

Out of the corner of her eye, she saw Ruby compress her mouth into a thin line.

"Just where do you think you'll go?"

"Ruby, please," Matthew said. "Let her talk."

"Matt, my children don't know who to obey. There are too many people telling them what to do." She avoided looking at Ruby. "They're feeling like they've lost both parents." Molly stood, clutching the back of her chair for support. She felt the way she had on the rare occasions when she'd taken a stand against her father. "The other day Arthur found us an abandoned cabin to live in and said he could fix it up for me. Now that Mr. Wolcott says he'll buy the coverlets—"

"What with the embroidery work and all, I think I can get five to seven dollars apiece for them."

Astonished, Molly stared at the storekeeper. "That much?"

He nodded. "And Arthur said you have blankets too?"

"Yes. Several."

Ruby grunted skeptically. "I still think the whole idea is foolish. A woman alone out in the wild . . ."

Arthur frowned at his wife and said, "It isn't out in the wild. It's a stone's throw from the town square."

"You know as well as I do that panthers roam the woods around town. Folks hear them screaming at night."

Luellen rose from the area under the stairs where she'd been playing with her doll. "Panthers?" She walked over to Molly, her face a picture of alarm.

Molly patted her cheek. "Never mind." She turned to Ruby. "We need a place of our own. Please keep your scare stories to yourself."

"It's not a scare story, it's—"

Arthur looked at her, holding up one finger in a warning gesture. Ruby subsided.

Matthew stood near the back door, his arms folded over his chest. "There's been Indian sightings in the area lately too. Even near town." He shook his head. "It isn't safe."

Molly stamped her foot. "Matt! There were Indians coming and going through St. Lawrenceville the whole time we lived there. You saw how Keokuk was when he brought me that corn last month."

"I also seem to remember you were afraid of him."

She dropped her eyes, a flush warming her cheeks. "I was wrong. He meant me no harm."

"Not every Indian is that peaceable."

"Then I have Samuel's flintlock if I need it."

"Do you know how to shoot it?"

"Well, no."

Her brother walked over and placed his hands on her shoulders. "You need to learn. After that, we'll talk about a cabin . . . maybe."

13

November 1838

Karl Spengler paused on the doorstep of his cabin in New Roanoke, arms full of firewood, and contemplated the early morning appearance of his surroundings. The settlement looked like an unfinished picture sketched in gray and black. Smoke from the few visible chimneys rolled along rooflines and pooled on the ground, signaling a change in the weather.

Karl's thoughts paralleled the smoke's performance. Instead of rising to greet the day, his emotions were bogged in an icy pool somewhere at his feet. The sight of the barren prairie town did nothing to lift his spirits. He missed the easy camaraderie he'd had with Matthew Craig, and now doubted the wisdom of his decision to live so far from Beldon Grove.

He knew he had no one to blame but himself for his loneliness— but in a community as small as Beldon Grove he couldn't have avoided Molly McGarvie's accusing eyes.

Those eyes were the reason he'd ridden past Matthew's house last month without stopping to deliver Betsy's message. Now guilt over that decision plagued him as well.

Once inside the cabin, Karl dropped the armful of wood into a box, then wrapped a cloth around his hand and lifted the coffee boiler from the hob. *Something hot's what I need.* Holding a filled mug, he stared into the fire. The flames sighed and hissed at him as they crawled over the logs.

A firm knock jarred his thoughts. When Karl opened the door, he saw a familiar-appearing man on the step, accompanied by a young woman he didn't recognize. *His wife? His daughter?*

"Well, Doc, are you going to keep us out here to freeze to death?"

The woman tapped his arm. "Papa! Don't be rude."

Karl swung the door wide to admit his first patients of the day. "Please come in." He scrutinized father and daughter. "Which of you is in need of my services?"

The heavyset man was about Karl's height. He had the ruddy skin that often comes to very fair individuals in middle age. In his case, however, the aroma of whiskey that clung to him went a step further to explain his flushed complexion.

The girl looked to be around twenty years old, with pale skin and hair. Not a beauty, but her eyes caught his attention. One blue and one green, framed with blonde lashes. He felt unsettled looking at her, not knowing whether to focus on the blue eye or the green one.

The gentleman leaned on a cane. "I'm the one that needs doctoring." He grabbed Karl's right hand and pumped it vigorously. "Name's Julius Fortune. This is my daughter, Lydia."

Lydia sent him a shy smile and lowered her lashes.

After offering them each a chair, Karl faced Mr. Fortune. "What seems to be the trouble?"

"You're the doctor, you tell me." His patient guffawed.

"This is no time to joke." Lydia frowned at her father. "Tell him about your feet."

"Consarn woman! Bad as her mama was. Always telling a fellow what to do." A fond smile in his daughter's direction negated his critical words. Julius bent over and lifted his trouser cuffs to reveal grossly swollen feet wrapped in bandages and stuffed into cloth slippers. "Been like this for a couple weeks. Tried soaking them in hot water, but it didn't help."

Karl picked up one of his patient's feet and propped it on his lap. After unwinding the bandage, he poked gently at the distended flesh. Every place his finger prodded left a pale indentation in the man's skin. When he looked up, he noticed the whites of Julius's eyes were stained yellow. "How long have your eyes been like that, Mr. Fortune?" The doctor pushed his chair back, facing the man and his daughter.

"I noticed it several weeks ago, Papa," Lydia said. "You remember I mentioned it to you."

"She's probably right. A fellow can't see his own eyes unless he spends all his time peering into a looking glass, and I don't have time for that."

"Any other changes in your health?"

Julius scratched his head, then smoothed his thick white hair back into place.

Karl noticed the gesture. *A careful man. He spends more time with a looking glass than he'd like me to think.*

Lydia watched her father and waited for his response.

Before answering the doctor's question, Julius glanced at his daughter. "I don't like to worry Lydia, but I've been feeling plumb wore out lately. It takes all I've got just to get up most mornings, and often as not I have to rest an hour or two after dinner. Reckon I need a tonic?"

Karl stood and walked to the hearth. The fire he'd started now blazed brightly. He grabbed a couple of pieces of wood and tossed

137

them on top of the flames, pushing scattered coals toward the center of the fireplace with the toe of his boot. Then he leaned an arm on the mantel and tried to think of the best way to tell his patient what was wrong. He glanced up to find Lydia studying his face with her disconcerting eyes.

"Is it serious, Doctor?"

"It can be." Karl took a deep breath. "Looks to me like you're suffering from fatty liver, Mr. Fortune."

Julius leaned back in his chair. "Want to tell me what that means?"

"It means you'll probably have to change your diet, get more rest, and avoid any heavy lifting."

"I've been after him not to work so hard ever since I came back out from Virginia," Lydia said.

"I've always worked hard. Made my own way in the world since I was a lad." Julius straightened his shoulders and inflated his chest. "In fact, it was me founded New Roanoke. Came out here and opened a stage stop fifteen years ago. When folks liked the look of the place and decided to settle here, I'm the one named it. Used to live in Roanoke, back in Virginia, don't you know."

Now Karl knew why his patient looked familiar. "You're the owner of Fortune House Inn. I should've recognized you sooner." He didn't add that the man's bloated features had disguised him.

Fortune House Inn stood at the south end of town on the main route between Quincy and Galesburg. Built of hewn stones, it stood two stories high, dwarfing the cabins around it. Karl smiled at his patient. "I enjoyed the hospitality of your inn when I first arrived in town."

"I remember you. You weren't one to complain about the food like some folks." Julius rubbed his swollen ankles. "Now, speaking of food, what do you mean about 'change my diet'?"

"I mean you'll need to adopt a bland diet, no fatty meats, and drink nothing stronger than spring water." Karl turned his gaze on Lydia. "See to it he gets a husky boy to help unload supplies and cut firewood at the inn."

Grumbling under his breath, Julius buttoned his coat over his prominent stomach. "How long will I have to live like that? If you call it living!"

"Come see me in a month. I'll wager you'll feel like a new man."

On his second visit, the much-improved Julius Fortune pumped Karl's hand. "Can't thank you enough, Doc! You'll notice I'm not needing a cane today." With a slight limp, he moved toward a chair. "How much longer do I have to keep up this 'changed diet'?" His voice twisted the end of the sentence with sarcasm.

Karl grinned at him, enjoying his contentious patient's spirit. "Forever, Mr. Fortune, forever."

Julius reared back in his chair. "I can't do that! If I don't share the victuals and raise a glass with my customers, they'll think there's something wrong with my inn."

"I doubt it. Has business dropped off over the last few weeks?"

"Well, no. As long as the road's clear, folks can travel."

Karl moved his chair closer and looked directly into his patient's eyes. "I saw people with your condition when my brother and I doctored together back in Philadelphia. It's ugly. Their whole body swells like your feet were doing, then they vomit blood and die."

"Tarnation, you don't mince words, do you?"

"You want to stay around to care for your daughter, don't you?"

Julius nodded, his bluster gone. "I'm all she's got. It weighs heavy on me sometimes, what's going to become of her. When Lydia was eight, Mrs. Fortune got consumption and went home to her folks. Took our daughter with her. After m'wife died, Lyddie stayed on with her Grandma Bell." He shifted in his chair. "Then after her grandma passed, I asked Lyddie to come back. We're just now getting reacquainted." Julius put a period to the personal disclosures by slapping his knees. "Well, that's enough of that! Speaking of my daughter, we'd like for you to come to supper tonight. Since you're a bachelor, guess you wouldn't mind a home-cooked meal, would you?"

☙

A routine developed between Karl and the Fortunes. At least twice a week he accepted a supper invitation from Julius and his daughter. Usually she served the same simple fare prepared for guests in the public room—hearty soups and stews, accompanied by squares of cornbread—but tonight, the fourteenth of December, was meant to be a celebration of Julius's fiftieth birthday. Karl had been promised something special.

With keen anticipation he walked through the dimly lit public area of Fortune House, surprised that it was full of travelers. Laughter and snatches of conversation swirled around the room. When he headed for the Fortunes' private apartment, Karl noticed two people walking toward him from the shadows. The man supported a middle-aged woman, who weaved drunkenly past him. The cloying odor of rum trailed behind her. Karl felt a familiar revulsion roil his stomach, closely followed by guilt for his unconscious reaction. *She can't help it. Show some compassion.* Karl repeated his brother's words like a mantra, but it did no good. *She can help it. She does it to herself.*

He turned away from the Fortunes' door and stepped outside until his heart slowed its pounding. Leaning against the frosty stone wall of the inn, Karl willed his thoughts back to Julius's birthday celebration. He wouldn't spoil their evening by brooding about something he couldn't change.

He strode back inside and knocked at the apartment door. Lydia answered, her pleasant smile widening when she saw him. Karl noticed she'd styled her blonde hair in a crown of braids that shone like gold in the light. The dark blue frock she wore emphasized her small waist.

He drew a deep breath before speaking. "Evening, Miss Lydia. That's a becoming dress you're wearing."

A pink flush brightened her cheeks. "Thank you. I've been working on it for a week."

She didn't have to add "in anticipation of your visit." He heard it in her voice.

A fire burned on the hearth at one end of the lamplit room, illuminating the comfortable furnishings. An open book sat on a table next to one of the upholstered chairs. Karl felt his earlier agitation diminish and slip away like a vanquished foe.

"Doc!" Julius strode toward him with no sign of the painful limp he'd had when he first visited Spengler's office. "Glad you could join us."

Karl shook the innkeeper's hand. "Happy birthday, Julius! How's it feel to be half a century old?"

"Pretty good. It's wearing Lydia out, though. She's been cooking all afternoon."

"Oh, Papa, I have not!" She smiled at Karl. "But I do have a few things to attend to in the kitchen. Please excuse me."

Julius clapped the doctor on the back. "Can't tell you how good I've been feeling! Look at my feet." He stuck out one foot and lifted his trouser leg. Instead of a cloth slipper, he wore shining leather boots. "Haven't had these on for months, and they fit perfect, thanks to you."

"All I can do is give advice," Karl said. "You're the one who has to follow it."

In a few minutes Lydia rejoined the two men. "Supper's ready."

They followed her to a table covered with a linen cloth. In the center sat a platter on which rested a boiled ham, its crumb crust delicately browned, flanked by sliced wheat bread and a bowl of mashed yellow squash. A pottery pitcher filled with water waited next to a decorated tin coffeepot. Lydia glanced up at Karl through her blonde lashes. "I remembered you liked coffee better than tea. I made some for you."

He smiled at her, appreciating her lack of guile. After Caroline, this girl with her fair hair and quiet speech came as a restful change. He'd even grown used to her different-colored eyes.

Julius stood at the head of the table. "Coffee smells mighty good. Be glad when I can drink it again." He grinned at the doctor. "Not to mention tapping some of the kegs out in the public room."

Karl shook his head. "Better not. You'll end up right back where you were—or worse."

"I'll be careful." Julius brandished a carving knife over the meat. "Smoked this myself," he said, carving thick slices off the steaming ham and placing them on pewter plates. "Got a secret mix of wood chips, don't you know. I wager you'll like it."

He passed a plate to Lydia, who added a scoop of buttery squash from the bowl in front of her and handed it to Karl. Her fingers brushed his. "Enjoy your meal. There's apple pudding for after."

While they ate, sounds of laughter and conversation drifted through the wall adjoining the public room of the inn. "Sounds like you have a full house tonight."

"We do. Got a coach full of passengers from Galesburg on their way to Vandalia to meet with the General Assembly. The capitol's moving to Springfield next year, but they've got business that won't wait." The innkeeper chewed a bite of bread. "We don't normally get all the rooms rented. This is a bonus, eh, Lydia?"

"Yes." She turned to Karl. "I enjoy the sounds of visitors to the inn. Life is so much quieter here than it was in Virginia. When I lived with Grandmother Bell, she kept a lively household—guests frequently coming and going." She pushed her food around on her plate. "You must find it awfully quiet here after the bustle of Philadelphia."

"It's quieter, to be sure, but I came to the frontier to practice medicine, not to participate in fashionable society."

"Oh, of course!" Lydia leaned toward him, a warm smile lighting her face. "I so admire your decision to come out here and help those less fortunate."

"Thank you." He returned her smile. She looked prettier this evening than she had when he first met her. *Must be that blue dress.*

14

December 1838

Molly watched Luellen twirl in her new blue dress. "I'm four! I'm four!" Her boots left circular marks on the hard-packed earth floor of their cabin.

James looked up from his schoolwork and grinned at his sister over the top of a bulky table crammed into a space under the window. "Careful! If you get dizzy, you'll fall in the fire."

"No, I won't." But she stopped and looked at her mother. "When is everybody coming?"

"They'll be here soon. Uncle Matthew said four o'clock." Molly's eyes burned from late nights spent altering garments to clothe her children. There'd been enough fabric in the skirt of her wool bridal outfit to sew the dress for Luellen. Samuel's work attire, cut down, was transformed into new shirts for James and Franklin.

The oiled paper tacked over the window openings allowed scant daylight into the cabin, making it difficult to gauge the time of day. Mentally, Molly added candle-making to her list of things to do. The supply she'd brought from St. Lawrenceville was dwindling fast.

The door latch lifted, admitting Ellie, carrying Maria, and Matthew, followed by their three boys. Ruby and Arthur pushed in at their heels.

"There's scarcely enough space in here to swing a cat." Ruby scowled as she gazed around. "Why don't you put that bed across in the other room?"

Molly's spirits fell. She hated defending herself against Ruby's everlasting criticism. "The loom takes up too much space. Besides, it's warmer in here."

Matthew broke the tension between them by grabbing Luellen under the arms and swinging her high in the air. "Looks like someone has a new dress for her birthday."

The child giggled. "Mama made new shirts for James and Franklin too."

The fire sputtered and snapped in the silence that followed her remark. Ellie was the first to speak. "A shirt for Franklin?" Her eyes searched Molly's face. "Why?"

Molly met her gaze without flinching. "By the time he gets back he will have grown. He'll need bigger clothes."

The adults were all staring at her, mixtures of astonishment and compassion showing on their faces. Matthew stepped forward.

Arthur put out a hand to stop him. "Don't hurt nothing to hope. Leave her be."

Hope? Was that all the voice had represented? Hope made audible? Molly's throat tightened. *It couldn't have been.*

James poked Luellen. "Mama said not to tell."

The child's face crumpled and two tears slid down her cheeks. She leaned into Molly's skirt and hugged her knees. "I forgot. Are you mad at me?"

"Not on your birthday." She dropped a kiss on her daughter's head and then walked to the hearth, avoiding her brother's eyes.

"Indian pudding's been steaming all day. We've been waiting for you to help us eat it."

Molly wrapped a piece of toweling around her hand and swung the fireplace crane toward her, then lifted the double boiler onto the edge of the table. She untied the string that held the pudding over the simmering water and transferred the cheesecloth bag to a waiting bowl. The sweet fragrance of molasses and raisins floated into the air.

Matthew's twins, with their younger brother Harrison, crowded to the table. Luellen stood on one of the benches and handed out filled bowls until everyone was served.

"I helped Mama take the seeds out of the raisins." Smoothing the skirt of her new dress, she settled onto a bench next to Molly.

"Raisins!" Ruby inspected her pudding. "Aren't they rather dear?"

Her husband lifted an eyebrow and frowned at her. "It's the child's birthday. She deserves a little treat."

Glancing at the paper-covered window, Molly noted that daylight had faded into dusk. *Good. They'll leave soon.* She didn't know how long she could tolerate Ruby.

After Luellen opened her gifts—a new hair ribbon and an apron for her doll—the family gathered at the door to say good-bye. When Matthew hugged Molly, he spoke softly in her ear. "You can always come back and live with us. I'm worried about you."

✑

The next day, Molly left James in charge of his sisters and hurried toward Wolcott's Mercantile, two blankets clutched to her chest. Now that she had a place to live, she needed to concentrate on saving enough money to buy Betsy. *I hope Mr. Wolcott will take these—they're my best ones.* Wrapped in thought, she didn't notice the blacksmith leave his shop and hurry across the road to intercept her.

"Mrs. McGarvie."

Molly jumped at the sound of Jared Pitt's voice. The man had an annoying habit of springing out from his forge whenever she passed by on her way to town. "Mr. Pitt. Good morning."

Lank, sandy-red hair drizzled down the back of his neck and drooped over his forehead. He backhanded it out of his eyes. "You oughtn't be out like this, unprotected. If you wait a minute, I'll hitch my buggy and take you wherever you're headed." The blacksmith took a step backward on his short bandy legs, prepared to dash to the stable and fetch his buggy.

Molly shifted the weight of the blankets and shook her head. "No thank you. I'm just headed to the mercantile."

"Then you'll need a buggy to carry home your supplies."

"I'll not be buying supplies."

Mr. Pitt was persistent, she'd give him that. The day she moved into the cabin he'd crossed the road and asked Matthew to introduce him, informing her that he'd been a widower—no children, he hastened to add—for over a year.

Now as he stood facing her, muscular arms hanging at his sides, Molly searched for a way to politely end the encounter. "I really must be going. I've left the children by themselves."

Mr. Pitt glanced behind him at her cabin. "I'll keep an eye out while you're gone. Next time, tell your boy he can come get me if he needs anything."

"Yes. I'll do that. Thank you." She hurried away, leaving him standing in the road.

When the store came in sight, she squelched a nervous flutter in her throat. *I hope Mr. Wolcott's not interested in these because he feels sorry for me—or obligated to Matt.* Molly pushed open the door and drew a deep breath for courage. A rich blend of aromas defined the mercantile—coffee, lamp oil, and leather, mingled with a winey smell drifting from a barrel of apples parked in front of the counter.

Mr. Wolcott looked up, a pleased expression on his face. "Mrs. McGarvie! Glad you came in today." He walked around the counter and stood in front of her. "I see you have some blankets with you. Good." He took them from her.

"I only brought two. Surely you don't need more than that."

"They're not just for me. Folks around here are mighty strained for blankets as well as clothing." At her expression of surprise, he explained. "You know this here's a new town. You've got the only barn-frame loom in Beldon Grove. I'd wager that you'd have all the business you could handle if you set up as a weaver. People have been depending on itinerants who bring looms with them and stay a month or two." He leaned against the counter, folding his arms across his chest. "If these blankets are anything like the coverlet Arthur showed me, you do better work than any I've seen."

Molly felt herself blushing at his praise. "I've just had a lot of practice, is all. My mama taught me to weave soon as I could work a loom."

"Oh, another thing. What with wolves and panthers getting at them, it's been a struggle to raise sheep around here. So we're kinda short on wool." He pointed to his leather trousers. "You've probably noticed folks wearing buckskin."

She nodded, waiting to see where he was leading.

"Matthew told me you grew flax in Missouri and how much you spun from that batch you brought with you. You'd probably have a market for any linen you can provide."

Molly's mind struggled to comprehend all that Mr. Wolcott

said. Set up as a weaver and raise flax too? How could she possibly do all that? The days were too short already.

One thing at a time. Planting season is months away. Her mouth quirked in a smile. *Matthew would call this a blessing. Well, I guess it is.* She looked at the storekeeper. "Can you make a handbill saying I'll do weaving for cash or barter?"

"I'll take care of it this afternoon. In the meantime, how many more blankets do you have to spare? There'll be a trader coming through from Springfield in a week or so. I have a feeling he might be interested in buying some to take west."

Molly remembered the roll of diagonal-weave wool twill she'd cut from her loom when they left St. Lawrenceville. "Two more, for sure." She thought of the others stored in her blanket chest. Winter had set in—she'd need to keep some for herself. "Maybe five. I'll have to check." She frowned as a sudden thought crossed her mind. "That would be all for a while, I'm afraid. I'll need to warp the loom to get started again. Might be a month or so before another one's ready, depending on how quick I get responses to the handbill."

Mr. Wolcott nodded agreement. "That'd be fine. We're in business then?"

She shook his hand. "We're in business."

He glanced over her shoulder at the sound of the front door opening. "Jared. What brings you here? Things slow at the forge?"

"Naw. I brought the buggy around so Mrs. McGarvie wouldn't have to walk home. I've heard talk of Indians lurking about. Didn't think she'd be safe out there."

Molly swung around when she heard the blacksmith's voice, noting that he'd taken time to remove his spark-scarred leather apron and run a comb through his hair. She sighed. The last thing

149

she wanted was to be courted by anyone, much less by a man near Mr. Wolcott's age.

"Mrs. McGarvie?" Mr. Pitt waited near the door.

A knowing smile flitted across Mr. Wolcott's face. "The notice will be posted this afternoon. See you tomorrow at church."

She wanted to tell him that things were not as they appeared, but how could she with the blacksmith standing right there? "Yes. I'll see you tomorrow."

Mr. Pitt held the door open for her and, face burning, she walked past him. A metallic smell of heated iron clung to his clothing.

When Molly reached his buggy, he gripped her elbow and assisted her up the step. She perched at the far edge of the seat and looked into his grey eyes. "You are kind, but this wasn't necessary. I'm able to look after myself."

"God didn't mean for us to be alone."

"I have my children."

He turned north on the stage road and didn't respond. Ahead, elms and wild plum trees fought with thorns and briars for space at the edge of prairie grassland. The creek that flowed along the western side of the road was bordered by a thick stand of oak and shagbark hickory. Molly's cabin sat a short distance ahead on the left, smoke rising from one of its chimneys. She studied the overgrown land behind it, wondering how difficult plowing and planting flax would prove to be. *I'll think about it come spring.*

She climbed out of the buggy as soon as it stopped in front of her home. "I thank you, but please don't feel obligated just because we live nearby."

He tipped his hat and half smiled. "That's not the reason I done it."

The following Monday, Molly had James help her carry the heavy roller from her loom into the main cabin. She measured and cut off two blanket lengths from the cream-colored twill. Spreading them over the top of the table to keep the wool clean, she lined up the selvages prior to joining the two sections down the center. If she could get these blankets hemmed quickly, she'd have a start on her savings.

Luellen sat on the edge of the bed, swinging her legs. Molly had given her the job of minding Lily to keep the baby from fussing. Right now, Lily slept in her cradle and Luellen stared across the length of the room, pouting. "Why can't I go to school with James? I'm big enough."

"I'll teach you at home until you're older, just like I did James and Franklin."

"Do you think Franklin's in school right now?"

Molly's stomach constricted. "Why, yes." She kept her voice light. "I'm sure he is."

"Then why can't I go?"

"That's enough!" She pushed loose tendrils of hair from her forehead. "You mind the baby. That's an important job. I need to get this blanket ready to sell so Betsy can come live with us again." Molly tried to concentrate on keeping her stitches tight and even. *Maybe I could send Luellen to school.* It was a tempting thought. But Mr. Newsome, the schoolmaster, had been firm when he said he wouldn't take four-year-olds.

Lily stirred in the cradle and sent up a tentative cry.

"Rock her, please, Lulie. I want to work on this a bit longer."

Luellen slid to the floor and tipped the cradle from side to side, humming a lullaby she'd learned from her mother. Lily's

151

cries subsided, but not for long. Soon she drowned out her sister's voice.

Molly sighed and anchored her needle in the woolen fabric, then walked to the cradle. She scooped Lily into her arms and laid her down on the bed to change her diaper before feeding her.

"Hush, now." Molly settled into the rocking chair near the fire, holding the baby in the crook of her arm. The quiet moment was interrupted by a sharp knock at the door. *Mercy sakes, now what?*

Luellen dashed to her side. "Can I see who it is?"

Mentally, Molly groaned. *It's probably Mr. Pitt.* She arranged the baby's blanket over her shoulder to cover the nursing child. Just in case, she glanced at Samuel's flintlock hanging on the wall for reassurance before nodding permission.

When Luellen opened the door, a stranger stood in the dogtrot area between the two rooms. His weathered face reflected surprise mingled with anger.

"What are you folks doing in my cabin?"

15

Molly stared at the stranger in the doorway, taking in his deep-set eyes, drooping mustache, and soiled clothing.

"Who are you?" She stood, supporting Lily's weight, and moved to the doorway. Luellen retreated to the far corner of the room.

"More to the point, who are you?" His voice sounded as if it started in his boots and gained strength on the way up. "This here's my place, and you don't belong here." He leaned forward, peering into the cabin.

Molly took a step backward. "I'm Mrs. McGarvie. We were told this place had been abandoned during the Black Hawk War."

"They tell you this is the Barker place?"

"Yes."

"I'm Zechariah Barker. This claim's mine. You and your young'uns are squatters."

Molly's legs turned to rubber. She leaned against the wall for support. "No. It's not possible."

He jerked his hat off and twisted the brim between his hands. "It most certainly is possible. My wife and sons are at the mercantile right now, getting supplies."

A stab of anger rocked Molly. Did he expect her to walk away without a fight? "Mr. Barker—"

Another figure appeared in the dogtrot.

Mr. Pitt. Molly sighed with relief. *I never thought I'd be glad to see him.*

"Mrs. McGarvie? I seen you had someone standing out here. Is everything . . ." Mr. Pitt's voice trailed off when he recognized her visitor. "Zechariah?" He stuck out his hand. "You're a sight for sore eyes! What brings you back to Beldon Grove?"

Barker tugged at the corner of his mustache. "This here's my claim, ain't it? I got a right to come back. Me and the boys are going to take up farming again."

Molly's mind raced. Where could she go? And how soon would she have to leave? Barker talked like he meant to move in that afternoon.

More than anything, she didn't want to return to her brother's house and abandon all her plans. There had to be a way out. She gazed at the blacksmith. "This is so distressing." Molly deliberately let her voice waver, as though she were on the verge of tears. She clutched Lily to her. "Mr. Pitt, could you take Mr. Barker to your place for a bit, while I tend to my baby?"

He flushed, apparently realizing for the first time that she was nursing an infant under the blanket draped across her shoulder. "Yes'm. Gladly." Grabbing Zechariah's arm, he walked toward the road.

Barker looked over his shoulder. "I'll be back directly. You start packing."

She pushed the door shut and leaned against it, fighting panic.

Luellen raced to her and clutched a handful of her mother's apron. "Mama? What's going to happen to us?"

Molly perched on the edge of a chair and looked into the child's brown eyes. "We'll be all right, Lulie. Don't worry." She tried to put conviction into her words, but Luellen's question echoed in her mind.

Mr. Pitt accompanied James when he arrived home after school. "I had a long talk with Barker. His family will stay with me while you get moved."

James moved to Molly's side. "How can he do this to us?"

She slipped an arm around his shoulders and shook her head.

Mr. Pitt answered for her. "By right of improvement, boy. He built this here cabin, so it's still his claim."

The cabin was dark and cramped, the dirt floor chilled their feet, but it was better than being beholden to her brother again. Molly pulled a chair away from the table and pushed the two halves of the blanket to one side.

"Please rest yourself, Mr. Pitt." She sat opposite him. "How long do we have?"

"I reckon a few days. If he knows you're leaving, likely he'll give you time to do it." He leaned forward, resting his hands on the table. "I'll do all I can to help." His gaze moved over her face, coming to rest on her mouth. A fire burned behind his eyes.

Molly pretended not to notice. Keeping her tone brisk, she asked, "Do you know of another vacant cabin hereabouts?"

He shook his head. "No, ma'am, I don't." A small smile curved his lips. "You and your children could rent a room from me. Soon's Barker leaves, there'll be plenty of space."

Molly squeezed her hands together in her lap, digging the

155

nails into her palms. James and Luellen watched with frightened expressions on their faces.

Speaking into the strained silence, the blacksmith continued. "I mean it honorable. I'd let the room in exchange for housekeeping."

Based on what she'd seen from the road, Mr. Pitt had a spacious home. No doubt he'd have space for her loom. She'd still be in town, able to take orders for her work. *But live in his house? Never.*

Suddenly, the prospect of returning to Matthew's didn't seem so unthinkable. Perhaps he would set up her loom in the unfinished space at the back of the upstairs hallway when the weather warmed. Molly blinked back tears. She'd counted on being able to fill orders as soon as they came in. Now she'd be delayed, and in the meantime an itinerant weaver might come through and take all her potential customers.

Molly lifted her head and saw the blacksmith watching her, one eyebrow raised. She had to decide. If only she knew where to find Franklin. If only she had Betsy with her. If only . . .

Betsy leaned against the curved top of a scrub board in the small laundry shed attached to Brody McGarvie's kitchen. Ever since Dr. Spengler's visit in October, she'd been grieving over the news about Franklin. The child had a special place in her heart. His mischievous ways were a trial at times, but he had the sweetest way of saying he was sorry afterward.

She groaned. "Oh Lord, why'd you have to take the boy? Ain't we had sorrow enough?" Under her breath, she sang phrases she remembered from a song she'd learned before they left Kentucky. ". . . Sickness and sorrow, pain and death, are felt and feared no more . . . I am bound for the promised land . . . Oh who will come and go with me? I am bound for the promised land."

Steam from the clothes boiler collected under the ceiling. Betsy continued to sing as she worked, pausing to wipe sweat from her forehead with the back of her arm. She picked up a long, forked tool and used it like a fishing gaff to lift a yellow garment from the simmering water.

The back of her neck prickled. Sensing she was being watched, Betsy glanced over her shoulder and saw Brody's wife, Patience, standing in the doorway.

"I know what you're doing." Patience spoke in a singsong voice. "I seen it ever since my husband brought you here."

"What d'you mean, Miz Patience? Doing what?" She turned to face her mistress.

The other woman took a step backward. "Don't come near me! You're a conjure woman!" She put her hands in front of her face, as though to ward off a blow.

Shocked, Betsy dropped the long-handled fork into the wash boiler. "Why, Miz Patience, I ain't! I been a Christian since I was a little bitty child."

"Don't play the fool with me! I just now heard you put a curse on my yellow dress."

Betsy stared into the woman's eyes. The pupils were pinpricks, giving her pale blue irises an unearthly glow. "Miz Patience, I wasn't—"

"One more word and I'll have Mr. Brody sell you next time a trader comes through." She pointed a shaking finger at Betsy. "Remember, I'm watching you." Patience backed into the kitchen, leaving as silently as she'd arrived.

Betsy's thoughts whirled. *Lord God, what'll I do?* Every black person had heard the horror stories of slave auctions. If she were sold away, there'd be no chance she'd ever see Miz Molly again. Brody was bad, but the unknown could be many times worse. Mechanically, she returned to scrubbing wet laundry. *I've got to talk to Reuben about this, soon's I see him.*

Once Brody McGarvie's family had finished supper, his four slaves gathered in the kitchen for their meal. Tildy placed a platter of fat bacon and corn pone in the center of the table before taking her place on a bench next to Betsy. The two men and two women reached out and scooped portions into wooden bowls.

Betsy looked with disgust at her food, an oily white chunk of bacon resting next to a square of corn cake. The others didn't seem bothered by the unappetizing meal, quickly downing their portions and reaching for more.

"Tasty supper, Tildy." Reuben helped himself to a third piece of pone, using it to mop grease off his plate.

"Thank you." Tildy smiled at the compliment. "Leave some extry for the rest of us, though."

Rueben swallowed a mouthful. "I worked up a powerful hunger today. Mr. Brody had me cutting some a' them trees behind Mr. Samuel's cabin."

Betsy's heart contracted when she heard Samuel's name. *Ain't nothing been the same since he been gone.* The frightening encounter with Patience McGarvie dominated her thoughts. She looked across the table at Reuben. "With all that wood cutting, did you get your stable chores done today?"

He smiled at her, his eyes telling her he understood what she meant. "Not yet. Still got work to do before it gets too late."

She nodded, communicating her intention to meet him in the barn with a motion of her head.

While Betsy scrubbed dishes and pots from the evening meals, Tildy sat in front of the fire, her feet on the fender. The McGarvies' supper of ham from a wild boar, boiled onions, and wheat bread stood in stark contrast to the servants' meal of fatback and corn pone.

"Wouldn't hurt 'em none to let the black folks have the leavings," Betsy said. She banged a cast-iron pot onto a shelf under the wash basin. "This be the last one."

Tildy raised her head. "Did you put them beans to soak?"

Impatient to be gone, Betsy asked, "Do it have to be done tonight?"

"Well, a' course." Tildy nestled further into the pillows lining the heavy rocking chair. "What's your hurry?"

Betsy didn't answer. She grabbed a brown pottery bowl from a shelf and tipped open a bin under the worktable, scooping the bowl half full of dried cranberry beans. After covering them with water, she laid a piece of cheesecloth over the bowl and left it on the table. "Anything else?"

"We be needing the wood box filled." Tildy's head drooped forward as she fought to keep her eyes open. "And some more kindling."

"I'll get right to it."

When Betsy entered the stable, she saw Reuben sitting on one of the feed sacks waiting for her. "Took you awhile."

"You know Tildy—she always finds something more for me to do."

"What is it now?"

"I'm supposed to be splitting kindling."

Reuben stood, grinning at her. "You'd best get to it, then." He took an ax from a peg and walked out to the woodpile. After grabbing a chunk from the stack, he lined up a maul and split

159

the wood into four pieces with one whack. Then he reduced the pieces into slivers of kindling.

"If Tildy sees you, she'll go telling tales to Mr. Brody." Betsy dropped the thin strips into a bucket as he worked.

"She ain't going to see me. Bet she's sleeping with her feet up in front of the fire."

Betsy chuckled. "She is."

"You had something you wanted to tell me?"

"Miz Patience come out to the wash room today whilst I was scrubbing clothes." Her heart pounded when she remembered the strange look on her mistress's face. Betsy moved closer to Reuben and lowered her voice. "She thinks I'm a conjure woman. Said she heard me casting a spell over her dress."

Reuben's eyes widened. Reaching out, he took one of her work-chapped hands in his.

He ain't never held my hand before. Betsy felt the strength trapped in his broad palm, promising comfort and protection. "What can I do?"

The big man shook his head. "It don't sound good. Miz Patience took a notion against a gal whilst we was still in Kentucky." He put his free arm around her shoulders and drew her to him.

She pressed her cheek against the rough cloth of his shirt, inhaling the sharp, sweaty smell of his body, relishing the sensation of his broad chest against her face. *It's been so long since I been held. Wish I could just stay here.* Sighing, she lifted her head. "What happened in Kentucky?"

Holding her close, he bent his face toward hers, near enough so she could see how his eyelashes curled above his dark brown eyes. Fear wrote itself across his features. "Miz Patience hounded Mr. Brody 'til he sold the gal. She don't trust no one around her 'cept Tildy." He traced Betsy's cheek with a calloused fingertip. "I'm afeard she'll get rid of you."

Betsy stepped backward. Somehow she couldn't think clearly next to Reuben's warmth. "But, what if I stay clean away from her?"

He shook his head. "Won't do no good. Conjure woman don't need to be close by to cast spells, you know that."

"I know." Her shoulders slumped. "But I ain't no conjure woman."

The barn door smacked open. Tildy stood there, a triumphant expression on her face. "Look at you, out here dallying with the stable boy! Mr. Brody's gwine hear about this."

16

"Why didn't I hear about this sooner?" Matthew faced Molly, a pained expression on his face. Crusted snow lay heaped in scattered piles around them in the churchyard. Tied to a railing, his horse stamped and blew clouds of steam into the air through flared nostrils.

He grasped her shoulder. "Ben told me what happened. Why didn't you come to me? You know there's always room in my house for you and your children."

Jiggling the heavily bundled Lily in her arms, Molly lifted her eyes to meet his gaze. It pained her to see her brother so upset. When she had accepted the blacksmith's offer, she made it clear they'd only stay until she found another cabin. In the meantime, he provided space for her loom, the compelling reason behind her decision. "I needed to stay in town. Surely you saw the notice in Mr. Wolcott's store about my weaving."

He stepped to one side to allow a man and a woman to pass. Their glances lingered on Molly a moment too long. Matthew lowered his voice. "It looks bad. The preacher's sister living in a house with an unmarried man."

"As a housekeeper. It's often done."

"People will talk."

"Are you worried about me? Or about yourself?" She turned her back, climbed the steps, and entered the church.

The building bore a faint aroma of fresh lumber although it had been completed nearly a year earlier. Tallow candles sputtered in sconces attached to the plastered walls, leaving trails of soot against the whitewash. Molly scanned the partially filled benches. Where were James and Luellen?

She started toward the front of the church when Charity Wolcott swooped over, enfolding Molly and Lily in a strong embrace. "There you are, my dear! My, you look lovely today. It's good to see you getting some color back in those cheeks."

Molly smiled at Ben's wife. Sturdy, with graying hair and sharp blue eyes, her practical appearance concealed a warm and caring personality. Molly knew Charity's public demonstration of affection would help squelch any gossip swirling around her move into Mr. Pitt's house.

"Where's Mr. Wolcott this morning? He's usually here early."

A guarded expression crossed the older woman's face. "A passenger arrived last night," she replied in a low tone. "He's escorting him to the next stop."

"A passenger?" Molly asked.

Just then, Ellie moved next to her and poked an elbow into her side.

Charity slid her forefinger over her lips, signaling silence. Then with her next breath, she raised her voice loud enough to carry to the ears of nearby worshippers. "Why don't you bring that precious baby to see me next week? I'd enjoy the company." She turned and bustled up the aisle of the church, leaving Molly staring after her.

Ellie tucked her hand under Molly's elbow. "Let's sit down. Mr. Foster's tuning his pitch pipe." She led the way to a bench where James and Luellen sat with their cousins.

163

While they walked, Molly unclasped Lily's fingers from her black grosgrain bonnet ribbons. "Did Charity mean—"

"I'll explain after church."

✑

Several days later, Mr. Pitt entered his cabin promptly at noon, as he'd done since Molly began keeping house for him. She watched from the hearth while he surveyed the room. Frowning, he pointed to the floor between the sawbuck table and the doorway to the room she shared with her children. "You forgot to sweep over yonder, looks like. Mrs. Pitt, rest her soul, kept her kitchen spotless. You could'a eaten off her floor."

Who'd want to eat off the floor, anyway? Molly stifled the quick retort. Grabbing the cornhusk broom that leaned in one corner, she swept the offending debris into a tin dustpan and tossed it out the back door. "I must've missed that when I cleaned up after breakfast. I'm sorry."

The blacksmith smiled at her indulgently. "No need to apologize. You're still learning." He slid a chair away from the head of the table and sat. "Whatever you're cooking smells good."

"It's venison stew and corn cakes."

"You didn't cook them squirrels I shot?"

Her back to him, Molly squeezed her left hand with her right until Samuel's wedding ring bit into her flesh. She would not defend herself again. Enduring Mr. Pitt's scrutiny of her every move was the price she paid for a place to work at her loom. Silently, she filled his plate and carried it to the table. "We're having the squirrel for supper."

"Fine, then. Don't want you wasting food." He picked up his spoon and filled his mouth with stew. Closing his eyes, he chewed slowly. "Pretty good." He put his spoon to one side and picked up a chunk of corn cake. "Ain't you going to eat?"

"Later."

"Well, sit with me." He pushed a chair out with his foot. "Tell me what you've got set for this afternoon." A scattering of crumbs decorated his beard.

Molly smiled, thinking of her plans. "Matthew's coming to take me to visit Charity Wolcott."

He raised an eyebrow in surprise, or anxiety. She wasn't sure which one.

"I'll be back before James comes from school—don't worry."

"Thought you was in a hurry to finish them blankets. Should you be gallivanting?"

Pushed past her limit, Molly folded her arms across her chest and glared at him. "I'm a grown woman. I'll decide whether I have time to call on a friend."

A wounded look crossed his face. "Just trying to make your life easier, Mrs. McGarvie. Thought you could use some advice."

Molly ignored his sulky expression. Walking to the hearth, she lifted the Dutch oven from the coals, using a corner of her apron to protect her hands. "More corn cake?"

Once he finished his meal and returned to the forge, she filled bowls for herself and Luellen, hurrying so they'd be finished quickly. Maybe there'd be time to work up the last of the wool twill before Matthew arrived.

Mr. Pitt was right. She didn't have time to go gallivanting, but she yearned for female companionship.

✑

December sun braved the chill air to shine through a cloudless sky as Matthew drove the spring wagon toward Wolcotts' farm. His disapproval of her living arrangement radiated from his body in waves.

Molly held Lily against her shoulder and turned to look at her brother. "Thank you for taking me to Charity's."

"Least it gets you out of Pitt's house."

She chuckled. "If you knew how he treats me, you wouldn't worry for a moment."

"That right?"

"Nothing I do lines up with the way his late wife did things. You'd think I was ten years old, the way he acts." She sighed. She'd been concerned about protecting her virtue once under Mr. Pitt's roof and instead found herself sharing a house with a man fixated on turning her into a duplicate of his dead wife. *No matter what I prepare for, life sends me something else.*

Molly's mind skipped to Charity's puzzling behavior on Sunday. She glanced at her brother over the top of Luellen's head. "Ellie told me not to talk about Mr. Wolcott being a conductor on the Underground Railroad. Why not? Illinois is a free state, isn't it?"

"Not everyone wants it that way. Governor Carlin hails from Kentucky and seems to support the Black Codes."

"Black Codes? What're those?"

"Mrs. Wolcott'll tell you." The tall barn that identified the Wolcotts' property rose from the prairie ahead of them like a watchtower. Matthew guided the horses toward the single-story cabin standing next to it.

Before they'd rolled to a complete stop, Charity opened the front door and waved at them. "Welcome! I'm glad you came." She bustled out to the wagon, holding up her arms. "Let me hold that baby while you get down."

Luellen watched anxiously while the older woman took the infant from Molly's arms. "Careful with our Lily."

166

Charity copied the child's serious tone. "Don't worry. She's safe." She looked up at Matthew sitting on the wagon seat. "Are you coming in, Reverend?"

"You ladies have your visit. I'll be back after a while."

Molly held Luellen's hand and followed Charity into the snug cabin. A pierced tin lantern cast light over a thick plank table in the center of the room. Steam rose from the spout of a kettle hung over the hearth.

"Sit down," Charity said. "The kettle's hot, we'll have some tea."

She turned to Luellen. "There's a stool just your size over by the fire." She pointed to a squat, three-legged seat at the edge of the stone hearth. "If you look in that basket next to it, you'll find some blocks and a little dolly to play with."

Charity put Lily back in Molly's arms and took a brown pottery teapot off a shelf. After measuring tea leaves, she added boiling water and set it aside to steep.

Molly surveyed the room. "What a comfortable cabin. Thank you for inviting me to visit."

"It's a blessing to have company. Folks are so spread out around here I can't do much neighboring." She glanced at the baby, fidgeting in Molly's arms. "I expect you'd like to put her down for a spell. I'll get a quilt for you." Charity disappeared into the adjoining room.

Molly heard a cupboard open, then Charity returned carrying a red and white quilt. She shook it out and folded it in half before laying it on the smooth pine floorboards beside Molly's chair. "This should keep her comfy."

After kissing Lily's cheek, Molly placed her on her stomach on the quilt. "She likes bright colors." She watched Lily push herself up to study the diamond shapes stitched into stars. "It seems a shame to put a beautiful piece like that on the floor."

Charity sat across the table from Molly. "That's my North Star quilt. We hang that out on the line when it's safe for a runaway slave to stop here."

"That's what you meant on Sunday when you said Mr. Wolcott had a passenger."

Charity nodded. "Did Ellie explain what he was doing?"

"She said he probably had an escaped slave hidden in his wagon. Where'd he go?"

"I don't know. Mr. Wolcott doesn't always tell me." She met Molly's questioning gaze. "Southern slave hunters often come through here looking for runaways. If he got caught passing a slave on, he could be fined or jailed. Even here in Beldon Grove, not everyone is antislavery."

Molly reached for the mug of tea Charity poured for her. "Matthew said as much a few minutes ago." Her mind went back to Ellie shushing her on Sunday. "Even people in church?"

"Even people in church."

She sat in silence for a moment, digesting the information. "When I asked Matthew, he said you'd explain 'Black Codes' to me."

"When Illinois became a state, they compromised on slavery. It's forbidden, but Negroes don't have the same rights as white people." Charity sipped her tea. "For instance, free colored folks can't come here to settle. The Legislature doesn't think they're smart enough to take care of themselves."

"Not smart enough!" Molly thought of Betsy, who could read almost as well as she could. "All you have to do is teach them, like my mama did Betsy."

"But you know your mama oughtn't to have done that. It's

against the law in Kentucky, for sure." Charity stood and removed a pan of gingerbread twists from a shelf under the window. "These are cool now. How about one for you, Luellen?"

She tucked the doll under her arm and took one of the proffered treats. "Thank you."

Charity smiled. "You're welcome." She placed the gingerbread on the table.

Molly brought the subject back to Betsy. "We've been friends since we were children. Betsy's no different from me, except for her skin."

"Mr. Wolcott told me about her when he came back from Missouri with you and your young'uns. Said your brother-in-law wouldn't let her come with you."

Molly straightened her shoulders and fixed a determined gaze on Charity. "I'm going to find a way to bring her to Beldon Grove and set her free. I need her so I can—" She broke off. "I need her."

"Have you thought about what she'd do then? A woman alone, and a colored one at that."

"Why, live with me, of course, just like she always has."

An expression of pity crossed Charity's face. "How do you know that's what your friend would want?" She shook her head. "Well, anyways, you can't bring a slave into Illinois just so's you can set them free. That's against the Black Codes too."

17

Christmas 1838

Shafts of sunlight slanted over the prairie, turning fencepost shadows into black brushstrokes painted across the road. The sight made Molly think of the bars over a jailhouse window. *How can it be against the law to free Betsy? There's got to be a way around it.* Charity's news closed the door on her plans to buy the Negro woman. Without Betsy's help, Molly couldn't imagine how she'd get away to search for Franklin.

Heavy clouds locked together and the sky grew prematurely dark. The smell of rain filled the air. Matthew flicked the reins over the horse's back.

"Get up!" He glanced skyward. "We should be back at Pitt's before the storm lets loose—not that taking you there is my choice, you understand."

"Matt, please. We've said all there is to say."

When the wagon passed a lane that turned to the east off the main road, Molly observed two small buildings set back from the roadway. One appeared to be a dwelling, but for the first time she noticed a squat kiln behind the second one. Above the kiln, heat waves danced in the winter air.

Molly tapped Matthew's shoulder and pointed. "That looks like the ones at Samuel's brickyard, only a lot smaller."

"That's Griffiths' place. He's a potter. Makes the brown crockery we use at the house," Matthew said. "Fact is, he makes all the crockery folks use around here." He turned toward her. "He gets the clay from along the crick bank behind Wolcotts' place, then once a year he travels up to Galena to buy lead for glazing." He waved at a black man who emerged from the pottery shed. "The Griffiths seem like good people, even though they don't come to church."

Molly stared at him, astonished. "The Griffiths are colored?"

Matthew snorted. "Don't let Mrs. Griffith hear you—she'd faint dead away! That's Charlie Richards. He's indentured to the Griffiths. Few more years, I guess he'll be free."

Indentured. Molly's mind pounced on an idea. *I won't say anything until I know more.*

When Matthew stopped the wagon in front of Pitt's cabin, he set the brake and clasped Molly's hand. "Just so you know, I heard about another place you and the children might move to."

"Where?"

"I don't want to say until I'm sure. Meantime, Ellie's expecting you to stay with us over Christmas."

Molly had done her best to put the upcoming celebration out of her mind. Her losses over the past months had been too great. She wished they could simply skip to January and forget Christmas entirely.

Luellen wiggled on the seat next to her. "I like being at your house, Uncle Matthew."

Her uncle patted her head. "We like to have you there." He

glanced back at Molly. "Christmas Day is on a Tuesday, so plan on coming home with us after church Sunday."

Molly snugged the blanket around Lily and resigned herself to the holiday. *What can't be cured must be endured.* "We'll be ready."

❧

Lily wailed, hiccupped, then wailed again. The rockers on her cradle squeaked against the bare wooden floor. Aroused from a deep sleep, for a moment Molly couldn't remember where she was. She sat up, aware of Luellen's sleeping form beside her.

We're at Matthew's house. She shook off the remnants of a dream in which she and Samuel had been dancing together, enjoying their first Christmas as a married couple. The memory of fiddle music faded, replaced by Lily's insistent cries.

In the silver dawn light, she saw James curled into a lump on the trundle bed. Three months ago, she'd had two little boys. Tears burned her eyelids. *Dear Lord, please protect Franklin, wherever he is.*

While she nursed the baby, Molly's mind traveled back to the previous Christmas in St. Lawrenceville. Before daylight, Samuel had gone with the other men in the settlement to ride from house to house waking families by firing guns into the air. He'd been almost childlike in his excitement that morning. Franklin and James had both clamored to accompany their father, but she refused. Now she wished she'd let them go. *I thought there'd be other Christmases.* Tears slipped down her cheeks and dotted Lily's dark hair.

She thought of Betsy, living at Brody's. He'd never been one to coddle his slaves, even on a holiday. "I've got to get her to Illinois," she said aloud.

James rolled over on the trundle. "Who are you talking to?"

Molly wiped tears from her face with a corner of the bedsheet. "Myself, I guess."

His face reflected concern. "Were you crying for Papa and Franklin?"

She nodded.

He wrapped himself in a blanket and sat with his knees clutched to his chest. "It doesn't seem like Christmas without them—and Betsy. There's nothing to be happy about."

He looked so lost that Molly forgot her own misery. Somehow she had to rally enough energy to make the day pleasant for her children. She glanced out the window at a ripe persimmon-colored sunrise staining the horizon. "Look. It's going to be a pretty day."

"Yeah."

Molly inhaled the aroma of cloves, cinnamon, and nutmeg that drifted into the room. "Smell the plum pudding? I can almost taste it from here."

James dropped the blanket and stood, pulling his pants on over his long woolen underwear. His smile appeared forced. "Smells good, all right. I like plum pudding." He climbed onto the bed and leaned against her shoulder.

She bent her head, dropping a kiss on his tousled black hair. "I have an idea. Why don't you tiptoe downstairs and fill the wood box? It would be a nice surprise for Uncle Matthew. When Aunt Ruby comes, she'll want a steady fire for roasting the goose, and that takes a lot of wood."

James frowned. "Why aren't you going to cook for us?"

"Aunt Ruby cooks in this house. She doesn't like it when I get in her way."

Tears welled in his brown eyes. "Nothing's right anymore!"

173

"No, Son, it isn't. But we need to be grateful for Uncle Matthew's help. He does all he can for us." Molly kissed his cheek. "Now, go fill the wood box for our Christmas dinner."

After James left, she rocked back and forth with Lily in her arms, staring out the window. The brilliant promise of sunrise had faded to pewter gray snow clouds.

❧

By noon, a festive atmosphere filled the house, but it failed to touch Molly's heart. The Craig and McGarvie children ran in and out of the kitchen, playing tag until Aunt Ruby banished them to the back porch.

"I don't see how a body can get anything done with all that commotion going on!"

Molly noticed she smiled while she said it.

Uncle Arthur had carried the two cradles into the kitchen and set them under the stairwell, allowing Molly and Ellie to keep watch over their sleeping infants while helping Aunt Ruby serve the dinner. A goose, its skin roasted to a crackling brown, rested on the worktable beside the stove. Ruby spooned savory onion stuffing into a bowl, Molly mashed turnips, and Ellie transferred chunks of pickled beets from a crock to a chinaware plate.

Arthur stopped on his way to the back door. "How much longer? The young'uns are mighty hungry."

Molly smiled at him. "Are you sure it's just the young'uns that are hungry, Uncle?"

"It won't be long," Ruby said. "You and Matthew can go wash up."

"Music to my ears!" The door banged behind Arthur as he left the room.

Once the food had been served, the two families formed a

circle around the table, holding hands while Matthew blessed their Christmas feast. Molly peeked around at the nine bowed heads: Matthew's wife, Ellie, standing next to him, then their twins and three-year-old Harrison, her own children, James and Luellen, Aunt Ruby, dear Uncle Arthur, and, finally, her brother, his wiry hair already springing loose from the watering down he'd given it. While Matthew prayed, she mouthed a silent petition for Franklin and Betsy. *Please, Lord, let them both be here before next Christmas.*

When the prayer ended, she sat, her children on either side of her. In the ensuing busyness of passing food and helping Luellen cut her meat, her mind barely registered a tap at the back door.

"Come in, and welcome!" Matthew called.

The door swung inward and Dr. Spengler stepped into the room. His vivid blue eyes searched the faces around the table, skipping over Molly, settling on Matthew. "Didn't want to be by myself on Christmas Day. Been riding since before daylight to get here."

For an awkward moment, he stood inside the door, twisting his hat around in his large hands. A fresh spasm of grief brought tears to Molly's eyes. *If not for him, Franklin would be here now.* She buried her face in her napkin, struggling to control the sorrow that swept over her.

Matthew stood. "This is a surprise! Great to see you, Doc."

Ruby jumped to her feet and pointed at the wall behind Dr. Spengler. "Hang your things on one of those pegs. You must be half froze—and starved to boot."

Scooping Harrison out of his chair, Matthew gestured at the empty spot. "Sit down right here. You're just in time." He moved Harrison's plate next to his own and tucked his son onto his lap.

Ruby lifted a thick, brown crockery plate from a stack in the cupboard. She hurried across the room and plunked it in front of their unexpected guest. "Forks are in the tray. Just help yourself to anything that looks good to you. We've got plenty."

Gradually the meal resumed its former rhythm. Molly kept her eyes on her plate.

Dr. Spengler cleared his throat hesitantly. "You're looking well, Mrs. McGarvie." He pointed to the cradles under the stairwell. "One of those must be your new daughter."

Molly nodded. Keeping her voice impersonal, she replied, "Lily's in the cradle on the right."

"She's what, three months old?"

You were there—you should remember. "Three months today. She was born on the twenty-fifth of September." Molly clipped off the words and took a bite of food, ending the exchange.

Once the plum pudding had been consumed, Ellie excused herself to take Maria upstairs to nurse while Molly and Aunt Ruby tackled the stack of dirty dishes. In honor of Christmas, Matthew lit the fire in the parlor and allowed the children to sit in there and play games. He and Dr. Spengler stayed at the kitchen table, talking.

"How'd you happen to pick New Roanoke?" Matthew asked.

Dr. Spengler tipped back in his chair, clasping his hands behind his head. "They needed a doctor. Simple as that." The front legs of his chair thudded back onto the floor. "I stopped in a couple of other towns on the way, asked around to see if they had a doc. They said yes, so I kept riding. When I got to New Roanoke, the answer was no, so I stayed."

"I told you before you left you could've hung your shingle out right here."

Dr. Spengler glanced in Molly's direction, then looked back at Matthew. "I'm better off in New Roanoke."

A soft whimper issued from Lily's cradle. Molly dropped her dishtowel over the pile of forks on the drainboard and hurried toward the stairwell. The baby had pushed herself up on her elbows, rocking her bed back and forth. Her whimper changed to a wail. When Molly scooped her up, Lily pushed her face into her mother's neck, making hungry noises.

The doctor's eyes rested on the infant. "She sounds healthy, Mrs. McGarvie."

"She is." Molly turned her back and climbed the stairs.

❧

By the time she rejoined the family, everyone had moved into the parlor. Yellow flames from the fireplace brightened the room and cast a glow over the children playing checkers on the hearth rug.

Uncle Arthur held his fiddle tucked under his chin. The bow carried the lively notes of "Joy to the World" into the room. Molly stood in the doorway and listened to the blend of voices harmonizing their way through the familiar melody. She struggled not to weep at memories of Samuel playing the dulcimer and his deep voice singing carols as part of their Christmas celebrations in Missouri. Molly put a hand on her chest, as though she could rub the pain away. *Smile. Don't spoil things for the children.*

"Come, sit!" Ellie whispered, patting a space on the black horsehair upholstery of the settee. "There's room next to me." Molly slid into the empty spot. Luellen climbed onto her lap and James scooted over to lean against her knees.

Ellie looked at her uncle. "Will you play 'Hark the Herald Angels Sing'?"

Arthur nodded and slid the bow into position. Tapping his foot, he filled the room with music. When the carol ended, he looked down at the tumble of boys lying in front of the fire. "Here's one for the little fellas," he said.

"All around the cobbler's bench, the monkey chased the weasel," the fiddle sang. The boys jumped up, Jimmy and Johnny joining hands to form a bridge. Luellen wiggled off Molly's lap to join in skipping between the twins and trying not to get caught when the weasel "popped."

Molly glanced up and caught Dr. Spengler gazing at her from his chair next to the hearth. She couldn't read his expression. Was it guilt? Anxiety? She turned away, staring into the fire.

He cleared his throat. "I need to talk to you privately." He spoke in a low voice that traveled under the gaiety of the fiddle and laughing children.

"I don't believe we have anything to talk about."

The doctor stood and stepped over to the settee. "I have a message from Betsy." He headed for the doorway.

Molly followed him into the kitchen and leaned against the worktable, her arms folded over her chest. Leftover aromas from the meal lingered in the air. Appetizing as they had been, they now sickened her. All she wanted to do was hear Betsy's message and then excuse herself as quickly as possible.

Dr. Spengler combed his fingers through his blond hair. An embarrassed flush rose in his cheeks. "I was in St. Lawrenceville back in October—"

"October! And you wait until now to give me the message? I pray it wasn't life or death!"

A spark of anger lit his eyes. "It wasn't." He jammed his hands in his pockets and held her gaze. "Are you ready to listen?"

"Yes." Molly jutted her chin in the air and looked out the window.

"I called on the Crosses while I was there. Betsy was working for them, on loan from Brody McGarvie. I told her about . . . about Franklin." He stopped and swallowed. "She said to tell you she's saving her money to buy her freedom so she can come to you."

Molly swayed forward, covering her face with her hands. The tears she'd fought back all day poured down her cheeks. "Betsy! If only she were here right now. I've never needed her more." Her shoulders heaved. She clapped one hand over her mouth to muffle her sobs.

Three steps and Dr. Spengler stood next to her, offering his handkerchief. Awkwardly, he slipped an arm around her and patted her shoulder. Without thinking, she slid her arms around his waist, seeking comfort from the warmth of his body.

What am I doing? Molly jerked out of his embrace. The two of them stared at each other for a long moment, then she turned and ran from the room.

18

January 1839

Karl Spengler stood in his office in New Roanoke, reliving the moment in Matthew's kitchen as he'd done dozens of times since leaving Beldon Grove. Molly's shoulders felt so small, so fragile under his hands. He told himself that as a physician he was concerned about her thinness. But deep inside he knew it was more than that. *Let it go, Spengler. Of all the women out there, that one can never be yours.*

Restless, he stepped outside, ducking to avoid melted snow dripping from the roof. *Too early to be this warm. Next thing we know it'll freeze and the whole town'll be covered with ice.* Karl looked up and down the state road that ran through the settlement to see if any patients might be coming his way. *Doesn't look like anyone's wanting a doc this afternoon.*

Back in the front room of his cabin he scribbled "Gone to Fortune House" on a scrap of paper. He tacked the message above the latchstring and walked south toward the inn.

When he pushed open the heavy door, the aroma of tobacco smoke and whiskey from the public room assaulted his nostrils.

Julius raised his hand in greeting from his station behind the bar. "Doc! Good to see you."

"You too." Karl settled into a chair next to a round table. Although it was late afternoon, the room was empty of patrons. "Where's all your customers? I hoped for a game of checkers."

"Dunno. Working outside, mebbe. Nice to have a bright day for a change." He picked up a rag and polished an already-clean glass. Giving Karl a sideways glance, he said, "Lydia's likely not busy. Some fresh air'd do her good. Why don't you see if she'd like a walk?"

Karl tried not to let his annoyance show. He'd come here hoping for some male companionship, not to escort the innkeeper's daughter along the board walkway that fronted Fortune House. Since his return from Beldon Grove, her fawning attention had lost its appeal.

Before he could respond, Julius stepped from behind the bar and opened the door to the apartment he shared with Lydia. "Lyddie! Company!"

The blonde woman appeared in the doorway. "Who is it, Papa?" Her expression changed from curiosity to pleasure when she saw Karl. "Doctor! What a nice surprise. Won't you come in?"

"He's come to take you for a walk," her father said. "Isn't that right, Spengler?"

"Uh, yes. That is, if you want to, Miss Lydia."

"Of course! I'll get my wrap."

Once outside, the two of them paced slowly along the boardwalk. Lydia slipped on a wet spot, and Karl reached out and grabbed her arm.

"Thank you." With her elbow, she pressed his hand tightly against her side. "It's so pleasant out here today, isn't it? Such a nice change."

He pulled his hand free. "Indeed."

"The weather here is harsher than it is in Virginia. It's difficult to get used to."

"You seem to have adjusted." Karl looked down at Lydia's face, which reflected the rosy glow of her bright red shawl.

She met his gaze. "This place gave my mother consumption. That's why she took me and went back to Virginia." Lydia pulled a handkerchief from her sleeve and dabbed at her eyes. "Mama died when I was just seventeen."

"Your father told me. I'm sorry."

She nodded, acknowledging his comment. "I stayed on with my Grandma Bell for two more years, until I finished at Miss Mowbry's School for Young Ladies. Then Grandma died. Papa said it was time for me to come home." She bit her lip. "Truthfully though, Doctor Karl, Illinois isn't home to me. It never will be."

They reached the end of the boardwalk and started back toward the inn. The sun had slipped behind a stand of cottonwoods and the air felt chilly. Karl buttoned his jacket. "I'm sure you'll change your mind after you've been here a while."

She smiled up at him. "I won't have to. Once we're married, we'll go back to Philadelphia, won't we?"

❧

In her living quarters in the blacksmith's house, Molly sat at her loom working on an order. She threw the shuttle and pulled the beater against the fabric with a *thunk*. Changing treadles, she raised a different set of warp yarns and threw the shuttle back, catching it in her right hand. The copperas-colored wool filled her nostrils with a faint odor of sheep.

In spite of her best intentions, her mind continued to return to the moment in Matthew's kitchen when Dr. Spengler had held her while she wept. The memory stirred feelings she thought had died with Samuel. Guilt surfaced. She felt disloyal, not only to her husband, but to Franklin. *I should be focusing all my thoughts on finding him. Why do I keep thinking about the doctor?*

The shuttle slipped from her fingers and hit the floor. "Drat! Now I have to rewrap the bobbin." Molly gathered the bluish-green wool into her lap and lifted the rod from its boat-shaped holder. She held the bobbin in one hand and rolled loose yarn around the shaft.

It took her a moment to notice the tapping at the door of her living quarters.

"Mrs. McGarvie?" Mr. Pitt called. "Are you well?"

She rested the bobbin on top of the warp yarn. "Of course." When she opened the door she stared at him, puzzled. "Why do you ask?"

"It's past suppertime and nothing's on the table."

"What!" Molly glanced over his shoulder into the kitchen area. "Where's James? When he comes from school, I start the meal."

"I ain't seen your boy."

Fear prickled through Molly. She pushed past Mr. Pitt and ran to the front door. Luellen followed. "Is James lost too, Mama?"

"Oh dear Lord, I pray not!" She grabbed her shawl from a peg and jerked open the door.

The blacksmith came to her side. "Where you going?"

"To look for my son."

"It's going on dark. It's not safe for you to be out there alone."

"Then come with me. Either way, I'm going." She turned to Luellen, whose eyes were wide with worry. "Lulie, sit with the baby. And stay put. I won't be long."

"Mama." Tears slipped over her cheeks. "I'm scared."

Dropping to one knee, Molly hugged her tightly. "It will be all right. Just do what Mama says." She kissed both wet cheeks, then patted Luellen's bottom. "Go on now."

Mr. Pitt waited at the door. Molly joined him and the two of them hurried along the road toward the school. Dusk settled over the village, turning trees and buildings into pools of darkness. Their footsteps on the packed earth sounded loud in the evening quiet.

"I can't imagine what might have happened." Molly walked so fast her words came out in short bursts.

Behind her, the blacksmith grunted acknowledgment of her statement. "Couldn't be anything too bad or we'd have heard."

A shape moved between buildings ahead of them. When it passed out of the shadows, the shape turned into a boy.

"Mama?" James ran toward her. "Why are you here?"

"Looking for you." She grabbed him in a fierce hug, holding him until he wiggled loose. "You're not hurt?"

James shook his head.

Mr. Pitt stepped next to Molly. "Where you been, boy? You done scared your poor mama half to death."

"I . . . I had to stay after school and clean the classroom."

Molly noticed the sound of tears in his voice. "After school? What on earth did you do?"

They started back toward the house. Molly waited for her son to respond.

"Answer your mama, young fella," Mr. Pitt said.

James's hand crept into his mother's. He sniffled. "One of the big boys dared me to climb on top of the outhouse, so I did." His voice wavered. "Trouble was, the schoolmaster was in there. He caught me, but the others ran off and he didn't see them." James moved closer to Molly's side and lowered his voice to a whisper. "I got a whipping in front of everybody."

184

Molly's heart tightened. James had never been in trouble before. Was it her fault? Was she neglecting him in her anxiety to find Franklin?

Mr. Pitt cleared his throat. "The lad needs a father, Mrs. Mc-Garvie." The tone of his voice left no doubt who that father should be.

That night, after everyone had fallen asleep, Molly stood beside the banked hearth in the bedroom, weeping silently. Was Mr. Pitt right? She knew he'd propose if she gave him the slightest encouragement. Should she marry him and let him take care of her and her children? Could it be that Franklin was indeed dead and she was deluding herself? Darkness cloaked the room, save for an edge of moonlight that slid under the drawn curtain. Molly dropped to her knees beside the bed, her wrapper snugged around her shoulders. "Lord, show me what to do! I can't go on like this." Silence enveloped her, deep and black. She kept her head bowed, waiting. Time slipped past. Her legs grew stiff, still she knelt.

"Franklin is alive."

Molly's head jerked up. The same voice she'd heard before. The edge of moonlight shimmered when she gazed at it.

Peace flowed through her, and a calm assurance that one day she would see her son again. She stood and lifted her hands toward heaven, as though she could touch the source of her consolation.

❧

One afternoon the following week, Molly heard a knock at the front door while she was settling Lily for a nap.

Luellen dropped the slate on which she'd been drawing and ran out of the room. "I'll answer it."

Wearily, Molly nodded assent toward her daughter's retreating back. Snowfall over the past several days had prevented the child from playing outdoors, and Molly was hard pressed to keep her occupied. Precious time at the loom slipped away while she helped Luellen with the alphabet and taught her simple rhymes.

"Mama! Come quick!"

What now? Molly scooped Lily into her arms and hurried out of the room. When she recognized their callers, her jaw dropped. "Marjolaine? Colonel Cross?" She couldn't have been more surprised if the governor of Illinois had been standing in Mr. Pitt's kitchen.

Marjolaine swept across the room, the skirt of her green silk gown brushing the floorboards. Her husband followed. "It's so good to see you." The older woman wrapped her arms around Molly and the baby. "When you left St. Lawrenceville I feared we'd never meet again, yet here we are!" She stepped back and held out her arms. "Let me see your Lily. Oh, so pretty! Such curls. Such eyes."

Molly stood dumbstruck.

"Quite a surprise, eh?" Colonel Cross took her hand and gallantly raised it to his lips.

"However did you find me?"

"We stopped at the mercantile and the proprietor told us you were living here." He glanced around the room. "A saddlebag cabin, eh?" He pointed at the central fireplace which served the two adjoining rooms. "Much nicer than the one you had in Missouri."

Molly bit her lip. "This isn't mine. Surely Mr. Wolcott told you I'm just the housekeeper here."

Marjolaine's expression clouded. "He did. I'm terribly sad to see you in such circumstances." She held Lily with one arm and

186

slipped the other around Molly's waist. "And we're oh so sorry to hear about Franklin. My dear, what a blow."

"Yes, but—" Molly stopped. She'd learned her lesson about trying to convince people that Franklin lived. She knew it, and that was enough.

Colonel Cross stepped toward the door. "I'll leave you ladies to visit. I want to talk to your storekeeper about suppliers." He winked at his wife. "Marjolaine has some special news for you. We're on our way to Vandalia for a political meeting but wanted to see you in person rather than try to send a written message."

Once the door closed behind him, Molly pulled a chair from the table. "Please, sit. Give me a moment to put Lily to bed and then I'll make tea."

While she tucked the covers around Lily's shoulders, Molly wondered what could be important enough to cause her friends to detour miles out of their way to see her. Luellen followed into their living quarters and Molly directed her toward the cradle. "Watch Lily, please. Mrs. Cross and Mama have to talk."

When she returned to the kitchen, she noticed Marjolaine staring up at the loft. "Is that where your employer sleeps?"

"It is."

Her guest drifted around the combination kitchen and sitting room, studying the furnishings. "Mr. Pitt must be very prosperous. This case clock is a costly piece—cherry wood. The painting on the moon dial is especially fine. And that Windsor." She pointed to an armchair fitted with rockers that faced the hearth. "That had to have come up from New Orleans."

"He's busy most of the time, that's all I know." Molly poured hot water over the leaves in the blacksmith's china teapot.

"And what do you do to pass the day?"

Molly pointed at the door to the other room. "Those are our quarters. I work at my weaving."

"The storekeeper showed us your handbill. How enterprising."

"It was your idea, remember? You said I should sell my work."

Her friend shook her head. "Yes, but I never really believed you would."

Molly smiled slightly. "I'm planning to buy Betsy as soon as I have enough saved."

Marjolaine whirled around, raising one blonde eyebrow. "I'm afraid you're too late. The colonel and I already bought her. She will come to live with us when we return from Vandalia."

The teapot lid slipped from Molly's fingers. "What?"

Obviously pleased with her news, the older woman nodded. Her satin bonnet bobbed over her curls. "Brody told everyone he was going to sell her to the next slave trader that came through. Said he couldn't afford to keep her—she'd been spoiled by your soft treatment and wouldn't work." Marjolaine paused, frowning. "I think Patience had something to do with it. That woman seems unbalanced."

Molly sank into a chair. "You bought her," she repeated, stunned. Absently, she pulled at a tendril of hair and twisted it while she spoke. "But I want Betsy here with me."

Marjolaine swooped into a chair next to Molly, putting an arm around her shoulder. "How were you going to be able to do that, my friend? Working as a domestic and weaving a coverlet now and then?" She didn't wait for a response. "At least with us she has a good home, a bed upstairs in our attic—not in a slave cabin, mind you—and plenty to eat. You know I'm very fond of her. She'll be treated well."

Molly freed herself from Marjolaine's embrace and stood, hands on hips. "But she's still a slave. That's not what she wants. It's not what I want, either."

The older woman faced her. For the first time, Molly noticed a flint-hard expression usually concealed by Marjolaine's soft smile. "What you want has nothing to do with it. I thought you'd be pleased that we saved Betsy from the slave market. But pleased or not, Betsy is mine."

19

February 1839

Betsy opened her eyes, startled to see daylight streaming through her bare window. "Mercy sakes! Why'd I sleep so long! Colonel Cross'll be expecting breakfast any minute."

She slipped out of her narrow bed under the eaves of the Crosses' upper story, her feet touching the braided rug Miz Marjolaine had provided. Wiggling her toes, Betsy took a moment to reflect on how her life had improved since she came to live with her new owners. She had a room inside the main house, with a wooden bedstead and chest to hold her belongings. True, snow sifted through gaps in the clapboards near the roof, but that only happened in winter. When spring came, she'd be able to enjoy the little window that faced the main road without wrapping herself in her Sunflower quilt to stay warm.

Betsy hurried into her dress, pulling the drawstring tight around her middle, then slipped an apron over her head. Tying her kerchief in place, she ran down the narrow stairs and into the kitchen. With quick movements, she opened the firebox on the cookstove and tossed in several pine sticks, gratified to see last night's coals immediately brighten and begin to gnaw at the edges of the resinous wood.

While the stove heated, Betsy filled the coffee boiler with water from a crock near the back door, then unwrapped a chunk of bacon and carved off a dozen slices. *Hope Crosses slept late too.* Still moving at top speed, she dropped the bacon into a skillet and measured flour and lard into a bowl for biscuits.

The kitchen door swung open and Miz Marjolaine swept into the room, wearing her morning gown of lavender silk moiré. "Betsy! The Colonel is waiting for his breakfast. What's keeping you?"

Betsy ducked her head. "Sorry, Miz Marjolaine. I slept past sunup this morning."

"You know we went to a great deal of expense to buy you from Brody McGarvie and give you this good home." Miz Marjolaine's lips pinched together. "The least you could do in return is see to it meals are on time. I didn't bargain on having to teach you how to be a house girl after all the time you spent with Molly's family in Kentucky." The ribbons on her lace cap jiggled as she spoke.

"Yes'm. I'll bring coffee right now." Betsy studied the floury mixture in the yellow crockery bowl. *Don't have time for beaten biscuits. I'll turn this into flapjacks.* After delivering the coffee to the Crosses' table, she poured sour milk foamed with pearlash into the flour, stirring the batter as it thickened.

Miz Marjolaine's words about Molly's family stung Betsy's heart. She'd been carefully taught in the ways of a house servant from the time she was old enough to help her mama in the kitchen on the Craig farm. *Miz Marjolaine make it sound like the Craigs was no-count folks.* Tears flooded her eyes at the memory of Molly's kind mother. *She was good to me—I should've been more grateful when I had the chance.* She sniffled as she poured a ladle of batter onto the hot griddle. *I can't figure Miz Marjolaine out. One day she sweet as pie, next day she hollering all the time.*

The door popped open again. "Betsy! How much longer?"

From the dining room, Betsy heard Colonel Cross's mild voice. "My dear, a few more minutes won't make any difference. Come back and sit down."

Ignoring him, Miz Marjolaine snapped, "Well?"

Betsy slipped the first flapjacks onto a platter, adding a rasher of bacon to one side. "Right now, ma'am." She hurried past her mistress to set the food on the table.

By early afternoon, Miz Marjolaine's humor seemed restored. She entered the parlor where Betsy applied blacking to the round stove at the rear of the room. "Have you been outdoors to enjoy the sunshine?"

"No'm. Not since emptying the chamber pots, leastways."

"Why don't we take the covers off my bed and hang them to air? The breeze will freshen them nicely."

Betsy followed her mistress into the large bedroom she shared with her husband. *Wish she'd thought of this before I made the bed!* Miz Marjolaine grabbed the top coverlet and tugged it loose, tossing it in Betsy's direction. Pillows spilled onto the floor. Sheets tangled in the center of the feather tick. Sighing at the thought of putting the linens back in order for the second time that day, Betsy trudged out the back door carrying the pile of bedclothes.

Miz Marjolaine stood near the clothesline and watched. "If you like, you may have the evening off. We won't be needing you for anything after the supper things are put away."

I can go see Reuben! "Thank you, ma'am." She threw a coverlet over the line.

"Don't mention it, Betsy. We're happy to do all we can to make your life here a good one—" Miz Marjolaine stopped, frowning at the bedding swaying in the breeze. "Take that one with the flowers and hang it inside out so it won't fade. Do I have to tell you how to do everything?"

The sparkle went out of the afternoon. "No'm." Betsy flipped the coverlet over. "I was getting to it." She ran her hands over the dark blue crewelwork embroidery, envisioning Molly's deft fingers stitching the design. The thought of Molly now working as a housekeeper was almost beyond imagining. *She surely did enjoy her weaving. I wonder does she still get to do it?*

Uncle Arthur called "Gee!" to the horses, and the buggy swung left onto a narrow lane that ran along one side of the town square. "About a half mile on," Matthew said to Molly.

She straightened on the rear seat, shifting Lily on her knee so she could peer between Matthew and Arthur. A rectangular cabin sat near the edge of a grove of bare oak and shagbark hickory trees. A broad stone chimney, framed by narrow windows on each side, rose above the roofline on the west end of the building. Dried grasses and weeds slumped in the deserted yard.

"Is that it?"

"Sure is," Uncle Arthur said.

"Where's the woods Ruby said was full of panthers?"

"Over there." He pointed to a stand of trees some distance beyond the cabin. "Don't let her worry you none. I've never heard of panthers coming into town."

Uncle Arthur reined the horses to a stop in front of the cabin. Molly took a moment to study the log structure before climbing out of the buggy. The chinking appeared solid and the shutters over the window at the east end hung straight and sturdy. *At least it looks better than the Barker place.*

Her brother jumped down and opened the thick plank door. "Come see." He walked back to the wagon, holding up his hands. "I'll take the baby while you get down."

Molly walked to the doorway, her gaze taking in the long, narrow building. The stone hearth in front of the wide fireplace extended nearly three feet into the room. Exposed log beams crossed overhead at spaced intervals. She hesitated, not yet willing to claim the space as her own. What if someone decided to take this one away too?

Matthew walked up behind her. "What do you think?"

"I'm afraid to get too excited. Are you sure about it?"

"Completely. It's the old schoolhouse—the school board met last night and granted it to you."

"Who's on the board?"

Her brother grinned. "Me. Ben Wolcott. And the miller out west of town." His eyes crinkled at the corners. "It was unanimous."

Molly threw back her head and laughed. She couldn't remember the last time she'd felt so lighthearted.

Matthew took her arm. "Go on in. Take a look at your home." He stamped on the floor. A solid *thunk* sounded under the heel of his boot. "Hear that? Nice and sturdy." He pointed at the beams overhead. "Those are strong enough to hold a loft if you want one."

"And I can put walls in to make this into separate rooms," Arthur said, joining them inside.

She turned toward him. "I'll think about that later, Uncle. We don't need walls." Molly paced the length of the room, stopping under a window at the southeastern corner. She turned toward her brother. "This would be a fine place to put my loom—plenty of light."

Peering through the grimy windowpane, she surveyed the

194

overgrown plot of land behind the cabin. "Matt, could you maybe plow this so I can plant my flax seeds this spring?"

Matthew and Arthur looked at each other, "She likes it!" written on their faces. Her brother replied, "Sure can. No trouble at all."

Puzzled, Molly faced the two men. "Why didn't you tell me about this a long time ago?"

"Guess I'm not so bright sometimes," Uncle Arthur said, a sheepish expression on his face. "I been looking for a house, not a school. I'm sorry."

She hugged him. "It doesn't matter now. How soon can we bring my movables over here?"

Matthew grinned at her. "How about tomorrow?"

☙

"The fireplace is going to be a problem," Molly told Matthew the next afternoon, once he'd finished setting up beds in the center of the long room. "It's made for heat, not cooking."

She stood by the fire, warming her aching back. Molly could feel every muscle she'd used to scrub the floor. While she worked, she'd mentally partitioned the cabin into three areas: kitchen, sleeping, and a place for her loom and spinning wheels.

Now Matthew joined her in front of the fire. "What's the difference?"

"No crane. I can cook in the coals, but how will I hang pots?"

Her brother surveyed the jumble of trunks and boxes surrounding them. "Aren't you putting the cart before the horse? I don't see any pots."

Riled, she faced him. "I wish you'd take me seriously!"

He held up his hand. "Settle down. You can have the smithy make a standing crane for you. It won't be the same as one that'll swing out, but it'll give you something to hang pots on."

She raised an eyebrow. "Ask Mr. Pitt for a favor? You know he's upset at my leaving. He's not likely to agree to help me now."

"Offer to sell him that black gelding of Samuel's. The horse is worth a fair bit. That way it won't be a favor."

She peeked over her shoulder to be sure the children couldn't hear them. "But James should have his father's horse. I can't sell Captain."

"Think about it anyway. You don't need him—he's been out in my barn since you got to Illinois."

After he walked away, Molly studied the open hearth. It would be like cooking over a campfire. *Matthew's right. It won't hurt to ask.*

❧

Back at Mr. Pitt's house at the end of the day, Molly's eyes swept the room she'd occupied, checking to see if she'd forgotten anything. Matthew waited out front with her children in his wagon. *No trace.* She sighed, relieved the awkward living arrangement had ended.

Footsteps crossed the living area and stopped behind her. She knew the blacksmith from the characteristic odor of smoke and stale sweat which clung to his clothing. "Mr. Pitt." Molly turned to face him.

His eyes drooped at the corners. "I'm right sorry you're leaving. You were coming along fine."

She decided to take that as a compliment. "Thank you."

"If'n you change your mind, you just come on back." He reached for her hand. "In fact, I'd be honored—"

"Could we talk business for a moment?" She folded her arms across her waist, tucking her hands out of sight.

Mr. Pitt blinked in surprise. "What?"

"I'll sell you a fine black gelding if you'll make a standing crane for my new home."

ༀ

When they turned onto the lane that began at Griffiths' pottery works and ended at her home, Matthew said, "Mrs. Griffith has a couple of nearly grown sons. Maybe you could work out something with her to get them to supply you with firewood. That stack I brought won't last out the month."

"I can cut firewood," James said.

His uncle turned and smiled at him. "You can chop branches, but it'll be awhile before you're big enough to cut trees down."

"But I want to help Mama."

Molly reached back and patted his knee through the heavy lap robe. "Don't you worry—there'll be plenty for you to do. Don't forget you're the man in the family."

Matthew stopped the wagon in front of the McGarvies' cabin. Excited, the children quickly scrambled down and pushed open the door. Molly joined them, carrying Lily. The fire had gone out, leaving the large room icy cold.

"I'll build a fire, Mama." James reached for pieces of kindling in the wood box.

"Here's some lucifers." Matthew handed James a small cast iron match safe. "Keep them away from your little sister."

James struck the friction match on one of the hearthstones and held it to the pile of kindling.

Molly patted his shoulder. "Thank you, Son."

She was rewarded by a proud smile. "You're welcome, Mama."

Matthew carried in the trunk full of blankets. "Guess this is it." He checked the basket of food resting on the table. "You're sure this is enough to hold you 'til I take you to the mercantile on Saturday?"

"It's more than enough to feed us for the next day and a half," Molly said. "Thank Ellie and Aunt Ruby again for me."

After Matthew left, she stepped back, glancing around the room. Her eyes lingered on familiar objects she'd brought from their home in Missouri. A flame of hope blazed in her heart. *I don't care what Marjolaine said. If I have enough money, I know she'll sell Betsy to me.*

That night she lay awake next to Luellen, enjoying the sensation of having her own walls around her after more than two months spent under the blacksmith's roof. Her daughter mumbled in her sleep, scooting closer. Molly slid an arm around her, glancing down at Lily asleep in her cradle and James lumped on the trundle bed. She closed her eyes.

Outside, a panther screamed.

20

As promised, Matthew arrived at Molly's cabin on Saturday. When Molly opened the door for her brother, a concerned expression crossed his face. "Your eyes look like two burnt holes in a blanket! Are you ill?"

"No. Just tired." She returned his hug and stepped back so he could enter.

Matthew surveyed the room. "You're all settled in." Admiration tinged his voice. "No wonder you're tired. You probably worked nonstop since I left Thursday."

"That's not it." Before she had the opportunity to say more, her children ran to greet their uncle.

Matthew placed a hand on James's shoulder. "It's clear today. Why don't you take your sister outside to play?"

"Mama won't let us. She's afraid a panther will eat us."

"Is that right?"

"You should hear them at night." Molly shuddered. "They sound like women screaming! What if they come in after us? I just know I couldn't get the flintlock loaded quick enough."

"Oh, Molly." He sat on a bench next to the table and patted the space beside him. "Come, sit."

He wrapped an arm around her shoulders, a slight smile twitching at the corner of his lips. "Panthers are afraid of people. Besides, how would they get in? This cabin is built like a fort." He hugged her to him. "Let the children out to play."

Luellen ran for the door. "I want to explore the woods!"

"No!" Matthew roared. He jumped to his feet, drawing himself up so that he looked taller than his five feet ten inches. Molly watched, startled. Her peaceful brother assumed a fierce expression and glared down at her children. "You can go outside, but no exploring. Stay away from those woods. You hear me?"

Cowed, they nodded. Luellen ran to her mother and hid her face in Molly's skirt.

Matthew sucked in a deep breath and settled back to his normal size. He dropped to one knee and held his arms out to Luellen, who walked toward him uncertainly. "I'm sorry to scare you, Lulie, but the panthers you hear live back in those woods. They won't come out in the daylight, so you'll be fine if you just stay close to the cabin."

James walked over to Luellen, placing a protective hand on her shoulder. "Don't worry, Uncle Matthew. I'll watch her." The two of them pulled on coats and dashed out the door.

Raising an eyebrow, her brother studied Molly quizzically. "Are you having second thoughts? Surely you've heard panthers before."

"Not this close."

Matthew leaned forward, resting his forearms on the tabletop. "You can always come back and live with us. No one would think worse of you for it."

Her mind pictured the smug expression Aunt Ruby would wear if Molly came cowering back to her brother's home. She stood. "I'm staying here. My children need to grow up under their own roof." *All of them.*

Matthew turned the wagon right at the east end of town and headed along the square toward Wolcotts' general store. Molly, cuddling Lily under her shawl as protection from the brisk wind, looked over the raw town forming on the Illinois prairie. Her brother pointed out a log building on their right.

"Post office is going in there. Pretty soon folks won't have to go to Rushville to get mail. Still going to cost twenty-five cents to get a letter, though." He turned left at the corner, stopping his team in front of Wolcotts' store.

Luellen and James scrambled off the wagon, eager to look at the merchandise displayed inside.

"Don't touch anything," Molly said. "If you're good, I'll buy you each a peppermint."

Luellen turned and sent her a sweet smile. "Thank you, Mama. I'll be good."

Mr. Wolcott looked up when they walked inside. "Mrs. McGarvie. Got any more blankets ready?"

"Just the two. I haven't had time to finish another one."

"Heard you're getting some orders from folks."

She nodded. "It's hard to keep up, but I'm glad for the work. I'm saving all the money I can."

He bent and lifted a black ledger book from under the cash box. "Speaking of money, I owe you for the coverlets you left with me, but it'll probably be some time before I can get you the cash."

Molly raised her eyebrows. "Why?"

A discordant clanging rang through the building and interrupted their conversation. Molly spun around and saw James standing next to a toppled pile of iron pots, shock written on his face.

Momentarily forgetting Mr. Wolcott, she hurried toward the commotion. "What on earth?"

James hung his head. "It was an accident, Mama. I didn't mean to. I just backed up and ran into them."

Mr. Wolcott joined them. "No harm done. Probably scared him more than anything." He turned to her son. "You're going to pick them up, aren't you?"

"Yessir."

"I'll help." Luellen squatted, righting a shiny round pot, then stacked another on top of it.

The storekeeper smiled at her. "Good girl. I need to finish talking to your mama." He guided Molly back toward the counter. "Here's the thing. Folks around here seldom pay in cash. It's mostly barter. I only get cash when I send goods to market in the cities, or when a trader comes through. If you want to do business here, that's the way it is."

She swallowed disappointment. She wanted to see the coins, to feel them in her palm. That way she'd know how close she was to having enough to get Betsy away from Marjolaine.

Mr. Wolcott flexed his fingers and then patted the ledger. "Don't worry. I keep track in here. When I get my money, you'll get yours."

Molly considered the folded list in her pocket. She'd come in hoping to have enough money from the sale of a blanket to cover necessities with possibly some left over for a blue-paper-wrapped cone of hard sugar. "But I need supplies."

Again the storekeeper patted the ledger. "I'll write down what you owe me. When we settle up, you'll get the difference."

When she'd moved to the Barker place, Molly still had a bit of cash left in Samuel's money pouch. Now that was spent and she'd have to trust Mr. Wolcott, both for her savings and for her daily needs. Why hadn't she asked about this before? How did she know he was honest?

Matthew must have read her expression, because he joined their conversation. "I've known Ben for many years. If he says he'll do a thing, it'll be aboveboard."

Molly hesitated, then reached into her pocket and drew out the slip of paper. "All right. Here's my list."

Shortly after Matthew deposited Molly and the children back at her cabin, she heard a knock at the door. She opened it, expecting to see her brother standing on the stoop with a last-minute admonition for her. Instead, a rawboned woman of medium height, her rust-colored hair eclipsed by gray, waited there. "The storekeeper says you do weaving. That true?"

"It is. Won't you come in?" Molly swung the door wide. "I'm Molly McGarvie."

"I'm Amber Griffith. We live up the road a piece."

The potter's wife. The one with the two sons Matthew told her might help with firewood. "Please come in. I've been wanting to meet you."

Amber settled herself in one of the two bentwood chairs next to the hearth, her gaze sweeping the converted schoolhouse. "You've made it cozy in here."

Molly glanced around the room and tried to see it through her neighbor's eyes. Since there were no walls, the view was unimpeded from end to end. Loom, beds, table, benches, cupboard.

"Thank you." She smiled. "If cozy means crowded, I guess it is." After filling two pewter mugs from a crock of water near the door, she offered one to her guest before taking the chair beside her.

While she sipped the water, Amber continued to look around

203

her. "You have a barn frame loom," she said, a sound of real interest in her voice. "We haven't had a weaver come through here since last spring. In November my husband took about fifty skeins of wool, already dyed, in trade for a pottery order. I don't have no loom. Could you work it up for me? We'd pay you, of course."

"I need a supply of firewood. My brother says you have sons? If they'd cut wood for me, I'd be pleased to trade it for weaving."

Amber beamed. "Got two boys, seventeen and nineteen. Both big and strong. It's settled, then?"

"I'm not sure how much firewood to ask for."

"How much do you need?"

"Well, half a cord can keep us going for some time."

"A full cord would be your rightful share."

Molly shook her head. "That sounds like too much."

"Not to me." Amber chuckled. "Having someone right down the road who can loom wool is worth more than that! Waiting all year for a weaver to come along can be mighty trying at times. You know how fast boys wear out their clothes."

Molly's mind flashed to Franklin. How much had he grown since last September? Was he being properly clothed? She closed her eyes for a moment and waited for his image to pass. Not talking about her son was a painful aspect of her determination to get him back.

"Molly? Is anything wrong?" Molly opened her eyes to see her neighbor bending toward her.

She shook her head. "No. Just dizzy for a moment." Molly relaxed as they firmed up the details of their barter, happy to have another woman to talk to even if she did need to avoid the subject of Franklin.

Before leaving, Amber promised to send her sons over right away so Molly could show them where to stack the wood.

Molly stared in dismay at the baskets filled with hickory-dyed wool that Amber's boys had delivered. *Fifty skeins!* Somehow she hadn't pictured it as being such a great amount. Her other orders would need to wait so she could repay the Griffiths promptly for the wood their sons had split and stacked. It had already taken the better part of a day to warp the loom before she could start on the faster process of actual weaving.

She flexed her shoulders and picked up the shuttle, sending it through the warp threads. Thankfully the sun had come out, so Luellen could stay outside and play. Lily slept and James would be in school for two more hours. Molly pulled the beater and changed treadles. The familiar activity had a hypnotic effect. The shuttle flew, the beater pushed the threads together, and the treadles changed the pattern. When she wasn't rushed, she relished the process.

She caught the shuttle, and then paused. What was that noise? Molly cocked her head to one side and listened. A panther's scream. Her blood chilled. In the daylight? Matthew said that didn't happen. She pushed back the stool and ran for the door. "Luellen! Come in now!"

No answer. Molly's breath caught in her throat. She hurried outside. "Luellen!" How long had it been since she'd heard the child playing? She couldn't remember. *Where is she?*

The panther screamed again. Then Molly noticed a trail broken through the dead grass behind the cabin.

"Oh, Lord, no!"

She turned and raced inside, grabbing the flintlock from its place on the wall. Her hands shook so much that she dropped the shooting bag and wasted precious moments gathering its contents off the floor. She leaned the rifle against the table, measured powder from the horn, and poured it down the barrel. Perspiration trickled over her temples. *This is taking too long. Why didn't I practice more?*

Molly found a patch in the bag and spit on it, laid it over the end of the barrel, and shoved the ball down on top with the round-ended ball starter.

How much time had passed? She heard the creature scream again.

"Lord, help me!"

Matthew's instruction came back to her: *Slow down. You'll make a mistake if you hurry. Use the ramrod and seat the ball good. Wait to prime the pan until you're ready to shoot.*

She seized the loaded rifle and dashed out the door, pausing to close it behind her to protect Lily. Then she raced toward the woods.

"Lulie! Answer me!"

The cry of the panther sounded closer. Molly slowed to a walk, taking one step at a time and listening for her daughter. She crept toward the trees until she stood behind a deadfall hickory. Scanning the forest, she thought she saw a touch of blue. Luellen had worn her blue dress that day.

Molly leaned forward, peering through the brush, her heart pounding so loudly it threatened to drown out all other sounds.

There. Luellen, staring upward.

On a branch above her head, a five-foot-long panther switched his golden brown tail and growled deep in his throat. Molly slid to her knees on the spongy forest floor. She had only one chance to kill the animal before it attacked.

With unnatural calm, she lifted the rifle until it was at shoulder level. *Now draw back the hammer and prime the pan,* she heard

Matthew's voice tell her. *Careful. Too much powder and it will blow up in your face when you pull the trigger.*

She angled the rifle upward, resting it on the hickory stump. The barrel lined up with the panther's chest. Molly sucked in a deep breath, then released the set trigger. The powder flashed and she heard a resounding explosion. Recoil rammed her backwards.

Through the gunsmoke she saw the predator slam sideways from the force of the bullet, then somersault out of the tree. It thudded to the ground two feet in front of Luellen.

21

Molly dashed through the trees and snatched her daughter off the ground. She pushed the now hysterical child behind her and approached the motionless animal, gripping the still-smoking rifle by its barrel. If the panther moved, she'd club it across the face with the stock.

She leaned close enough to see blood spilling from a ragged hole behind the animal's right shoulder. Tentatively, she poked the rifle against its side. Not a twitch. Molly backed away, clutching her daughter's hand, then turned and ran. Glancing back at the woods to be sure they weren't being followed by another panther, she tore across the open field toward the cabin, tugging her daughter behind her. Once inside, she dropped the rifle on the table and collapsed into a chair. Every nerve in her body vibrated.

"Come here." Molly held out her arms. "Let me look at you." She turned Luellen around searching for wounds, but found none. "Are you hurt?"

"N . . . no." She shook her head, sobbing.

Molly rocked the trembling child back and forth, covering her cheeks with kisses. She couldn't hold her tightly enough. Later there would be time to decide on punishment for her disobedience. Right now, she rejoiced in her daughter's safety.

Gradually, Luellen stopped crying and stared up at her mother, her face still white with fear. "Mama. You shot that panther."

"He would have killed you, Lulie." Molly's voice shook.

It had happened so fast. Across the room the shuttle rested on the warp yarns of her loom. Lily napped in her cradle. Nothing looked out of place, yet if a few more minutes had passed before she heard the panther, Luellen would be gone just like Franklin was gone.

Heightened awareness suffused Molly's mind. You could lose a child even when you thought you knew exactly where they were.

Oh, Lord. Molly squeezed her eyes shut. *I must apologize to Dr. Spengler!*

Banging at the door interrupted her thoughts. "Miz McGarvie! Are you all right?"

Molly put Luellen down and moved to answer the door. Amber Griffith's sons, Landon and Daniel, stood on the stoop. Both young men were as rawboned as their mother, but much taller.

Landon studied her, worry lines impressed on his forehead. "We heard a shot. Ma sent us over here to check on you."

Molly pressed her hands to her temples. "I killed a panther. Luellen was in the woods. It was ready to . . ." Her voice caught in her throat. "I shot it."

Admiration crossed their faces.

"Well, if that don't beat all!" Daniel said, with a cheek-splitting grin. "Where is it?" He gazed around the cabin.

"Not here!" Molly shuddered. "It's right where it fell, back in the trees."

Landon cleared his throat. "Ma'am? Begging your permission,

could we have the hide? I'll tan it for you, and give you whatever Wolcott thinks it's worth."

The thought of handling the dead animal made Molly light-headed. "Take it. Do what you want."

Daniel turned and stepped into the yard, apparently eager to head for the woods, but Landon paused. "You and the girl ain't hurt?"

Molly shook her head.

He looked over her shoulder. "You want I should clean that rifle for you? It'll foul if you don't swab it out."

All Molly wanted was time alone to think. "I know how to do it. Thank you, and thank your mama for her concern."

Once they'd gone, she tucked the exhausted Luellen in bed for a nap and then sat at the table staring at the rifle. All her accusations against Dr. Spengler rolled through her mind. *He didn't deserve any of them.* She cringed, remembering the way she'd yelled at him.

How could she make it right, especially after the encounter in Matthew's kitchen at Christmas? She'd have to find a way to apologize without sounding like she was setting her cap for him.

◠

"Someone's coming, Mama! Hear the wagon?" Luellen ran to the door.

Molly slid her feet from the treadles and stood, rubbing the back of her neck. She'd stayed up late the previous night working on an order, and today she had hoped to complete it. There wasn't room in her plans for interruptions.

She lifted the latch and looked outside. A wagon carrying an odd-looking contraption rounded the corner and rattled down the lane toward her. Its wheels crunched on the frosty ground.

Who could that be? She straightened, clutching her shawl around her chest, and waited.

When he drew closer, the driver raised his hat in greeting. "Mrs. McGarvie. How are you this afternoon?" Mr. Pitt said. James stood behind him in the wagon bed, holding the back of the seat.

"Mr. Pitt. I didn't realize school was out already. How kind of you to bring James home." She hoped he didn't intend a long visit. Since she'd settled into the former schoolhouse, the blacksmith had found reasons to drop by every few days.

"That's not all I brought you." He pointed at the horseshoe-legged black apparatus, positioned lengthwise in the back of the wagon. "Here's your standing crane. I finished it this morning."

Her hand flew to her mouth. "But the horse is still at Matthew's. I'm not able to pay you right now."

"It don't matter. You can have your brother bring him by next week." Mr. Pitt climbed off the wagon seat. "Come see if it'll do."

When she walked over to the wagon to inspect the sturdy forged iron crane, Molly felt a momentary tingle of pleasure at the prospect of being able to cook without stooping over coals in the fireplace. Then guilt enveloped her. *I shouldn't give up Samuel's horse. Our sons ought to have him.*

She remembered the day eleven years ago when Samuel had first ridden to her father's farm to court her. Captain had been newly broken and Samuel had to fight to keep him from rearing at the sound of her father's barking hounds. She could still picture his strong hands gripping the reins until the horse calmed.

Molly sighed. *Letting go of the past is so hard! It's not just the big losses, it's all the little ones.*

211

She swallowed her memories and reached out to pat James's shoulder. "Are you going to carry our new crane into the cabin for me?" She forced lightness into her voice.

The blacksmith laughed. "It's going to take more'n me and a boy to move that thing. It's near as big as you are. James, how 'bout you go down to Griffiths' and see if their sons could be spared to give us a hand."

In a short while, Amber's two sons loped down the road toward them, James hurrying to keep pace.

"James here says you need help, ma'am," Landon said, looking worried. "Is something wrong?"

Molly smiled reassurance. "No, we just need some muscles to get this iron crane into the cabin and set it in the fireplace."

"Well, we got muscles, don't we, Landon?" Daniel said, punching his older brother on the shoulder. "We dig clay for Pa all the time. We can carry that crane with no trouble at all."

After a large amount of grunting and hefting, the brothers got the crane out of the wagon. With the blacksmith supporting the crossbar, the three of them worked it through the door. Molly followed them inside. They eased it down with the front portion of the horseshoe legs resting on the hearth and the back slightly into the glowing pile of coals.

Mr. Pitt wiped his forehead with the back of his arm. "Whew! Wouldn't want to do that every day." He turned to Molly. "Leave it sit like this for a bit. New iron needs to heat slow—you wouldn't want it to crack."

She nodded and looked at the Griffith boys. "Since you were so good to help us, would you like some coffee? The pot's nearly full. And there's a bit of johnnycake left from dinner."

212

"No thanks, ma'am," Landon replied. "Pa needs us to help fire an order of jars. We'd best get back."

Daniel flashed his wide grin. "Send for us when you're ready to move that crane into the fireplace."

After they left, the blacksmith chuckled. "Old Ridley Griffith's got himself a couple of good boys. One of these days he'll be turning his pottery business over to them." He wiped his hands on his buckskin trousers and gazed meaningfully at James. "A man needs sons to carry on his trade."

Molly watched as he slid a bench away from the table and sank down on it. It appeared he was settling in for a lengthy stay.

"That offer for coffee still good?" he asked.

Weaving waited on her loom, but she couldn't refuse him hospitality after the effort he'd expended to craft and deliver the crane. "Of course." She poured a mug and handed it to him.

Luellen went to the cupboard and put plates on the table. "You said we could have some johnnycake, Mama."

"So I did." Biting her lip, she lifted a linen towel from the pan of corn bread and set it in front of Mr. Pitt. After he served himself, James and Luellen each took a wedge. They sat in silence, munching on their snack, their eyes darting between their mother and the blacksmith.

He flicked crumbs from his straggly beard. "This'd be better if you made it with milk instead of water."

Lord, give me patience. "I don't have a place to keep my cow. We get by without milk for now."

"What you need's a barn raising."

"It's still too cold."

Mr. Pitt looked at James and Luellen. "Why don't you young'uns go play over by the fire? I want a word with your mama."

Molly bristled. "They can sit here if they want."

"It's warmer by the fire," James said. He stood and tapped Luellen on top of her head. "C'mon. I'll read you a story."

The blacksmith waited until both children had settled in front of the hearth, then he leaned across the table. "It pains me to see you so tired. I heard you're wanting enough money to buy a slave gal you left behind in Missouri. You know this here's a free state, don't you?"

Stunned, Molly stared at him. How had he learned of her plans? Then she glanced at Luellen and knew the answer. Little Miss Chatterbox.

She took a deep breath and met Mr. Pitt's eyes. "Once Betsy is with me, she won't be a slave. There's no law against indentured servants."

He opened his mouth to say something else, but she held up her hand to stop him.

"Betsy and I grew up together. Until now, we've never been apart." Of course, this wasn't her entire reason for wanting Betsy in Illinois, but the rest of it needed to stay secret.

The blacksmith reached across the table and placed one of his calloused hands over hers. He lowered his voice. "If we was married, I'd be pleased to give you the money to buy that gal."

For an instant, Molly considered his proposal. Marriage to the blacksmith would mean no more long hours hunched over the loom, plenty of food for herself and her children, someone to protect them from harm . . .

But she didn't want Betsy just to have Betsy. She needed her to stay with the children so Molly could search for Franklin. Without asking, she knew Mr. Pitt would never allow such a thing. He'd probably lock her in a room if he even suspected her plans.

She drew her hand away from his. "Mr. Pitt. I couldn't marry

214

you under such circumstances." *Or any other circumstances, for that matter.*

He smiled at her, unruffled. "Think on it. You'll get mighty weary of working so hard for so little." He pushed back from the table and walked to the door. "I'll come by again. Maybe by then you'll want that Betsy enough to want me too."

❧

Betsy and Reuben walked toward the Des Moines River. Reuben carried a fishing pole and creel, Betsy toted her Sunflower quilt and a tin bucket filled with corn biscuits and bacon.

"Sunday afternoons are the bestest time, ain't they?" Reuben said.

She nodded agreement. "Half a day to do what we want."

They passed through a thicket of closely spaced willow trees. The earth beneath their feet changed from heavy loam to the sandy-textured soil deposited by years of seasonal flooding. Shafts of early spring sunlight dappled the clearing. The flutelike call of a wood thrush competed with the song of the river tumbling over rocks.

We never been this far away before. Betsy's heart beat faster at the thought.

Upon reaching the bank, Reuben baited his hook while she spread the quilt and placed their dinner pail next to it. Sitting behind him, Betsy watched the muscles in his upper arms flex as he cast the line into the water. His dark skin shone in the afternoon light.

With a fisherman's intensity, Reuben kept his eyes on the cork he used for a bobber. When it ducked beneath the surface, he set the hook and stepped back to work the fish to shore. Betsy leaned forward to observe.

"A pike," he called over his shoulder. "Got a power of fight in him."

After he'd landed two more pike and a catfish, Reuben left the wicker creel at the water's edge and walked over to the edge of the quilt.

Betsy blinked up at him. "I'm just about to fall asleep. It's nice sitting here."

When he lowered himself next to her, she noticed how his muscular thighs strained at the cloth of the homespun pants he wore. The sight of him triggered warmth in the center of her belly. She scooted to one side, uncomfortable with the direction her thoughts were taking. Reuben looked puzzled when she moved away.

"How 'bout I make us a fire and cook up a mess of fish?" he asked. "Won't take long."

❧

The remains of the fire cast a muted glow in the twilight. Reuben lay back on the quilt, hands behind his head. Betsy sat near his feet, watching changing patterns of orange and blue flicker over the coals. Gray smoke spiraled upward through the trees.

"We'd best start back before it gets full dark," she said. "Wouldn't want no one to think we'd run off."

Reuben stood, stretching. He reached out and helped Betsy to her feet, but instead of letting go he drew her toward him. Her heart pounded so hard she felt sure he could hear it. Bending his head, he kissed her on the cheek, then his lips found hers. For a moment she yielded completely, wanting nothing more than to be as close to his body as possible. He kissed her again. His lips were surprisingly soft—somehow she'd expected them to be muscular, like the rest of his body.

Trembling with awakened desire, Betsy pushed herself away from his embrace. "We can't. It wouldn't be right."

He groaned, taking Betsy by the shoulders and leaning his forehead onto the top of her head. "I cares for you something fierce. I watches you all the time when you're coming and going from the Colonel's."

She rested against his chest and felt his heart thud against his ribs. "Reuben, I cares for you too. I feel safe when you're around." She stepped back, studying his face in the growing twilight. "But we can't just roll around here in the woods. Man and woman need to do right in the eyes of God. We ain't animals."

Reuben sat on the quilt again, folded his legs in front of him, and reached for Betsy. She knelt and they faced each other.

He gazed into her eyes. "I wants you to marry me. We kin get the blacksmith to say the words. He's a preacher when we ain't got a real one around here."

Betsy hugged herself around her middle, feeling if she let go she'd crumble like crushed pottery. "No, Reuben, I ain't going marry you. I ain't going marry nobody lessen me an' him both be free." When she saw his stunned expression, she yearned to reach out and comfort him, but she feared where that would lead. Instead she said, "We can't never be sure one or the other of us won't be sold off. Look what happened to Tildy's man."

He reached across the quilt and pulled her into his lap. "Then what're we going to do?"

22

March 1839

Molly stood on her doorstep and drew her shawl close around her shoulders against the tang of not-yet-departed overnight cold. Matthew's wagon, followed by Uncle Arthur's buggy, rolled to a stop in front of her cabin. To her surprise, several other families she'd met at church arrived after Uncle Arthur.

Amber Griffith, accompanied by her husband, sons, and their indentured man, Charlie, walked toward the gathering. Molly surveyed the crowd, hoping Mr. Pitt hadn't come, but there he stood next to his wagon. She turned her head and pretended not to notice him.

Early morning sunlight glittered on the frost-covered grass. Horses stamped and blew steam from their nostrils, their harnesses creaking. Luellen hid behind her, peering out at the growing crowd. "What's everybody doing here, Mama?"

"They're going to build a shed for our cow." Molly hugged her daughter to her side. "I had no idea so many folks would turn out."

James elbowed past her and ran toward Matthew's wagon.

"Flossie!" He rubbed the forehead of the black and white cow tied at the back.

Molly blinked back tears. Flossie had been Franklin's pet. He'd hand-raised her from the time she was a newborn calf. She followed him around like a puppy until Molly had to forbid Franklin to go into the pasture for fear the cow would run to him and knock him down. *When I get him back, I'll let him spend all the time he wants with Flossie.*

She walked to her brother's wagon, still thinking about her son. She smiled at Ellie, who sat beside Matthew holding their daughter, Maria. "It's a treat to see you."

"You too."

"It'll be good to have fresh milk and butter again, Matt." Molly glanced into the wagon bed. "With all the grass around here, she may not need that hay."

"Better to have it and not need it than to need it and not have it."

With a nod, Molly acknowledged his often-repeated maxim.

Aunt Ruby hurried over to them. "Ellie, you need to get that baby out of this cold air." Glancing over her shoulder at her husband, she called out, "Arthur! Bring that basket of food with you. We're going inside."

People climbed down from wagons. The men formed a group around Matthew. The women, carrying food baskets, walked toward the door of McGarvies' cabin.

"Put everything on the table until later," Ruby told them. She glanced around the rectangular room. "Looks like you're doing the best you can to make this a home, Molly."

What's that supposed to mean? She opened her mouth to respond when Landon appeared, carrying a large Dutch oven wrapped in toweling.

219

"Where d'you want this, Miz McGarvie?" he asked. "Ma made you a pot of stew."

She pushed a trivet into the coals. "Right here—it'll keep warm without burning."

After setting the oven near the fire, Landon stepped sideways, stopping near Molly. "Is there anything else I kin do for you? Bring in firewood, maybe?"

He stood close enough for her to notice the smell of damp clay mingled with sweat hovering about him.

She moved back a pace. "Thank you, no. I'm sure the men could use your help outside."

"Well, you holler if you think of something." Landon moved a step closer. He bent his head toward her, an earnest expression on his face. Speaking just above a whisper, he said, "I can take care of most anything you need."

Although he appeared freshly shaved, dark shadows of beard outlined his square jaw. Landon's thick, russet-brown hair stood out slightly from his head, giving him a wild appearance. Broad-shouldered and at least six feet tall, he towered above her.

Molly took another step backward and glanced nervously toward the chattering group of women standing inside the door. For once, she was happy to see Aunt Ruby headed in her direction.

"Molly, I hope you're not expecting me to do everything today. You need to make more space for all this food."

She slipped around Landon and placed her hand on Aunt Ruby's shoulder, guiding her toward the table. "I'll take care of it, but I'd appreciate your help." With Ruby around, Landon wouldn't be able to get her alone.

She watched him as he left. He closed the door with a last meaningful glance in her direction. *Why me? I'm thirty years old, with four children!* She remembered a conversation she'd overheard recently between Matthew and Mr. Wolcott. They were discussing the shortage of marriageable women in Beldon Grove. It had been Mr. Wolcott's opinion that they'd have to attract more settlers or risk losing the single men to bigger towns. "A man gets close to twenty," he'd said, "he's going to be wanting a wife."

Maybe Landon didn't realize her age. After all, Ellie was ten years younger and she, too, had four children. Molly considered her appearance, compared to Ellie's. They were similar in height and weight. Neither one had the matronly appearance of some of the other women in the room, although Molly was fairly certain she'd noticed gray hairs this morning when she brushed out her hair before braiding it.

She bit her lip. *I'll just have to keep my distance.*

☙

The thud of axes ringing against hickory logs provided harmony to the flute of women's voices in the cabin. Outdoors, children ran and shouted. Through the thick glass of a south-facing window, Molly saw that the riven walls of the cowshed had reached shoulder height. The rounded sides of the logs had been shaped with an adze to flatten them for stacking, which helped the work go faster.

Aunt Ruby joined her at the window. "It's warming right up today. I'll get Arthur to put up a table outside for the food. It's near dinnertime."

She smiled and nodded agreement with herself, hurrying off without waiting for a reply. Molly heard her hollering "Ar-thur!" when she stepped outside.

Once a makeshift table was assembled from spare boards, the women placed their contributions along its length. Not since leaving Kentucky had Molly seen such a feast: venison, hominy, ham, beans, squirrel stew, even real wheat bread and honey.

After Matthew asked the blessing, Molly looked at the towns-folk. "I can't thank you all enough." She brushed tears from her cheeks. "I never dreamed . . ." Her voice caught in her throat.

Matthew patted her shoulder. One of the men called out, "That's what we do around here, Mrs. McGarvie—look out for each other."

Another voice added, "C'mon, let's dig in. We got a lot to do before nightfall."

The families lined up to fill plates. Molly waited until last, tak-ing enough to share with Luellen. She walked to a bench near the cabin wall and sat down to cut the food into small bites.

"Mind if I sit here?" Mr. Pitt stood in front of her, holding a heaped-up plate in one hand. Without waiting for an answer, he settled next to Luellen.

"Of course, sit," Molly replied, as though he hadn't already done so. She looked around hoping to see someone else heading her way. Everyone seemed occupied with eating—no one paid any attention to her. Luellen bounced on the bench between her mother and Mr. Pitt, swinging her legs while chewing on a chunk of bread.

After swallowing a mouthful, he turned toward Molly. "Have you been thinking about—"

"There you are. I been looking for you." Breathless, Landon settled near Molly's feet and balanced his plate on one knee.

Mr. Pitt glared at the young man. "You'll get your backside wet, sonny, sitting on the ground."

"These is oiled britches. I won't get wet." Landon glared back. He busied himself with his knife, cutting hunks from the slab of venison on his plate. He cleared his throat. "You got a fine cow there. I'd be happy to see to the milking."

"Uh, no. I've got James for that."

Landon gestured at the tops and limbs of cut hickory trees piled behind the shed. "Looks like he's got more'n enough to do already. Ain't he supposed to be cutting them limbs into firewood for you? Don't seem he's making much progress." He jabbed a piece of venison with his fork and shoved it into his mouth.

"You and Daniel do enough for me as it is. But it's kind of you to offer." Molly took a breath. *Lord, please send someone else over here.* She tried to catch Matthew's eye.

Mr. Pitt cleared his throat. "Hope you know you can call on me for anything needs doing around here. Seems like you've got boys trying to do a man's work."

Landon scooted closer to her feet. Ignoring the blacksmith, he shot Molly a soulful look. "I'd do just about anything to help you out. It just don't seem right, a pretty lady like you alone with these young'uns." He wiped his mouth with his fingers. "Maybe you'd—"

His brother Daniel whapped his hat against Landon's back. "Here you are. I'm all done eating and you're just poking along." He squatted on his haunches next to Landon. "They want us to start shortening logs for the gables. I brought your bucksaw." He held out the tool.

"Landon! Daniel!"

Both young men sprang to their feet.

"That's Pa," Landon said to Molly. "I better go." He sent her one final calf-eyed gaze and loped toward his father.

Molly frowned after him. Things were complicated enough with the blacksmith hovering around, but Amber's oldest boy considering her an eligible woman left her stunned. James, now nine years old, still wasn't big enough to cut down trees and buck logs. Matthew had done more than his share, Molly couldn't ask him to take on the job of providing firewood too. She needed Landon's help, along with that of his brother, to remain in her home.

Late afternoon sun streaked through the narrow windows that flanked the fireplace. Outside, the men had fastened the last clapboard onto poles, completing the roof on Molly's new cowshed.

Uncle Arthur entered the cabin where the women had gathered to gossip and tend babies. "Well, we've got 'er licked, Molly. Your Flossie has her own little barn. We've made it big enough to hold a calf too, if you want to put your cow with a bull this spring."

"Arthur!" Aunt Ruby blushed to her hairline. "Such talk. Stay outside if that's the best you can do."

Molly walked over to Uncle Arthur and patted his arm. "It's all right, Uncle. I'll walk out with you to see Flossie settled in."

The area out back had been trodden flat by men trimming and hoisting logs to construct the outbuilding. Molly savored the damp, earthy aroma rising from the muddy ground. *Smells like spring. Next month it'll be time to plant the flax.* She pushed down an apprehensive quiver at the thought of more chores. *Not now. Think about it later.*

Arthur led her to Flossie, closed inside one of the two stalls. The cow had her head down in a manger chewing the hay Matthew provided.

Molly leaned over the side of the stall and stroked the animal's neck. "She looks content in her new home."

A warm breeze passed through the small building, filling the interior with the fragrance of fresh-cut hickory.

"You'll still have to chink the walls." Arthur pointed toward bars of sunlight filtering through narrow spaces between logs. "But with the cold weather about over, you'll have time to get it done before next winter."

"You've helped me so much." Molly squeezed his arm. "How can I ever repay you?"

Arthur acted as though he hadn't heard, but by now Molly had learned to interpret his silences as meaning he felt there was nothing he needed to say.

What a dear man he is! I've been so blessed to have his help.

A voice cut into the quiet. "Well, forevermore! Here you are." Ruby stood at the entrance, hands on hips. "I've been hunting all over for you. It's time to load the wagon—folks are leaving." She turned and preceded him toward the house, talking all the while. "I declare, you're always so busy helping Molly, you forget your other responsibilities."

Arthur paused in the doorway and turned back to Molly. Keeping his voice low, he said, "Don't let her bother you none. She's all bark and no bite."

She shrugged. "Ruby is Ruby."

Nevertheless, once Uncle Arthur walked away, Molly leaned against Flossie's stall, arms folded across her waist. "He's not always busy helping me," she said to the cow. "He hasn't been here for weeks." She glowered at Aunt Ruby's retreating back. "Old biddy!"

Flossie continued to crunch hay, chewing as if to let Molly know there were more important things in life than Ruby Newberry.

Through the doorway, Molly watched various families loading tools and food baskets into wagons. She started out to repeat her thanks to each one when she heard voices coming through the back wall.

"When're you going to go courting and find yourself a wife,

Landon?" Molly didn't recognize the speaker's voice. The man added, "There's probably a dozen girls between here and New Roanoke that'd be glad to get married."

Her breath caught in her throat when she heard Landon's answer.

"I've already found someone. Just have to talk her into it."

☙

Amber poked her head through the open doorway. "Hello, Molly! I cooked up some dried pumpkin yesterday. Thought you and the young'uns might like a bit of pudding." She placed a brown crockery bowl on the table.

Molly's nose caught the spicy aroma of ginger and cinnamon that drifted up from the bowl. "Thank you! It smells delicious." She smiled at her neighbor. "Sit a spell. We haven't had a good visit for a couple of weeks."

The woman took a chair next to Molly, and held out her arms. "Let me hold that baby! I swan, she gets bigger every day."

Lily gurgled and cooed, rocking on Amber's lap while Amber grasped her chubby hands.

"The children will be pleased to have something special after supper. I don't take time to make treats much—about all I do is work at the loom."

"And it's lovely work you do! I sewed pants for Ridley and the boys out of some of what you wove for me. A nice tight weave it is. Should wear a long time." Amber tickled Lily's round belly, drawing a giggle from the baby. "I sure do thank you."

"I've been thanked enough with all the firewood and having logs cut for my cowshed."

"Talking about wood, I notice you still have all them treetops piled out behind your place." She shifted Lily to a sitting position. "Wasn't young James supposed to cut them up for you?"

Molly looked out a window toward the bristly pile of hickory limbs heaped near the edge of the nearby grove. "He's been working at it, but it takes him almost as long to carry the cut wood up here as it does to saw it into pieces."

"How about I have Landon come take care of them? Wouldn't take him more'n a day or two."

Molly swallowed. *What'll I say? The last thing I want is Landon over here.* "That's kind, but James would be crushed if he felt I was taking away his job. He wants to be the man of the house."

Lily lunged across Amber's lap, reaching for her mother. "Whoa there, little one!" Amber handed the baby to Molly and then leaned back in her chair apparently pondering Molly's response. "Well, how about I send Landon over to drag them tops up here? He can use one of our horses. That way James won't have to waste so much time carrying the wood."

"Couldn't Daniel do it just as well? I know your husband needs Landon's help in the pottery works."

Amber studied her, one eyebrow raised. "Is there something wrong with Landon? Hasn't he done a good job for you?"

What could she say that wouldn't alienate her neighbor? At that moment, Luellen dropped the tin plate from which she'd been pretending to feed her doll. It clattered on the stone hearth, startling Lily into tears.

"Lulie!" Molly spoke more sharply than she intended. "Now see what you've done. Can't you play quietly?"

Her daughter's lower lip trembled. Wailing, she ran for the trundle bed and threw herself across it.

A headache squeezed between Molly's temples. She turned to her guest, raising her voice to be heard over her children's howls.

227

"Landon's work is fine. It'll help James if one of your boys hauls those tops up by the cabin. I just hate to be beholden to you any more than I already am." Molly jiggled Lily, tickling her neck to coax a smile out through the tears.

Amber patted her shoulder. "Don't you worry about being beholden. Landon'll be glad to do it. He's been asking me if there was more chores he could do for you." She smiled complacently. "He's a good boy, is Landon."

✑

A candle burning in the center of the table cast wavering shadows over the walls. Darkness outside turned the windows into mirrors. Molly noticed her reflection as she sat tallying the chits Mr. Wolcott had given her. *I look like a drudge. I need to take better care of myself.* Loose hair straggled down her neck, her dress was carelessly tied, her apron had food splotches across the front. *Samuel wouldn't recognize me.* Straightening, Molly ran fingers through her hair, pushing stray tendrils under the coil of braids at the back of her head, then picked up a pencil and wrote: "Four blankets—twenty-eight dollars." She studied the total, then added a question mark. Mr. Wolcott had yet to settle accounts with her.

Although she'd been paid with provisions—potatoes, ham, a sack of beans—for some of the weaving she did for people in the community, occasionally a settler's family had ready cash. Molly shoved the pencil behind one ear and dumped an assortment of coins out of the tin box where she kept her savings. She pushed them into a pile, counting. "Not quite thirteen dollars. At this rate, it'll take me to the end of the year or longer to get Betsy." Her voice sounded loud in the quiet room. What would become of Franklin in that time? Where was he now? Her thoughts fragmented with worry. *There's got to be something more I can do.*

Molly scooped the money back into the box, laying the notebook and chits on top of the pile, and walked to the bed. She pulled her nightgown from under the pillow and was about to step out of her dress when she saw a flash of white at the window behind her loom. Cold fear tingled through her body. *Someone's out there!*

Keeping her movements casual, Molly walked to the door, heart pounding in her throat. She tugged the latchstring inside, then shot the wooden bolt in place. When she blew out the candle, a faint glow from the banked fire spilled onto the hearth. Molly grabbed the money box and stepped backward, blending into the darkness.

After a moment, the face appeared again. Molly gasped. Squinting, she tried to discern who it might be. Without light reflected from inside, all she saw was an indistinct shape. Was that long hair, or shadows?

She studied the flintlock rifle hanging on the wall. She'd left it loaded. The bag containing gunpowder dangled below the weapon. All Molly needed to do was prime the pan and fire.

She turned back to the window. The face had disappeared.

23

"Thank you for taking me to the mercantile," Molly said to Matthew. "It's a long walk, and those blankets were heavy." She arranged her cloak to cover Lily, who slept against her shoulder. "Looks like we're in for some rain."

He checked the sky and urged the team into a faster trot.

"Ho there! Matthew Craig!" A horse and rider approached from the west. The stranger overtook their wagon, then slowed his horse to a walk alongside.

Molly peered around her brother and tried to see the rider, but he was wrapped in a heavy overcoat with his hat worn low on his forehead. "Who . . . ?"

The man swept off his hat, smiling at the passengers in the wagon. With a start, she recognized Dr. Spengler.

Matthew pulled the horses to a stop. "Doc! Haven't seen you since Christmas. What brings you down our way?"

Molly looked up at the doctor. His blond hair whipped back from his face in the brisk wind. His clean-shaven cheeks had reddened in the cold, emphasizing the blue of his eyes.

"Good to see you, Mrs. McGarvie," he said.

"Yes, you too." Molly's face felt hot in spite of the chill air. She wasn't prepared to offer the apology she knew she owed him. She needed more time. Somehow, looking at his face, all she could think about was his arms around her in Matthew's kitchen. *What can I possibly say that won't sound like I'm interested in him?*

Dr. Spengler turned his attention to Matthew, answering his question. "I'm on my way to Fox River, but couldn't pass by without saying howdy."

Her brother whispered in her ear, "It'd be sociable to offer him a hot drink and some food. Can I invite him to follow us to your place?"

She nodded and swallowed hard. Part of her hoped there'd be no opportunity for a private word with the doctor. But in her heart she knew an apology was long overdue. How he accepted it was not up to her. She needed to do the right thing.

Once they reached her cabin, Molly tucked the still-sleeping Lily into her cradle and moved it close to the fire. James and Luellen crowded near the hearth to warm their hands and backsides.

After the men carried in her supplies, they joined the children in front of the fireplace. Avoiding Dr. Spengler's eyes, she asked, "Will you have a bite to eat before you go on your way? I'll fry some cornmeal mush." She pointed at the coffee boiler, which sat on a trivet at the edge of the fire. "Coffee's still hot."

Dr. Spengler blinked in surprise at her cordial tone. He shoved his hands in his pockets, stretching his shoulders and rolling his neck from side to side. "Thank you. I am kind of empty after riding all morning."

Matthew went to the door and squinted at the sky. "Probably be awhile yet before that rain gets here. I'll be glad to stay too."

Molly tipped the contents of a square earthenware pudding dish onto a cutting board and divided the stiff cornmeal mixture

231

into five thick slices. Luellen crowded under her elbow. "Let me help you, Mama."

"You can get the butter out of the cupboard and bring it to me."

Luellen marched past James. "I get to help Mama."

"I always help Mama," he said. "I'm the man of the family."

"That's enough, children. Remember, we have a guest."

Self-importantly, Luellen brushed by her brother and thumped the butter crock on the tabletop next to Molly's cutting board.

"Thank you, Lulie. Now why don't you play a game with James while I cook?"

Matthew turned to the doctor. "Long as you're in town, you're welcome to stay at our place. Ellie would be glad to see you."

"Appreciate it, but I'm anxious to get to Fox River. Besides checking on my . . . parents, I'm hoping to talk my brother Joseph into taking over my practice in New Roanoke."

After tapping a dollop of lard onto a three-legged griddle, Molly grasped its long handle and pushed it over the coals to heat. Straightening, she looked at the doctor, puzzled. "Why do you want your brother to take over? What are you going to do?"

He leaned toward her, folding his hands together on the tabletop. "I've decided to open a practice here in Beldon Grove."

Molly felt her heart thud in her throat. Now she'd have to apologize. She'd be seeing him often once he was settled in the community. "We do need a doctor." She kept her voice noncommittal.

Matthew clapped him on the shoulder. "That's great news, Doc! Be good to have you around." He tossed a glance at his sister. "Don't you think so, Molly?"

She picked up the cutting board, pretending she hadn't heard her brother's question. With a cake turner, she slid mush slices onto the heated griddle. Staring into the coals, she remembered the devastation and guilt written over Dr. Spengler's face when she'd first accused him of losing Franklin. *How could I have been so cruel?*

Molly kept her back to the room, trying to calm the fluttering in her stomach. In spite of the appetizing aroma of roasted corn rising from the griddle, she knew she wouldn't be able to swallow a bite.

Luellen appeared at her side. "Can I help some more, Mama?"

"You're supposed to be with James."

"He doesn't want to play."

Molly cupped a hand over her daughter's curls. "Then you can put the plates around the table." She looked at her son. "Go outside and wash. Food's almost ready."

⌒

The men did most of the talking during the meal, while Molly pushed a small square of browned mush back and forth across her plate. Her mind raced, searching for the best way to speak to the doctor before he left. She looked at her now-cold food. *There is no best way. I just have to do it.*

Dr. Spengler placed his fork on his empty plate and pushed back from the table. "Thanks for the meal." He lifted his coat from a peg near the door and shrugged his arms into the sleeves. "It's getting late. I'd best be on the road."

Matthew stood. "Before you go, tell us why you've decided to settle in Beldon Grove. It's a real surprise."

"To make a long story short, New Roanoke didn't suit me." He turned toward the door.

Molly jumped to her feet. "Dr. Spengler."

He regarded her, eyes wary. "Yes?"

She knew he expected another of her accusatory tongue-

233

lashings. After all, how else had she ever addressed him? "May I speak with you a moment? Privately?"

Molly ignored Matthew's startled expression. She wrapped her cloak around her shoulders and opened the door. When she stepped outside, a gust of wind whipped through her hair and caught at her skirts.

The doctor followed her, shutting the door behind them. "Not a good day to linger in the cold." Clutching the brim of his hat, he moved toward the edge of the stoop. "If it's about your son, I don't think there's anything more to say."

She put her hand on his wrist. "Just one thing. I'm sorry."

"*You're* sorry?"

"You weren't at fault in Franklin's disappearance. I know that now." Molly searched his face. "Can you ever forgive the awful things I said to you?" Tears flooded her eyes and she blinked hard to prevent their falling. "It could have happened to anyone."

He stepped to the ground, so that his eyes were level with hers. "Why the sudden change of heart?" His expression hadn't softened.

"I'd like to say my better nature took over, but that wouldn't be true." The wind tore at them, billowing her cloak and threatening to send his hat sailing. Molly wrapped her arms around her middle. "A couple of weeks ago, Luellen disappeared while I was weaving. I thought I knew right where she was, but . . ." Molly shuddered at the memory. "She wandered into those woods back there, right under the nose of a panther."

Dr. Spengler dropped his guarded expression. "Thunderation! What happened?"

Molly couldn't help the proud smile that lifted the corners of her mouth. "I shot it."

He didn't return her smile. "That was brave." His blue eyes remained frosty. "But you got her back, didn't you?"

"Yes. Thank the Lord, I did." Molly drew a deep breath. "But it was the same thing, don't you see? I believed I knew where she was, and she'd wandered off."

"It's not the same thing at all." Dr. Spengler pushed his hat on and turned to leave. "I know it was difficult for you to speak about this. I appreciate that. Good day, Mrs. McGarvie."

Watching him ride away, Molly wondered why she felt hollow. What had she expected?

◯

The community of Beldon Grove fell away as Karl rode south on the road leading to Missouri and his parents' home in Fox River. The hurt expression in Molly's eyes rode with him. *I didn't need to be harsh.* He wished he could go back and have the conversation over again. This time he'd listen and not bristle.

On the other hand, life had taught him that women were duplicitous creatures. One minute they were all sweetness and the next they turned and showed their true natures. *Just like Lydia Fortune.* He felt a flash of anger. *Using me to get back East! I'll have to warn Joseph about her.*

Drops fell, then the sky opened, sending drenching rain in sheets across the landscape. Karl stopped his horse, slipped his oilcloth cape from his saddlebag, and threw it around his shoulders. Then he tugged his hat down and urged the mare on toward his parents' home. As always, he dreaded the visit.

◯

Karl's mother lay unconscious on the bed. Her head lolled to one side, drool from her open mouth left a wet spot on the pillow.

Karl clenched his teeth and looked at his younger brother. "I hate this! I should've stayed in Illinois. It's the same old thing—she's drunk as a lord."

"I'm worried she's not going to come out of this one," Joseph said. "She's been like this since last night. Pretty soon her body won't take it anymore."

"Then let her die!" Bitterness etched Karl's words. "When did she ever worry over us?"

"Ah, you don't mean that." Joseph put an arm around Karl's shoulder. "She can't help it. She never could stop once she got started."

Karl stalked onto the porch. He found his father sitting in a rocking chair, gazing out at muddy fields. The sky was a brilliant wash of frothy white clouds lit by a vermillion sunset.

"Look at that sky, boy," his father said. "An artist couldn't paint anything prettier."

Karl glanced at the glowing horizon and made no comment.

Ambrose Spengler pointed at the steps. "Sit and calm yourself. It doesn't do any good to get worked up about your ma. The devil's got ahold of her and he's not letting go."

After he settled on a step near his father's chair, Karl tipped his head up. "How do you stand it, Pa—never knowing what will set her off?"

"We've been together going on thirty-five years." He shrugged. "Guess I've learned to live my own life in spite of what she's doing." The rocking chair creaked. "I think you should take your brother with you when you leave. He's wearing me out trying to find a cure for inebriety. There ain't no cure. He needs to let it be."

Karl studied his father. His white hair seemed thinner but his farseeing blue eyes were undimmed. A wave of affection for the man who had been his bulwark throughout his youth brought

236

sudden tears to his eyes. He stood and clasped his father's shoulder. "I'll talk to Joseph. Fact is, that's why I came home."

Ambrose covered his son's hand with his own. "You've grown into a fine man. I'm proud of you."

The two of them walked into the house when the sunset faded. "Light a lamp, Joseph," Ambrose called. "Karl wants to talk to you."

When his brother brought the lamp, Karl looked around the tidy room. *Pa hasn't lowered his standards one bit. He's been more of a mother to us than Ma ever was.* Clean curtains hung over the windows and a wooden utensil box stacked with knives and forks rested on the linen cloth covering the table. A kettle of water steamed on the hearth.

While their father poured hot water into a copper teapot, Joseph turned in his chair and pointed at the closed bedroom door. "Ma's awake—she's going to be all right."

Karl snorted. "Until next time."

"Maybe there won't be a next time."

Ambrose thunked three empty mugs on the table and set the teapot on a trivet. "Joe, this ain't your worry," he said. "I want you to listen to Karl—he's got a proposition for you."

❧

Headed toward the Mississippi River and Illinois, Karl and Joseph trotted their horses south through St. Lawrenceville. After riding in silence for some time, Joseph blurted, "I still feel guilty about leaving. Somehow it doesn't seem right."

"It's time you left. You haven't changed things by staying, have you?"

"Well, not yet."

"Pa's accepted the way she is, and he doesn't want you to waste your life trying to doctor someone who can't be doctored. He told me so himself." Karl looked at his brother. "Maybe what Ma really needs is less help from you." He weighted the word "help" with heavy meaning. "Could be she'd stop if she knew you wouldn't be there to smooth things over."

"What are you talking about?" Joseph slowed his horse to a walk, turning his head toward his older brother.

"Ever since we were boys, you tried to hide what she was doing—even from Pa." Karl leveled his index finger at Joseph. "You clean up what she breaks or burns, so she doesn't have to face it later. You treat her like an invalid when she's coming out of one of these spells." He slapped his thigh. "She doesn't need to be waited on. She needs to face what's happening."

"It's easy for you to preach. You left home as soon as you could. You didn't have to come to Fox River with us."

"I thought things had changed. She was fine on the trip out here." Karl shook his head. "It seemed like a good chance to start over after . . . Philadelphia."

"And Caroline." Joseph's natural empathy shone in his blue eyes. "That woman treated you like dirt."

Reaching across the distance between them, Karl patted his brother's shoulder. "Ah, Joe. Ma always called you the 'good' one. On that she's right." He straightened in the saddle. "Anyway, Pa thinks it's for the best if you leave."

Joseph shrugged. "I guess we'll see, won't we?" He kicked a heel against his horse, urging it to a trot. "Tell me more about New Roanoke."

Karl summed up the town, giving his brother details about patients he'd seen and their illnesses. "There's one person you need to watch out for," he concluded. "A young woman named Lydia Fortune . . ."

When they neared Colonel Cross's white frame house, Karl impulsively decided to stop. From what Matthew told him, the news that Crosses bought the slave Betsy had left Molly greatly distressed. Maybe he could make amends for his rudeness by bringing her fresh news of the woman. He guided his mare toward a hitching post.

"Why're we stopping here?"

Karl didn't want to explain his actions, so he temporized. "Thought we'd pay our respects to the Colonel. He's been real good to Pa."

Betsy opened the door in answer to his knock. "Dr. Spengler!"

"Morning, Betsy." Karl noticed she'd filled out since he'd last seen her. Her mahogany skin glowed with health. But the sun's candid light revealed sadness on her face that hadn't been apparent when he'd first met her at Molly's the previous September.

"We're on our way back to Illinois and decided to stop and say hello to Colonel and Mrs. Cross," Karl said. "They home?"

Betsy's round cheeks lifted in a smile. "Sure are. They finishing breakfast. Wait just a minute—I'll tell them you folks is here." Her bare feet made almost no sound on the polished pine floor as she left them standing in the entry and walked toward the back of the house.

Within moments, Colonel Cross pushed through a door at the rear of the hallway. "Spengler! Good of you to stop by. Come on back and have coffee with us." He led the way to the dining room, where his wife sat at the table.

Karl introduced Joseph to them, then at the Colonel's invitation, he and his brother seated themselves.

After the customary pleasantries, Marjolaine asked, "What brings you gentlemen to St. Lawrenceville?"

"We're just passing through. Joseph is going to take over my practice in New Roanoke," Karl said. "I'm going to set up in Beldon Grove."

The lavender ribbons on Marjolaine's lace cap trailed across her shoulders as she turned her head toward Joseph Spengler. "It is easy to see you are brothers." Her French accent set her words to music. "You are both so fair." She tapped a finger against her cheek, frowning slightly. "But how do your parents feel about the two of you leaving at the same time?"

A shadow crossed Joseph's face. "It was Pa's idea. He thought I'd be better off in a bigger community."

The door between the dining room and the kitchen swung open, and Betsy came in carrying a tray laden with cups, saucers, and a silver coffee biggin.

"Once you've served our guests, you may stay in here if you wish," Marjolaine said. "I would imagine you'd like to know if there is any news from Molly's family."

Karl glanced between Betsy and her mistress, trying to gauge how much the Negro woman knew of the animosity between Molly McGarvie and Marjolaine Cross. "I stopped in Beldon Grove on my way to Fox River," he said, deciding to act as though he'd heard nothing of Molly's feelings about the Crosses' purchase.

At the mention of Beldon Grove, Betsy looked at him. "Did you see Miz Molly?"

Marjolaine leaned forward, resting her forearms on the linen tablecloth. "Yes, do tell us how she's faring." Coolness crept into her voice.

Karl smiled at the memory of Molly's converted school-to-home dwelling. "Reverend Matthew invited me to share a meal with them in his sister's cabin."

Betsy blinked. "Miz Molly have a cabin?"

"She does. It was an abandoned schoolhouse about a mile east of town. Her brother Matthew made arrangements for her to move into it."

"A schoolhouse!" Marjolaine said. "However did she make it livable?"

"By working hard, it looks like. Her weaving business keeps her table supplied with food."

Colonel Cross entered the conversation. "I thought sure she'd give up and go back to Kentucky."

"Don't think she will." Karl turned to Betsy. "She seems to be planning to stay right where she is."

"I wish—" Betsy broke off, swallowing whatever she'd been planning to say. She darted a glance at Marjolaine.

Her mistress gave her a keen look. "Well, we can send word to Molly that you are very happy here, can't we?"

Betsy nodded. "Yes'm."

Karl couldn't get Betsy to meet his eyes. *Something's wrong, and she can't tell me what it is.*

24

Bright light from the window above her loom illuminated the pale wheat color of linen warp yarns. Molly threw the shuttle, caught it in her left hand, beat the web, and sent the shuttle back across the warp, adding one thread at a time. The bobbin contained the last of her wool supply, dyed with a concoction of simmered hickory nuts and potash. Her back ached from hours of steady weaving. *Hope this'll be acceptable.* She studied the striped blanket panel accumulating on the roller at her knees. *Mr. Wolcott said he wasn't sure about linsey-woolsey.*

James walked across the room and stood under the window. "Mr. Pitt said I could help him groom Captain today. Can I go?"

Resting the shuttle on the warp yarns, she flexed her shoulders. "Yes, if you take Lulie with you." From experience she knew her son's visits to the blacksmith's shop would keep him busy for a couple of hours. If Lily didn't need tending, Molly might be able to complete a blanket length before they returned.

Her son scowled. "Luellen will only be in the way."

"You take her or you don't go."

242

With a martyred sigh, James grabbed his sister's hand and walked to the door.

"Be back in time for supper." Molly picked up the shuttle and returned to her task.

The gathering of women during the barn raising earlier in the month had brought Molly more weaving orders than she could handle. Reluctant to refuse work, she'd added hours to the day by staying at her loom long after the children were settled for the night.

The afternoon slipped away, lost in the steady clack and thump of the sturdy apparatus. When a knock sounded at the door, Molly looked up, startled. *The children should be back soon, but they wouldn't knock.* She hurried to see who it was and found Dr. Spengler and another man standing on the doorstep.

"Dr. Spengler. Come in." Molly kept her voice neutral, surprised at the visit.

He stepped inside, followed by the younger man. "This is my brother, Joseph. Thought you'd like to meet him." The two men favored each other—she would have known they were brothers without the introduction. But Joseph's hair went beyond blond to nearly white, and his pale eyebrows and lashes made his eyes look like splashes of indigo on bleached linen. Judging by the pallor of his skin, he spent most of his time indoors. "Joseph's on his way to New Roanoke to take over my practice."

"Happy to meet you, Dr. Spengler." After the way his brother had responded to her apology, she expected he would keep his distance. *Why is he here?*

The younger doctor gripped her extended hand. "Two Dr. Spenglers is too confusing. Call me Doctor Joe. You can call my brother here anything you want." He chuckled.

243

"How about Doctor Karl?" The other man's tone sounded conciliatory.

"Fine." She still felt unsure of his intentions, but if he could be cordial, so could she. "Come, sit down. There's coffee left from breakfast."

After serving the men, Molly joined them at the table, hoping the visit would be brief. She didn't often have time to work without both of her older children around.

Joe picked up his mug with his left hand and took a sip. "Karl showed me where he's going to open his practice here in Beldon Grove."

"You found a place already? There's not much to choose from around here."

"I'm going to rent the upstairs portion of the new post office. Worked it out before we came here today. Soon's I get Joe introduced around in New Roanoke, I'll be back to stay." Karl gestured toward the door with a nod of his head. "Won't be far away, if you need me." He cleared his throat. "Medically, I mean."

Molly stared at the tabletop, feeling a flush redden her cheeks.

He glanced at his coffee, then back at Molly. "I stopped at Crosses' while I was in St. Lawrenceville. Figured you might want news of Betsy."

"Oh, I do! How is she?"

A reflective expression crossed Karl's face, and he paused a moment before responding. "Well, she looks healthy and well cared for. You must realize I didn't have any time alone with her."

"There's something you're not saying, isn't there?" Molly raised an eyebrow. "What is it? You don't need to shield me."

"She seemed unhappy." Karl shook his head. "I had the impression that between Brody McGarvie and Mrs. Cross her spirit's been broken. She acted like most slaves I've seen—afraid to have a thought of her own."

Molly put a hand over her mouth. "Oh, poor Betsy! She was never treated like a slave. Even though she helped in my mama's house—and in mine—she was always able to say and do what she wished."

"Maybe that's the trouble," Joe said. "With all due respect to you, she's a colored gal. Colored gals are slaves."

"She won't be if I have anything to say about it!" Molly set her mug on the table with such force that a few drops of coffee flipped over the brim. "We've talked about her being free ever since we were old enough to know there was a difference between us."

Joe leaned forward. "That's what your brother Matt told Karl. All I'm saying is, don't get your hopes too high."

"There's nothing wrong with hope," Karl said. "Sometimes it's the one thing that keeps us going."

If he only knew. Molly thought of her plans to hunt for Franklin once she purchased Betsy. "What other news do you have of St. Lawrenceville?"

"The blacksmith told me Brody's about to abandon the brick-yard. Can't get anyone to work for him. Heard he's doing a lot of drinking." Karl looked at her. A concerned frown creased his fore-head. "It's sad to see the place now. It's looking tumbledown."

"Samuel worked so hard to build that brickyard." She drew a breath and glanced at her loom. "I wouldn't be spending day and night weaving if Brody'd done the decent thing by me and my children. We'd never have left Missouri." Her eyes stung with unshed tears. "I'd still have my Franklin—and Betsy."

At that moment, the door swung open, admitting Luellen and James. They both looked tousled and grimy from their afternoon

245

in Jared Pitt's stable. Molly forced a smile. "Looks like you had a fine time."

"We did, Mama." Luellen hurried to her mother's side, holding a book next to her chest. "Mr. Pitt sent you a present." She held out a leather-bound volume.

Molly took it, reading the gilt lettering on the spine. "*The Betrothed*, by Sir Walter Scott." She knew he sent more than a book—it was meant to be a message. True to his word, the blacksmith had continued to press her to marry him and didn't seem discouraged by her refusals. He'd even repeated his offer to buy Betsy and bring her to Beldon Grove.

"Mr. Pitt said it was one of his wife's favorites," James said. "He thought you might like the story."

"I'm sure I will." Memories flooded back, warming her. "My mama read Scott's poems to me when I was a child. I loved them." Glancing up, she noticed that Karl had one eyebrow raised. Why did she feel the need to explain Jared Pitt to him?

When the brothers prepared to leave, Karl pointed at the latchstring on the open door. "We saw Indians on the move while we were traveling to Beldon Grove. A large number. I hope you're careful about keeping the door bolted."

Molly's mind flashed to the night she'd seen the face at her window while she counted her savings. She'd bolted the door then, but had grown careless over subsequent days. What if the person had pushed his way in, rather than peering through the glass?

"Yes, of course I am," she lied. "But thank you for your concern." *From now on, I'll secure the door.*

After they left, Molly stood next to her loom gazing at the grove of trees that stood between her home and the cemetery. Knobby branches seemed to tremble in their eagerness to unfurl spring leaves. By squinting, she could see an aura of green hovering over the treetops.

Suddenly, her eyes caught a movement at the edge of the grove. Startled, she stepped back from the window. *Someone's watching!*

☙

Several mornings later, Molly heard a tap on the door. Opening it, she saw Landon on the step, hands tucked into his pants pockets, sleeves rolled up to reveal hairy forearms. "Ma said you wanted me to drag them treetops up here so's li'l James could get at them easier." A straw hat shaded his eyes. "I'll be glad to do it. Like I told you, anything you need, just holler."

She glanced over his shoulder. "Daniel didn't come with you?"

"Nah. No need for help on a piddling job like this. Just show me where you want 'em." He moved to one side.

Luellen came to the door and leaned against her mother's leg, staring up at Landon. Molly took the child's hand, grateful for a buffer between herself and the young man on her doorstep. Leading her daughter, she walked through ankle-high grass next to the road, Landon close at her heels.

She indicated a spot about fifty feet away from the house. "If you pile them here, they'll be out of the way and still handy for James to work on."

Griffiths' dapple-gray plow horse waited at the edge of the road, head down, grazing. A coil of rope hung from a battered saddle. Landon walked over and picked up the trailing reins. "I'll get right to it. Sure you don't want me to cut them into firewood while I'm at it?"

247

"No. That'll be James's job."

As the morning wore on, she could hear the clop of hooves and the screeching sound of treetops being dragged past the house. Each time she looked out the window above her loom, the pile behind the cowshed had grown smaller. *He's a hard worker, I'll say that for him.*

Molly threw the shuttle back and forth across the warp, working as fast as she could to finish the blanket she'd promised Mr. Wolcott. Lily played on the trundle bed, grabbing at her feet and babbling. For once, Luellen sat still, occupied with wooden farm animals Samuel had carved for James and Franklin.

"Miz McGarvie?" Landon called from the open doorway. "Got 'er done." Hat in hand, he wiped his sweating forehead with his sleeve. "Could I trouble you for a cup of water? It's mighty warm."

She scooped Lily into her arms and went to the door. "Wait there." She pointed to a bench outside in the shade. "I'll bring it right out."

Landon dropped onto the bench, resting his back against the log wall. When she handed him a mug, he patted a spot beside him. "Want to sit?" His gaze traveled down her figure.

Molly backed away, shifting Lily to her hip. She shook her head. "I've been sitting all morning."

He sipped at the water, watching her over the brim of the cup. Once again she was struck by the contrast between his muscular arms and the smallness of his hands. Almost daintily, he set the empty cup on the bench next to him and stood. "Friend of my pa's got married last week," he said, his voice casual.

She waited for him to continue.

"Yep. Met a widow woman over in Rushville. She's a tad older than him, but it don't matter none if they're suited to each other, does it?"

Molly swallowed. "Truthfully, I haven't thought about it." She picked up his empty cup. "Thank you for your hard work." She gestured toward the swell of treetops resting next to the road. "James'll appreciate it." Turning, she headed toward the door.

"Miz McGarvie."

"Yes?"

He stood with one hand on the horse's mane. "You planning to go to the Spring Recital at the schoolhouse next Friday evening?"

"Of course. James is going to recite." She looked at him questioningly. "Why do you ask?"

"Well, Daniel's got a piece to say, so we're going. Thought maybe you'd let me take you."

By effort of will, Molly kept herself from rolling her eyes. "No, thank you. Mr. Pitt has offered to transport us."

Landon swung onto the horse's back. Lips set in a half smile, he said, "Be seeing you."

⟲

Toward the end of the afternoon, Molly heard a wagon squeak to a stop.

A rap sounded on the doorframe. "How do, Mrs. McGarvie."

She looked up from the pot she stirred over the fire. "Good afternoon, Mr. Wolcott. Come on in."

"Smells like something's dead in here." The storekeeper wrinkled his nose. "You must have indigo in that pot."

Molly nodded, lifting a skein of spun flax with a long fork. When the wheat-colored yarn hit the air, it turned pale blue. She held it aloft until it stopped dripping, then dunked it back into the dye pot. "That's why the door's not shut, to help with the stink."

"It's warm today—why don't you build a fire outside and dye the yarn there?"

Molly hesitated. She believed she was being spied upon, and being out in the open made her nervous. *Should I tell him about the watcher?* She cleared her throat. *No. He'll think I'm a hysteric.* "You came for a blanket?"

"Aye-yuh, that I have. Your son stopped in after school yesterday and told me I could pick it up."

She laid the dye fork on the side of the hearth and walked to her blanket chest. "I hope it will be suitable. You know I'm out of wool. I had to use linen yarn for the warp." She handed a tan and brown blanket to the storekeeper. "The other's almost ready to come off the loom. You'll have it by the end of next week for certain."

He unfolded the checkered bed cover, fingering its thickness. "Won't be nearly as warm. Still, I suppose it would do for spring-time, but I can't pay you as much for this. The value's not there."

Molly ducked her head to hide her disappointment. *That's what I get for counting my chickens before they're hatched.* "You don't want it?"

"Didn't say that." He examined the stitching in the center seam and hems. "Perfect as always. Say maybe three dollars apiece?"

"I'll take it. Thank you."

Mr. Wolcott eyed her sympathetically. "Might be you could keep part of folks' spun wool in trade for weaving their goods. You know, like a miller keeps some of the grain. That way you could gather enough for more blankets by next winter."

Then I'd lose out on cash money for my work. Molly's brain whirled trying to find a solution to her dilemma. Unbidden, a thought crossed her mind. *I wonder if Jared Pitt really would buy Betsy if we were married?*

Molly hurried back to the dye pot and lifted the flax into the air, the blue darkening while she watched. "I just wish it didn't take me so long to finish an order. Sometimes the children keep me so busy, a whole day goes by and I haven't got to my weaving."

Mr. Wolcott paused in the doorway, the blanket tucked under his arm. "Now that the weather's warmer, I expect people won't be thinking about bedcovers for a spell. Once you get that one done, you should have a chance to slow down a bit." He turned to leave.

Impulsively, Molly called after him. "Wait! I need to ask you something." As soon as he turned around, she regretted her action.

"Is anything wrong?"

She dumped the flax back into the dye and took a breath. "Has there ever been talk of a Peeping Tom in Beldon Grove?"

"Never!" He dropped the blanket on the tabletop and faced her, a concerned expression on his face. "Tell me why you ask."

Molly hugged her arms together across her stomach. Her face felt hot. "It's probably nothing . . ."

"Let me decide that." Mr. Wolcott seated himself on one of the benches next to the table.

"Late the other night I could swear I saw a face at the glass." She took a deep breath. "Then recently I think someone was standing at the edge of that grove of trees back there. Seemed like he was staring at the cabin." Molly clenched her fists. "I'm frightened."

Mr. Wolcott rested his chin in his hand and studied her face. Doubt hovered behind his hazel eyes. "Could it have been an owl? Maybe a raccoon?"

"I do know the difference between a person and a raccoon!"

251

"Sorry. I meant no offense." He stood, frowning. "Let me know if it happens again. I can have a dozen men out here in short order. We'll catch him."

Molly put a hand on his arm. "Please don't say anything. I'd rather not worry the children."

He gave her a long look. "Then I'll stop by from time to time to see how you're doing." Mr. Wolcott covered her hand with his. "You're a brave woman."

25

April 1839

Molly spent the afternoon prior to Spring Recital seeing to it that her children had baths and clean clothes. After filling a large tub with heated water, she rotated them through in reverse birth order: Lily first, then Luellen, and finally James. By the time he'd finished, soap scum floated on the surface of the water like curdled milk. Her work dress and apron were nearly as wet as the toweling draped over a rack in front of the fire.

Franklin was never far from her mind, and now as she stared at the cloudy bathwater, she wondered whether the people who found him had enrolled him in school. Six months had passed since his disappearance—he'd be seven now and in the second level. But worrying about school wasn't as important as praying he was still near the Mississippi. What if he'd been taken by a trapper on his way north? She'd never find him.

"Mama?" Luellen tugged her hand. "Can I go outside?"

Molly forced her thoughts back to their cabin in Beldon Grove. "No. Stay indoors and keep clean. James, you mind Lulie while I change my dress. Mr. Pitt will be here soon."

Afternoon sun glowed behind the tow cloth curtains Molly had tacked over the windows. Inside, the air felt thick with moisture. *Bath day was so much easier with Betsy's help. I never dreamed there'd be so many ways to miss her!* Perspiration slid down Molly's temples and she stood a moment in her shift fanning herself before slipping her good black dress over her head.

"Can I open the door now, Mama?" James asked. "It's hot."

She nodded. "Then come here and let's practice your piece again."

James crossed his arms over his chest and frowned at her. "Do I have to? I've practiced 'til I'm sick of it."

Luellen skipped over to her mother. Her hair, tied with a blue ribbon, hung in damp ringlets over her shoulders. "I know a rhyme, Mama. Want to hear it?"

"You said it to me while you were in the bath." She glanced toward the trundle bed. "Go keep an eye on Lily—she's acting kind of puny this afternoon."

By the time James began the concluding paragraph, "We, therefore, the Representatives of the United States . . ." of his recitation, the blacksmith's buggy had pulled to a stop in front of the cabin. Lifting Lily to her shoulder and taking Luellen's hand, Molly led her family out the door. Jared helped her onto the seat while the older children scrambled in back. "You look mighty fetching this evening, Mrs. McGarvie." He studied her approvingly.

Molly tilted her head and studied him. Jared's hair had been freshly trimmed and he wore a clean shirt and trousers. He smelled faintly of soap. *I must be getting used to him. He doesn't seem nearly as bad as he did at first.* "Thank you," she murmured. "We appreciate your driving us to the schoolhouse."

"Anytime. Just ask."

The buggy turned right at the corner of Beldon Grove's town

square and rolled past the building housing the post office. A small red-lettered sign hanging next to an exterior staircase read Dr. Karl Spengler, Physician.

"We'll probably be seeing the new doc tonight," Jared commented when they passed the sign. "The whole town generally turns out for Spring Recital."

Griffiths' wagon turned off the main road and rolled toward them, Landon at the reins. A few other wagons and buggies were lined up along the hitching rails surrounding the square.

"Gracious, we're not late, are we?" Molly asked. "I want to have a word with Mr. Newsome before the program begins."

The blacksmith fished his watch out of his pocket and clicked open the lid. "Nope. It's just quarter till. Plenty of time."

❧

The schoolmaster stood near the door, hands clasped behind his back, watching his pupils and their families enter. Glowing lanterns hanging from the ceiling illuminated the walls of the schoolroom, decorated with boughs of greenery. A broad desk sat at one end with chairs behind it for the students. Benches in the center of the room were already filling with parents and other spectators.

The teacher's pockmarked face appeared cratered in the flickering lantern light that played across his self-satisfied expression. Molly sailed in his direction, pushing her way past other early arrivals.

"Mr. Newsome, I will not have you tormenting my son James," she blurted without prelude.

"Mrs. McGarvie. So good you could be here tonight." Oliver Newsome's bland smile couldn't disguise the irritation in his voice.

His glance flicked over her shoulder, possibly to see whether she'd been overheard.

Molly ignored his unctuous tone. "James told me you whipped him in front of the class again yesterday. You blamed him for something he didn't do."

"Oh, but he did do it. I saw him with a frog at recess, and then I saw the same frog in our bucket of drinking water."

She shifted Lily to one arm, placing her free hand on her hip. "Didn't he tell you one of the big boys took the frog away from him?" Molly stared straight into Mr. Newsome's eyes. "James told me he didn't put it in the bucket, and I believe him."

The teacher shifted his gaze from her face to a point behind her head. "That's the same story he gave me, but I know a trouble-maker when I see one."

Molly cocked her head and studied him. Oliver Newsome stood no taller than she did and was foppishly dressed in a black frock coat and black silk cravat. A thin blond mustache fuzzed across his upper lip.

She lowered her voice. "Could it be you picked on James because any one of the older boys could whip you?"

He backed away from her. "Mrs. McGarvie . . ."

"My brother is on the school board with Mr. Wolcott. I haven't mentioned this to them . . ." She paused for effect. "Yet." Turning toward the center of the room, Molly said over her shoulder, "They'll decide next month whether you'll be rehired for next year or not."

Her heart pounded in her throat so fiercely she felt she couldn't breathe. Dragging Luellen by the hand, she marched to a bench and plunked her daughter between herself and Jared Pitt. *I can't believe I lectured a teacher!* Her hands trembled.

The blacksmith leaned over and whispered, "You're quite a

spitfire." His voice sounded admiring. "But that boy does need discipline. It's not right that he's fatherless."

Molly gritted her teeth. Just when she thought Mr. Pitt's good qualities outweighed the bad, he came out with a remark like that. She glared at him. "It's not his fault!"

"No. It isn't." He looked at her, his meaning plain.

Ellie and Matthew entered the schoolroom and headed in their direction, the twins joining James on the platform at the front of the room. Molly smiled at her sister-in-law and patted the space beside her on the bench, relieved to have someone besides the blacksmith to talk to.

Ellie sat, fixing concerned eyes on Lily. "Her little cheeks are so flushed. Is she ill?"

Patting the baby's back, Molly nodded. "I'm afraid she's coming down with something. She's been listless all afternoon." She sighed. "I shouldn't have brought her out this evening, but James has worked so hard on his piece, it would have been a shame to miss it."

The Griffith family came through the door, followed by Karl Spengler. Landon started toward her but stopped when his mother grabbed his sleeve and said something to him. He frowned, obviously anxious to break away.

Moving around the Griffiths, the doctor seated himself on the bench in front of Molly and her sister-in-law. "Evening, Mrs. McGarvie, Mrs. Craig. Are your young'uns ready for tonight's recitations?"

"James has been practicing all day. I think I could recite his piece myself," Molly said.

Karl tilted his head, observing Lily. "Your baby looks feverish. Is she teething?"

"Maybe. But she's never had a fever with it before." Molly felt a tap on her shoulder and turned to see Amber smiling at her.

Landon stood next to his mother, his hat brim clutched in one fist. "How do, Mrs. McGarvie," he said. "You're looking awful pretty this evening."

On her right, Jared turned and scowled at him. "Thought you'd be up there with the rest of the young'uns, sonny."

Landon's face reddened. "I'm done with school. Have been for a whole year."

His point made, the blacksmith smirked at him and faced forward.

Karl rose and held his hand out to Landon. "Don't believe I know you. I'm Karl Spengler, the new doc in town."

"These are the Griffiths," Molly said. "They own the pottery works down the road from me. Their sons have been helping out with firewood and such."

Amber spoke up. "My son Daniel's reciting tonight." She beamed toward the front of the room, where the pupils were assembled. "Hope he don't forget his piece."

Molly surveyed the row of students and saw Daniel sitting at one end of the platform next to two other boys his age. James sat near the other end of the ranks, one of the smaller children. She folded her arms across her chest and watched grimly while Mr. Newsome called the assembly to order. *He'd better mind how he treats James!*

⌒

Molly put out an arm to hug her son when he descended from the platform. "You were perfect! I'm so proud of you!"

"I could recite too, if I was bigger," Luellen said. " 'Oh! The dust on the feather, and the feather on the bird—' "

"Yes, Lulie," Molly cut in. "That's lovely." She patted the top of her daughter's head.

Ellie's soft voice interrupted. "Wasn't it nice of Mr. Newsome to praise James's performance?"

Molly met her sister-in-law's gaze with a half smile. "Yes, wasn't it?"

Karl stood, joining the conversation. "Tell you what impressed me—young James here knowing the whole *Declaration*!" He squeezed James's shoulder. "With a memory like that, you'll go far in life."

People flowed out the door, heading for home.

"Dark of the moon," Matthew said to Molly, as they walked together across the shadowed lane toward the waiting wagons. "Tomorrow will be a good day to plant your flax. Me and Arthur will be over early to do the plowing."

❧

Lily coughed and whimpered as Molly and her older children entered their cabin after bidding the blacksmith good night. Once the door closed, the coffee-sweet fragrance of molasses mixed with ginger enveloped them.

"James, light the lamp, please, while I see to the baby." Molly smiled at him. "I made a treat for you. Since this is a special occasion, we'll have Indian pudding before we go to bed."

She placed Lily on the trundle and then hooked a covered pan out of a pot of simmering water. Two faces turned toward her, grinning with anticipation. Luellen ran to the cupboard to get bowls. Putting a generous serving of the sweetened cornmeal mixture in front of each child, Molly said, "While you're eating I'll feed Lily."

When she lifted the listless child, heat from the infant's body radiated through her clothing. Alarmed, Molly cupped a hand around Lily's flushed face and tipped her head back. "Her nose is all stopped up. Lulie, please bring me a handkerchief from the cupboard."

Luellen dropped her spoon into her bowl and ran to the freestanding cupboard at the back of the room. When she returned to her mother's side, she held a soft linen square. "Is the baby sick?" she asked, watching while Molly cleared Lily's nostrils.

"She is. Her skin's very hot."

After trying unsuccessfully to get Lily to nurse, Molly dressed her in a flannel gown and tucked her into the middle of the big bed, praying a night's rest would effect a cure. She supervised James and Luellen's nighttime preparations, listened to their prayers, then blew out the lamp and settled into bed next to her dozing baby.

In the middle of the night, a strange noise disturbed Molly's sleep. For a moment she thought it was the wheezy cry of a barn owl hunting somewhere near the house. Fully awakened, she realized the sound was Lily's labored breathing. The baby's small fists clutched at her mother's nightgown. A barking cough tore out of her throat as she struggled to roll over in the bed.

Molly scooped her daughter into her arms, standing beside the bed in almost the same motion. Lily's cough sounded like crows cawing. Holding her over one shoulder, Molly walked to the fireplace and dropped more wood onto the coals, then lit a candle. By its glow, she rummaged in the cupboard until she found a crock of rendered goose fat and a small piece of folded linen.

With Lily seated on her lap, Molly opened the neck of her baby's nightgown and placed the grease-covered linen cloth over her throat. The touch of cold, congealed fat against her skin brought a bellow of outrage from Lily, followed by another bout of harsh, wheezing coughs.

James pushed himself up on one elbow and looked at them. "What's the matter, Mama?"

"She's croupy, and we're out of turpentine. Run to Mrs. Griffith's and see if she has some. Tell her Lily's having trouble breathing."

He jumped out of bed and pulled on his pants and boots. Outside, the scream of a panther slit the darkness. James stared at his mother, open mouthed.

Molly met his frightened eyes. "It'll be all right. He's back in the woods." She patted Lily's back, willing her to breathe. "Her throat's blocked, Son. We've got to have turpentine for a poultice. The goose grease isn't helping."

By now, Luellen was awake and stirring. She rolled out of the trundle bed. "Mama?"

Molly rubbed her daughter's tousled black hair. "Get back in bed, Lulie. I don't need you underfoot." She turned to James. "Go now! Run!"

James grabbed his coat and opened the door. Molly looked up at the carpet of stars glittering above the horizon. "Follow the road. You can do it."

Quickly, she closed the door behind him to keep cold air from Lily. Shivering, Molly slipped her plaid wrapper over herself and the baby and tied it as tightly as she could using one hand. To track how long James might be gone, she counted her steps as she paced from one end of the cabin to the other and back again. *Thirty-five. Must be about a minute.* She had counted to over a hundred and seventy when a pain-filled scream tore through the night air.

"Dear Lord! A panther!" Molly ran to the door and peered into the darkness. She heard James's voice screaming in a way she'd never heard a human scream before. Then she heard voices coming from the direction of Griffiths' house. Straining to see, all she could do was wait as she listened to running footsteps, the murmur of voices, and James's howls. When the sounds drew closer, she recognized Ridley Griffith running toward her, James's body lying over his outstretched arms.

As soon as he reached the doorway, Molly took one look at her son and felt herself grow hot, then cold.

Blood rolled from the left side of his face and dripped onto the floor. A clear, jelly-like substance oozed from under the tightly closed lid of his left eye.

26

Molly gripped Lily against her chest and ran to the high rope bed. She flung the blankets back. "Bring him here!"

Mr. Griffith leaned over the bed and settled James on the exposed linen sheet, cradling the boy's head with one hand as he did so.

James's howls subsided to shuddering moans. "Mama, it hurts!"

She squeezed his hand. "I'm right here."

Amber hurried through the door carrying a lantern, a shawl wrapped tightly over her nightdress. Her sons crowded in behind her. "We heard him clear up to the house," she said to Molly. "It's a good thing, too."

Molly clutched Lily with one arm while stroking the top of James's head with her free hand. "What happened? A panther?"

"No!" her son gasped, a catch in his voice. He clapped a hand over his injured face and writhed on the bed, sobbing. "It burns!"

Amber lifted Lily from Molly's arms. The baby took a shallow breath, which exploded into a series of barking coughs. "Land sakes! D'you have any turpentine for her chest?"

On the verge of hysteria, Molly almost laughed. "No. That's what James was going to your house to borrow."

Amber met her gaze, the expression in her eyes acknowledging Molly's ordeal. Patting Lily's back, she shot a glance at her sons standing in the doorway. "Daniel, run home and get the turpentine—hurry!" She turned to Molly again. "Appears young James poked his eye out with one of them hickory limbs you got piled next to the road. He was rolling around on the ground there when Ridley found him. We got him here quick as we could."

"Poked his eye out!" Molly forced James's hand away from his face, and stared at the bloody flesh surrounding his left eye. She reached a tentative finger toward his eyebrow, her heart pounding with fear.

"I wouldn't touch it, was I you," Amber said. She jerked her head toward her husband. "Ridley, take the lantern and go get us some slippery elm bark. You know where the trees are." When he left the cabin, Amber said, "We'll pound it down and make a poultice for that eye. Meantime, let it be."

Luellen sat on the edge of the trundle bed. In a small voice, she asked, "Mama, shouldn't we get the doctor?"

With a sense of seeing life repeat itself, Molly's mind flashed to the day Samuel had asked her to fetch Karl Spengler. Then, she'd refused. *I won't make that mistake again!* "Oh, Lulie, of course." She looked at Landon, who stood rooted to a spot just inside the door, worry lines etched across his forehead. "Go tell Dr. Spengler we need him."

He hesitated.

"Don't stand there gawking, do it!" his mother snapped.

Landon ignored her and asked Molly, "D'you think we need him? My ma's good at doctoring."

"I need him," Molly said. "Now please go!"

Muttering to himself, Landon turned to leave the cabin, almost colliding with his younger brother.

Daniel rushed past him into the room. "Here's the turpentine, Ma." He handed her a cork-topped brown flask.

Amber held the baby and paced back and forth in front of the fire, the turpentine poultice on Lily's chest filling the air with the sharp tang of pine sap. "I think it's helping, Molly. She's breathing easier."

"Thank God for that." Molly knelt at James's bedside, her left hand holding his.

Luellen burrowed close to her side. "James is crying," she whispered. "He never cries."

"No, he doesn't, not since your papa died."

"I'm scared, Mama."

"Me too." She wrapped her free arm around the frightened child. "Let's pray." They bowed their heads. "Lord, please heal our James. Help us through this."

Her son quieted while she prayed, his injured eye concealed under a covering of pulped bark. In the dim light thrown from a lamp on the table, the streaks of blood on his face looked like dark trails winding into his matted hair.

Luellen stood. "Why isn't the doctor here? It's been forever."

Molly patted her shoulder. "It just seems long. He's not that far away. He should be here soon." An uneasy thought entered her mind. *What if Landon didn't fetch him?*

Karl Spengler turned over in his narrow bed, the straw-filled tick beneath him crackling. He clasped his hands behind his head and stared into the darkness. *I must be leading a pretty dull life if a school program keeps me awake at night.* His lips curved in a wry grin.

He knew it wasn't the stimulation of the Spring Recital that kept him from sleep. The evening spent near Molly McGarvie filled his thoughts with images of her lively face glowing with pride at her son's accomplishment. The gold flecks in her eyes had sparkled when she congratulated James. Karl puzzled over what had seemed different about her, then realized it was the first time he'd seen her look happy.

I wonder why I thought she reminded me of Caroline Moore? They're nothing alike. The only strength he'd ever known in Caroline came from her determination to marry well. Beyond that, she'd always seemed content to let others, especially her father, take charge of her life. Karl couldn't imagine anybody taking charge of Molly. She was the kind of woman who'd survive no matter where she found herself.

Slow down, Karl. Just because she's not like Caroline, and certainly not like Lydia, doesn't mean she'd want anything to do with you. In spite of Molly's apology, guilt for losing Franklin burdened him. He and Molly could never have a future together. He rolled on his side, punching his pillow and willing his mind to sleep.

Footsteps clattered on the outside stairs leading to his combination office and home. Then someone pounded on the door. "Doc Spengler? You there?"

"Hold on. I'm coming." He threw off the covers, shoved his legs into his trousers, and hurried to the door in his stocking feet.

Landon stood at the threshold, the lantern he carried splashing shadows across his features. "Miz McGarvie sent me. Appears her boy stabbed his eye out."

Karl pulled his boots on and then grabbed his black leather

satchel from the table beside the door. He dashed down the stairs, outrunning the light thrown by the lantern.

He pictured James standing on the platform in the schoolroom earlier that night, flawlessly reciting the Declaration of Independence. Karl remembered the first time he'd met the boy, outside Molly's cabin in St. Lawrenceville. James had been only eight years old, yet he shook Karl's outstretched hand like a full-grown man. It didn't seem fair that something so serious could happen to such a fine lad. *I wonder how Mrs. McGarvie's holding up.*

Landon's feet pounded behind him like an echo. "Hurry up," the doctor called over his shoulder. "It's black as coal out here tonight. Bring that lantern out in front of me."

"It's not that big of a hurry, Doc," Landon said. "Couple more minutes won't matter to James—his sight's probably gone."

"How do you know? You're not a doctor."

Landon didn't answer, but he picked up his speed to match Karl's pace.

When they reached the cabin, Karl pushed the door open and hurried inside. "Mrs. McGarvie! I came quick as I could. Landon says James hurt his eye?"

"He fell against a broken limb." Her voice trembled. "He won't let me touch his face." She grasped Karl's forearm. "Can you help him?"

He laid his hand over hers. "I'll do my best." He turned toward Landon, who stood next to the fireplace warming his hands. "Carry that lantern over here. Hold it up so I can see the wound."

⌒

In spite of her fear for her son, Molly noted a change in Karl Spengler. Since coming to Beldon Grove, he'd been subdued in her presence, almost hangdog. Now he displayed professional confidence as he bent over the bed and carefully removed the poultice from the wounded eye.

Molly gasped when she saw the ragged, oozing flesh. Yellow light cascaded from the lantern, illuminating each scratch and gouge on her son's face. The flow of blood seemed to have stopped, but his eyelid appeared grossly swollen.

"Bring me some hot water and clean rags," Karl said. "I'll need to wash the blood off before I can see how bad it is."

On the bed, James stirred and whimpered, "No. It'll hurt."

Karl squeezed the boy's shoulder. "Don't worry. I'm going to give you some laudanum first." He opened his satchel and drew out a square brown bottle, then turned to Molly. "Bring a cup of water too."

When she handed him a filled pewter mug, the doctor carefully measured ten drops of thick brown liquid into the water. Supporting James with his left arm, he held him upright so he would be able to drink.

James made a face as he swallowed, but after the doctor laid him back on the bed his features began to relax. "I'll wait a moment, then get started," Karl said. He took his watch out of his pocket and counted James's pulse.

By the time he snapped the watch shut, Molly had returned to the bedside with a basin of warm water, linen toweling, and a chunk of soap.

The doctor looked at her, concern showing on his face. "Do you think you're up to this? I don't want you fainting in the middle of things."

She squared her shoulders. "He's my son. I won't faint."

At the head of the bed, Landon fidgeted and set the lantern on the floor. "My arm's getting tired. Ain't there another way to keep light on him?"

Holding the croupy infant, Amber approached the group around the bed.

Molly turned to her. "Can you stay a bit longer, until the doctor finishes with James?"

"I'll stay as long as it takes. I just come over to give Landon what-for." She drilled her son with a look. "You'll hold that there lantern where the doc tells you. No more complaining. You want this boy to lose his eye?"

Landon lifted the lantern, holding it so the light landed directly on the left side of James's face. "Seems like he's already lost it," he muttered.

Karl glared at him. "Not in front of the patient!" He smoothed James's tangled hair from his forehead. His hand rested on the top of the boy's head for an extra moment. "I'll do everything I can, James."

Amber shifted Lily from one arm to the other, then turned to Luellen, who leaned over the foot of the bed staring at her brother. "C'mon, young'un. I might need your help." She shepherded her toward the fire.

Karl gestured to Molly. "If you'll stand right here and hold the basin, I'll get started." He selected a piece of toweling and swished it through the warm water. Beginning at the hairline and work-ing downward, he swabbed dried blood from James's temple. Drowsy by now, the boy didn't react when the cloth moved over his face.

"Doesn't look quite so bad now, does it?" the doctor asked Molly.

The abrasions on her son's skin resembled claw marks, but he was right. With the excess blood washed away, she saw that most of her son's face had been spared. However, the cleansed skin em-phasized the torn area below his left eye. Molly swallowed hard.

Karl studied her. "Are you all right? Want Mrs. Griffith to take over?"

She shook her head. "Go on," she said, aware of the shakiness in her voice. "I'm fine."

"This is going to be the worst for you. Turn your head away if you must, but hold the basin steady." Bending over her son, the doctor carefully lifted the lid away from the injured eye. The white portion appeared completely filled with rusty red fluid. "Bring the lantern closer." Tilting his head, he peered closely at James's eyeball.

Molly waited, afraid to breathe.

Karl straightened and eased the lid down over the damaged eye. He looked at Molly, a smile lighting his face for the first time since he'd arrived. "It's a clean wound. Nothing's embedded under the surface." Relief filled his voice. "I'll put a poultice back on, then wrap a bandage around it." He reached for a fresh piece of linen. "He'll have to stay down until it heals. Might be a couple of weeks. We won't know until then if the sight in that eye's been spared."

Molly leaned over and placed the water basin on the floor with trembling hands. "I'm glad you're here, Doctor." She gritted her teeth to keep them from chattering.

He touched her arm. "Why don't you call me Karl?"

❧

James lay bandaged on the bed, sleeping. Amber had persuaded Luellen to crawl under the blankets on the trundle, "so you'll be out of Mama's way," and the child immediately succumbed to weariness. After the Griffiths left, Molly slumped in a chair next to the fire, all strength drained from her body. Karl sat in a chair on the opposite side of the fireplace and sipped at a mug of coffee. Purple shadows stained the skin under his blue eyes.

"It's almost dawn," Molly said, noticing the dark sky had turned pewter gray. "I'm sorry to have cost you your rest."

"It's part of being a doctor, Molly. Accidents don't always happen at noon."

Her heart warmed at his use of her first name. Rising, she tiptoed to the bed and looked down on James, then checked Lily.

Karl joined her. "He should sleep for a few more hours. Remember, keep him flat in bed with his eyes covered. I'll be back this afternoon to change the bandages."

❧

It seemed to Molly she'd barely fallen asleep when she heard a rap on the door. Still wearing the plaid wrapper over her nightgown, she pushed herself off the trundle and stumbled to answer the knock.

Mr. Wolcott stood on the step, one hand resting on Landon's shoulder. Behind him, her brother and Uncle Arthur sat on the seat of Matthew's farm wagon. Early morning sunlight glittered on the shiny blade of a plow resting in the wagon bed.

"What . . . ," she started to say, then remembered it was Saturday—the day Matthew and Arthur had promised to plow her garden plot so she could plant flax. She ran her fingers back along the sides of her head, smoothing her hair. "Oh, Mr. Wolcott, I've got to tell you what happened last—"

"In a minute," he said. "Landon here has something to tell you." His grip tightened. Landon winced.

"I didn't do nothing," the young man blurted. Mr. Wolcott squeezed harder, his fingertips showing white beneath his

271

nails. "Honest, Miz McGarvie. You got to believe me." Landon's frightened eyes met hers.

Molly's sleepiness fled. "What's happened?" She looked from Mr. Wolcott to Landon.

Mr. Wolcott answered. "I thought I'd walk over to check the ground before we started plowing this morning. What should I see but this . . . this . . . lout trying to peer in your back window!"

"I wasn't!"

"Mrs. McGarvie told me someone's been spying on her, and I caught you in the act. Don't try to lie your way out of it." Mr. Wolcott's tone was contemptuous. "What were you doing behind the house?"

"Checking the wood supply." Landon shuffled his feet. "Been a while since I cut any."

Molly stepped back, her hand at her throat. "You're the one who's been watching me?"

"I never done it, I swear."

"I don't believe you." She turned to Mr. Wolcott. "Does Amber know about this?"

"Nope. Just now caught him at it."

Landon's fingers kneaded the brim of his hat. Pleadingly, he looked at Molly. "You can't tell my ma. It ain't true."

Matthew and Arthur walked up behind him. "Why don't we let her decide?" Matthew said. "Let's go."

27

Molly watched Landon walk away between her brother and Uncle Arthur. *Poor Amber! She's so proud of her sons—she doesn't deserve this.* "I wish I could go comfort Amber," she said to Mr. Wolcott. "She's been good to us."

"Aye-yuh, she's a good woman. Sorry things happened this way." Silence fell between them while they watched the three men walk toward Griffiths' property.

When the men reached a point beyond the pile of hickory limbs, they stopped, evidently having a spirited discussion. Landon waved his arms as though making a point, and Matthew stepped back and shook his finger at him. Then Matthew and Arthur turned toward her cabin. Landon hurried on toward home.

Matthew arrived at Molly's door first. "He said he wanted to talk to his ma by himself." He shrugged. "Doesn't matter to me, long as he tells her."

Face pink with exertion, Arthur trudged up behind Matthew. "That's a lot of running back and forth so early in the day!" He grinned at Molly. "Don't suppose you have the coffee on?"

She took a deep breath, the events of the previous night flooding her mind. "Not yet." She stepped back from the doorway. "Come in, I'll make some."

Matthew scrutinized her. "What's the matter? You look all raveled out."

Molly held her finger to her lips and said in a low voice, "Keep your voice down. The children are still sleeping. I'll tell you all about it while the coffee boils."

By early afternoon Molly had a freshly turned half acre behind her cabin. Dizzy with exhaustion, she surveyed the wide furrows of dark earth, open and ready for sowing. Overwhelmed, she looked from the field to her loom and then at James. How would she be able to do it all?

Matthew sat on the edge of the bed and laid a hand on James's shoulder. "I've got some news that'll cheer you, boy."

He turned his head. "Tell me, Uncle Matt."

"A group of us are going to build a community sheepfold. One of the members of my congregation arranged for a flock to be driven here from Quincy—they should be in Beldon Grove in a few weeks." Matthew patted the boy's shoulder. "We'll need someone to lead them out to pasture and gather them up at the end of the day. A boy like you, maybe."

"Did you hear that, Mama?"

Molly stopped dinner preparations and joined Matthew beside the bed. "I heard."

"Would they pay me? That'd be a help to Mama."

"Well, more likely you'd get a share of the wool at shearing time." He looked at his sister. "That would be just as good, wouldn't it, Molly?"

"It would be a great help." She bent and kissed the top of James's head. "Lie still now. We'll talk about it later." Molly walked to the fireplace where a kettle of squirrel stew steamed. "Come sit down, Matt. Dinner's ready." Using an iron pot lifter, she set the kettle on the table next to a bowl of boiled hominy and a stack of tin plates.

"This smells mighty good." Uncle Arthur smacked his lips. "I sure do thank you."

"It seems so little compared to everything you've done for me." Her gaze encompassed Arthur, Matthew, and Mr. Wolcott.

"It's no trouble," Matthew said. "Helping each other is what families are for."

"Ah, Matt." Molly squeezed his shoulder, love for her brother lifting her heart. "There's Indian pudding left from last night for a sweet—I know you like it." She turned to Luellen who dawdled with her food. "There won't be any pudding for you if you don't clean that plate." She rested Lily on her lap, thankful that her fever had disappeared.

James pushed himself up on one elbow, bandages bound around his eyes. "It smells good, Mama. Will you bring me some?"

"Lie down. I'll get it right now."

Arthur turned on the bench next to her. "Let me hold the baby whilst you help him." He slipped his hands around Lily and settled her on one of his plump thighs.

Molly scooped a ladleful of stew into a bowl, then cut the meat into small bites. After raising her son's shoulders slightly by propping two pillows against the headboard, she sat on the side of the bed, noticing a pinkish stain had seeped through the bandages. *I wonder if it's supposed to do that?* She hoped the doctor would arrive soon. She smiled at the thought. *I never dreamed I'd look forward to having him come through my door.* Molly stabbed a chunk of squirrel meat and placed the fork in James's hand. "Eat. This'll help you get better."

Luellen slipped away from the table and stood next to Molly. "Let me feed him, Mama."

James waved a hand in the direction of her voice. "Go away! I ain't no baby."

Even though her brother couldn't see her, Luellen put her hands on her hips and scowled at him. "Mama's feeding you."

Molly put another piece of meat on the fork and gave it to James. "Luellen, please. You can help me more by eating your own dinner."

Luellen looked at her, dark eyes filled with hurt. A tear trickled down one cheek. Sniffling, she walked to the trundle bed and dramatically threw herself upon it.

Molly bit her lip in frustration. "You're tired, Lulie. Why don't you take a nap?"

"I'm not tired!" She flounced back to the table and shoved a bite of food into her pouting mouth.

Uncle Arthur stood, holding Lily away from his body. "You need to tend to this'un, Molly. She's leaking." Molly saw a wet spot on the leg of his homespun trousers.

"She'll just have to wait. We're almost done here."

Restlessly turning his head from side to side on the pillow, James asked, "How long do I have to stay in bed?" Her son's bare feet had worked themselves free of the blankets, toes wiggling like they could do his running for him.

Molly rested the fork on the plate and stroked his hand. "A couple of weeks, Dr. Karl said."

"I wish Betsy was here. She could take care of Lily so you'd stay with me." James groped for his mother's hand.

"I wish it too!" she replied fervently. *For many reasons.*

Molly hooked the curtains back from the windows so Karl could see James's face. Late afternoon sun illuminated blond hairs on the back of the doctor's hands as he eased the stained linen cloth from her son's face. At the sight of the torn skin around James's bruised eyelid, Molly's stomach lurched. A gasp escaped her before she could quell it.

"Mama?" James's voice squeaked with fear. "What's wrong?"

Karl glanced at her and shook his head.

Molly patted her son's hand. "Nothing. It looks better already." She smiled brightly and handed the doctor a clean bandage.

He wrapped the linen strip twice around James's head, covering both eyes. "It's important that you lie still," he said as he worked. "Until that puncture heals, any pressure behind that eye could start it leaking fluid."

He looked at Molly. "How about I see if Charity Wolcott could come by in the mornings to give you a hand? Maybe she could watch the other two so you'd have time to sit with James and read to him. It'd help him stay quiet."

James smiled, the scratches on his face wrinkling. "That's a fine idea. I like it when Mama's close by."

Happy as she was for the promise of help, Molly recognized that for the next couple of weeks there'd be little time to weave. She'd have to take over the milking and fetch the water and firewood. Her shoulders sagged. Hard as she tried, it seemed her plans to buy Betsy were doomed to failure.

Luellen ran barefoot into the cabin, her feet leaving dusty tracks on the floor. "Mama! Uncle Matthew said to tell you he's ready for the flaxseed." She darted to the cupboard, opened a lower door, and pulled out a squat crockery jar. "I'll plant it for you."

Molly rescued the jar from her daughter's hands. "Thank you, but sowing flax is a job for grown-ups. You have to be careful it doesn't blow away." She patted the top of Luellen's sunbonneted head. "Why don't you stay with Lily while I'm outside? Make sure she doesn't roll off the bed." The baby sat in the center of the trundle, gumming the edge of a spoon.

Luellen removed her bonnet, hanging it on a peg by the door. "I'll watch her. Don't worry." She picked up her rag doll and plopped herself on the low bed next to her sister.

Turning back to Karl, Molly said, "I shouldn't be too long planting these seeds. Help yourself to coffee if you have time. I know Matthew would like to visit with you."

Karl stood next to his open satchel, a corked flask in his hand. "I'll be awhile here—I need to make up a diachylon plaster for the scratches on James's face."

She walked to the bedside and peered at the flask. "Di-ack what?"

He opened a box containing something that looked like reddish dirt. "Lead oxide—mixed with the oil in this flask, it'll prevent corruption."

Molly watched while he measured the powdery lead compound into a cup-sized marble mortar, then added a few drops of oil. His long fingers curled around the pestle, blending the concoction into a paste. After he spread the mixture onto a square piece of linen, Karl laid it over James's cheek.

Molly thought of the first time she'd met the doctor and how much his skillful hands had reminded her of Samuel's. She studied Karl's face. A lock of blond hair had fallen forward, hanging in his eyes. *He's different from Samuel, but he's a good man in his own right.* She gripped the jar of seeds with both hands to keep herself from reaching out to brush the hair off his forehead.

"I'd better get these in the ground." She turned and hurried out the door.

❧

That evening, Molly stood in front of the fireplace and lifted the lid on a pot hanging from the crane. She tumbled a bowl of freshly picked dandelion greens into the boiling water. With fried salt pork and leftover cornbread, it would be a quick meal. Fatigue caused her knees to tremble when she bent to turn the slices of pork frying in a footed skillet over the coals. *I should finish that blanket for Mr. Wolcott, but I'm too tired to stay up tonight.*

Luellen skipped around the table, laying bowls and spoons at each place. "Is it ready yet, Mama?"

"Almost. Go wash."

Once the meat browned, Molly carried James's bowl over to the bed and raised his shoulders, feeling a stab of sorrow at the sight of his face. Covered by the rust-colored plaster, with a linen bandage wrapped around his head, he looked like the drawings of Egyptian mummies he'd shown her in his schoolbook.

"You're being very brave, Son." She bent over and embraced him. "I'm proud of you."

He clung to her. "I'll be helping you again before you know it. When did Uncle Matt say they'd need someone to herd sheep?"

"Probably next month. Don't worry over it now."

❧

After supper, Luellen sat on the trundle bed playing peek-a-boo with Lily while Molly washed the dishes. Her daughters' giggles made Molly smile. *It's good to hear laughter after everything that's happened.* She felt herself relaxing. *A night's sleep will make us all feel better.*

Molly walked to the trundle and ruffled Luellen's dark hair. "After I feed the baby, it'll be bedtime."

"Aw, Mama, it's still light outside."

"Not for long. Put on your nightgown."

Molly scooped Lily up, kissing her on each cheek. "You're going to sleep tonight, aren't you?"

Lily babbled in response, saying something only she could understand.

On a chair near the fire, Molly untied the binding at the neckline of her dress. While the baby nursed, warmth from the coals caressed the back of Molly's neck. Her eyelids drooped. *Just a few more minutes and I can go to bed.*

The next moment someone pounded on the door, calling her name. She snapped awake.

"Let me get it, Mama!" Still fully dressed, Luellen ran to the door.

Before Molly could stop her, she threw the bolt back and Amber pushed into the room. "Is Landon here?"

Apprehension tightened Molly's shoulder muscles. *Didn't he talk to her?* "Not since early this morning. Why?"

Her neighbor slumped on a bench next to the table. "I thought he'd be at your place. When he left this morning, he said you'd asked him to come work today."

Mystified, Molly studied Amber's face. "He was here early, but I didn't ask him to come." She paused, unsure of how much to say. "Uh, after my brother arrived to do my plowing, Landon went home."

Amber's expression changed from worried to puzzled. "We haven't seen him all day. One of our horses is missing and we thought he rode it over to haul more wood from the grove for you." She looked at Molly, bewildered. "Where could he have gone?"

Luellen leaned on the arm of Molly's chair. "Maybe a panther ate him."

Their neighbor's face blanched. "I didn't think of that."

"Lulie, I told you to get ready for bed. Now scat! This is grown-up conversation."

Sticking out her lower lip, the child took a few steps toward the trundle bed. Then she stopped and turned around, tears rolling down her cheeks. "You're mean! I wish Betsy was here. She's nicer than you."

❧

Betsy cocked her head, hearing a sound at the window of her attic room. There it was again. Tick, tick, rattle. She slid out of bed and padded barefoot across the wooden floor. After pushing up the sash, she leaned out and peered into the darkness.

"Who's there?" she called in a loud whisper.

Reuben's voice answered. "Help me! I'm hurt."

Betsy flung a dress over her head and dashed toward the stairs leading into the kitchen. Her pulse throbbed in her throat. She tiptoed down and slipped out the back door.

In the southern sky, gauzy clouds smeared the light of the waxing crescent moon, turning the yard into pools of light and shadow. At the foot of the steps, dew-wet blades of grass gleamed like newly sharpened knives.

"Where are you?"

"Over here."

Betsy followed the sound of his voice and discovered him silhouetted against the white wall of Crosses' house. Even in the dim light, she could see dark stains on his shirt. *Blood!* She swallowed to settle rising nausea. Her hands trembled. "Oh Lordy! What's happened?"

"Mr. Brody. He whipped me for hurting that stallion he prizes." He slumped to the ground.

Blood streaked the clapboard siding behind him. Betsy crouched, squeezing one of his hands. "You wouldn't hurt no horse—he knows that."

Reuben rested his head against the wall. "The horse hurt hisself on a nail today trying to get at a mare. I was going to tell Mr. Brody about it in the morning." A shudder ran through his body and he sucked in a ragged breath. "But he come home drunk around midnight. He must of seen the torn hide when he stabled the gelding. Anyways, he come raving into my cabin and hauled me out of bed. Said he'd teach me what it felt like to have my hide torn."

"I don't want to hear no more!" Betsy lifted his hand to her face and kissed it, rubbing her cheek against its roughness. "Let me get some water an' salve for your back."

She groped her way through the dark kitchen to a cupboard under the sink, holding her breath while she pulled out a basin. *Got to be quiet. If Crosses hear me, they'll send Reuben back to Mr. Brody.* Her sleeve caught on the long handle of a cast-iron posnet, which banged against the basin and hit the floor with a thud.

Betsy froze, waiting to see if the sound had carried to Crosses' bedroom at the front of the house. Stillness, save for the ticking of the case clock in the entry. After a long pause, she tiptoed over to a pottery crock against a wall. She filled the wash basin with water, careful not to tap its sides with the metal ladle.

What else do I need? Clean rags. The wooden hinges on the linen cupboard screeched when she opened the door. Her heart pounded while she listened again for a reaction from the front bedroom. *Hurry! What if Mr. Brody comes looking for Reuben?*

She slipped a jar of ointment into her pocket and grabbed one of Colonel Cross's shirts from the laundry, then stole back outside. Between each step she paused and listened. *Good. Nobody stirring.*

Reuben hadn't moved.

Betsy knelt on the grass next to him. "Take off your shirt before it sticks to your back."

He raised his arms to remove the blood-soaked garment, catching his breath as it dragged across his lacerated skin.

Betsy gingerly sponged each welt, wringing the cloth frequently to rid it of blood and bits of flesh. She felt him tremble beneath her hands. "Hope I'm not hurting you too much," she whispered.

"Your touch takes away the pain."

After she cleaned his wounds, she dabbed the ointment on his raw flesh. Then she sat back on her heels and took Reuben's calloused hand, lifting it to her cheek. "Wisht I could do more—you needs a doctor."

"Black folks don't get doctored. They gets better or they die." He stood, slipping Hector Cross's soft linen shirt over his head. "I ain't going back to Mr. Brody's."

"What?"

"This be the last time he flog me. If he touches me again, I'm afeard I might kill him." Reuben grabbed Betsy's hands and turned her to face him. "I'm going north. Tonight. I wants you to go with me." Placing a thumb under her chin, he tipped her head up and looked into her eyes.

"Reuben, I'm scared. You know what'll happen if they catch us."

"I know what'll happen if they don't. We be free. There's plenty white folks up north that helps black folks get away—like that Mr. Wolcott what came to Miz Molly's."

283

At the mention of Molly's name, Betsy caught her breath. *Miz Molly! If we goes north, I'd never see her again.*

Then she studied Reuben's face, his broad shoulders, his sturdy legs. Could they do it? "What if Mr. Brody or the Crosses send dogs after us?"

"I knows how to fool dogs."

"Then what about slave catchers? Can you fool them?"

He let his breath out in a long sigh. "I don't know." He dropped his arms to his sides. "Are you coming or not?"

28

Late April 1839

Molly bent over newly emerged spears of flax in the plot behind her cabin, pulling weeds. When Landon first disappeared, she'd kept watch on the grove of trees behind her whenever she went outside, fearful that he'd creep back to spy again. But as his absence stretched into its second week, she'd relaxed. Now, glancing toward the pile of shagbark limbs next to the road, she watched Daniel saw wood into fireplace-sized lengths.

As if sensing her gaze, he rested the bucksaw on the ground and removed his hat, wiping sweat from his face with his forearm. He grinned at her. "Ain't you hot in that black dress, Miz McGarvie? I'm 'bout to render out, m'self."

Molly smiled back. "It is pretty warm. Let's go get a drink of water."

Once inside she glanced around the room, her gaze lingering on her son, a bandage still wrapped around his eyes. The scratches on his face had healed, leaving red tracks where scabs had been.

"Mama?" James called, alerted by their footsteps. "Is Dr. Karl here?"

Daniel walked to the bed. "Nope, it's just me. If you stay in that there bed long enough, I'll have all them branches cut into firewood."

James laughed. "Wish you would! But the bandages come off today. I'll be helping Mama again real soon."

After removing her bonnet, Molly filled two mugs with water from the crock next to the door. She carried them to the rope bed, handing one to Daniel and sipping from the other.

Luellen staggered over, carrying Lily, whose feet dangled almost to her big sister's knees. "She's been fussing, Mama. I think she's hungry."

"Give her to me." Molly put her mug on a chest next to the bed and rested the baby on her hip.

Luellen hung over the footboard, tickling James's bare feet. James kicked at her, missing. "You just wait," he said. Luellen tickled him again.

"Stop bothering James," Molly said. "Go outside and watch for Dr. Karl."

"I'd best be getting back to work." Daniel drained his cup and followed Luellen out the open door.

James propped himself against the headboard and asked, "Will you read to me after you're done with Lily?"

"Of course." Molly settled into a chair at the side of the bed. "Pretty soon you'll be reading to yourself again."

His voice assumed an anxious tone. "Do you think so, Mama?" James hesitated. "What if I'm . . . blind?"

He'd hit on her deepest fear. *What can I say to him?* She swallowed and tried to sound reassuring. "You only hurt one eye, Son. Of course you won't be blind."

"But—"

"We'll just have to wait until the bandages come off. Now, what story do you want me to read?"

"How about Samson? He got blinded."

☙

Luellen poked her head inside the cabin. "Mr. Pitt is coming down the road."

Oh, bother. Molly set the Bible aside and walked to the door.

"I come to see how your boy's doing." He held up a paper-wrapped parcel. "Brought him some peppermint sticks."

Molly gestured toward James. "Go on over. He'll appreciate the treat." She peeked out the open door, hoping to see the doctor coming.

She refrained from offering the blacksmith any refreshment, wanting to speed him on his way. He hadn't called on them since the night at the school. Molly believed that if he sincerely cared about her and the children, he'd have been there as soon as news of James's accident got out. No matter what he offered now, it wouldn't be enough.

Jared stood next to the bed, shifting from one foot to the other. His efforts at conversation met with monosyllabic answers from James.

Molly stepped to the opposite side and faced their unexpected guest. "You'll have to forgive us. Today's the day the bandages come off, and I'm afraid James is a little distracted right now."

"Well, you enjoy those peppermints, boy. I'll come back another time." Sounding relieved, he turned to go as Karl entered the cabin.

Molly hurried toward the doctor. "James has been waiting for you all afternoon." She clasped her hands together, lowering her voice. "He's been fretting that he'll be blind in that eye."

Karl enclosed Molly's hands in his. "We've known that was a possibility." He released his breath in a long sigh. "Let's go find out."

Jared frowned, then strode to the door. "I see how it is. Good day, Mrs. McGarvie."

Startled, Molly watched him go. *See how what is?* She wanted to defend herself, to tell him Karl was there as a physician, nothing more.

She followed the doctor across the room, then held her breath while he uncoiled the bandages from around James's head. The eyelid had healed well, looking healthy and pink.

"You can open your eyes now," Karl said. "Tell me what you see."

James sat up and blinked several times, turning his head from side to side. He studied his hands, first closing one eye, then the other. An expression of alarm crossed his face.

"What do you see?" the doctor asked again.

A tear slipped down James's cheek. "I can see fine with my right eye." His voice caught in his throat. "But my other eye only sees shadows. Everything's gray." He hunched over and sobbed. "Will it be like this forever?"

"I'm afraid so."

Molly covered her mouth with her hand and fought the impulse to weep with him. She bent over the bed, stroking her son's hair and kissing his forehead. "Oh, Son, I'm so sorry. I'd give you one of my eyes if I could." She knew that was small comfort, but it was all she had.

James cried harder.

She sat beside him and rocked him in her embrace, looking up when she felt a gentle hand on her shoulder. Karl moved next to her and wrapped his arms around the two of them. His voice rumbled in her ear. "Go ahead. Cry if you want to. You've been carrying a heavy load—it's time you let go."

◠

That evening, once the children slept, Molly headed for the cowshed to return the empty milk bucket to its shelf. A full moon washed the landscape with silver. The shed stood in bold silhouette against the prairie, and nearby her garden plot twinkled with dew.

Flossie stirred and pushed her nose against the boards when Molly walked to the stall. She reached into her apron pocket and brought out a handful of dried apples, dropping them into the cow's trough. "There you go, girl." She stroked the animal's neck. "James will be back to milking you soon. I know you miss him."

She leaned against the stall and listened to Flossie chew. Cricket and frog songs sounded from the grassland around her cabin. The tension of the day melted as she relaxed and let the peace of the prairie wash over her.

"McGarvie's woman?"

Molly jumped, dropping the bucket. It rattled on the earthen floor. Whirling, she stared into the face of an Indian. She gaped at the intruder. The woman wore a short buckskin garment with fringed leggings and moccasins. Her unbound hair flowed down her back. She held out her hands, palms up, showing she was unarmed.

Molly's heart pounded so fiercely she had trouble speaking. "What do you want?" Her voice squeaked.

"You are McGarvie's woman?"

Molly nodded. The milk bucket lay at her feet. *I could hit her with it and run for the cabin.* She moved her foot so her toe nudged the bucket's wooden side. "How do you know who I am?"

"I remember you from across the big river. I find you. I am Red Moon, from Chief Keokuk's clan."

Red Moon moved out of the light into the partial shadow of the shed door. Again she held out both hands. "Your man helped my people. Now I help you."

Molly's mind jumped to the face she'd seen at the window. *That was Red Moon. Landon really didn't spy on me!*

The Indian woman spoke from the shadows. "I bring your son."

Molly thought her heart would explode. "Franklin? You have Franklin?"

"Fox people have Franklin." She pronounced his name "Frahn-kleen." "I take him, hide him, give him to you."

"Where is he?" Molly ran to the door, looking in all directions. "How do I know this isn't a trick?"

Red Moon remained in the shadows. "No trick. He not here." She reached into a pouch tied at her waist and pulled out a folded piece of cloth, offering it to Molly.

When Molly took it, she saw it was the sleeve of a boy's shirt. She ran her fingers over the linsey-woolsey fabric, feeling the ribbed weave. A shock of recognition tingled through her. "I wove this. I know my pattern."

Red Moon nodded. "Franklin have this when I take him away. I cut piece for you. Now I know you are here, I give him tomorrow night." She pointed in the direction of the woods. "Fox people angry I take him. We hide. You come in dark. I will have your Franklin." Red Moon moved toward the door.

"Wait!" Molly held out her hand. "Why would you do this for me?"

"McGarvie was our friend. He gave corn when Great Father forget us."

Her *s*'s sounded like *th*, but Molly understood every word.

"He gave us . . ." Red Moon hesitated. "He gave my people honor." Moonlight glittered in her dark eyes. "Tomorrow. I bring Franklin." She slipped out the door and ran toward the trees.

☙

The setting sun hovered over the horizon, sending shards of crimson through scattered clouds. Near the barn, James swung the ax into the chopping block with a solid thud. "I'm getting the hang of it, ain't I, Mama?"

"Aren't I," Molly said. "Yes, you sure are. Look at all the kindling you've split." With a touch of sadness she studied his face. A jagged red line, formed by scar tissue, pointed to his sightless eye. "Come in and rest now. Supper's ready."

While he put the ax away, Molly shaded her eyes and searched the edge of the forest for movement. Never had a day passed so slowly. *Another hour and it'll be dark.* She turned and paced back to the cabin, clutching the piece of linsey-woolsey in her apron pocket. *It could be a trap. We might be attacked.* Somehow, she didn't think so, but how could she be sure? She wished she had someone to confide in. What if her decision brought death to them all?

The sound of horses' hooves on the road drew her attention. Mr. Wolcott whoa'd his matched chestnut team next to the hitching rail in front of the cabin and climbed out of his buggy. Reaching up, he helped his wife descend.

"Mr. Wolcott, Charity. This is a surprise." Puzzled, Molly looked at her visitors. "You picked up the last blanket on Monday. Do you have another order?"

"Nope," he said. "I come to take you to our farm. Charity here'll watch your young'uns while we're gone."

Molly's breath caught in her throat. "What's wrong?" Her gaze jumped from Mr. Wolcott to Charity. "Has something happened to my brother? To Ellie? The children?"

Mr. Wolcott moved close to Molly so James couldn't overhear. "It's your Betsy. She and Reuben are in a hiding place in my barn."

One hand on her chest, Molly stared at him. "How can this be?"

Charity took her arm and she and Mr. Wolcott walked her away from the cabin.

"They arrived last night," Charity said. "They ran away after Brody McGarvie beat Reuben. He was in a bad way when they got to us."

Molly glanced between them. "But . . . they can't stay here, can they?"

"No." Mr. Wolcott put his hands on her shoulders. "That's why I came for you. I'm taking them to the next station tonight. They're headed for Canada. Betsy wants to see you before they go."

Tonight!

Molly swayed as a surge of dizziness rocked her.

Mr. Wolcott grabbed her arm. "What's wrong? I thought you'd be anxious to spend time with her."

Tears blurred her vision. "I can't. I'm sorry. Tell Betsy . . . tell her I love her." She turned and ran toward the cabin. She knew the villagers feared an Indian attack—how could she explain her decision to trust Red Moon? If she mentioned anything about Indians, Mr. Wolcott would have armed men camped around her cabin by dusk.

The Wolcotts followed her inside. "I'm disappointed in you, Molly," Charity said. "I thought you were made of sterner stuff."

They think I'm afraid to go! Molly hung her head, praying for a way out of her dilemma. She couldn't risk losing Franklin again, if indeed the Indian woman had told the truth, so she said nothing. Still, the thought that Betsy was so near shattered her heart. She met Charity's sorrowful gaze.

"Forgive me. I have no choice," Molly whispered.

Anger sparked in Mr. Wolcott's eyes. "We're taking a risk too." He kept his voice low. "I'm willing to show you our hiding place. No one but Charity knows where it is."

She placed a trembling hand on his arm. "I won't forget your kindness. Now please leave—and Godspeed." Molly turned her back to hide her tears.

Once they left, she sank into her rocking chair and stared at the floor. When James came in he looked at her curiously. "What was Mr. Wolcott mad about, Mama? He shouted at his team when he drove off."

She stood and wrapped her arms around him. Holding him close, she rested her cheek on top of his head. "He asked me to do something I couldn't do. One day soon I pray he'll understand."

❧

Molly waited until the moon rose. Before leaving the cabin, she checked to see that her daughters slept, then roused James and led him to the glowing hearth. "I'll be gone for a time."

Wide-eyed, he looked from his mother to the flintlock laying on the table. "What—"

"I'll tell you about it when I come back. Now listen. Bolt the door after me and don't open it for anyone else. If you hear anything outside, take your sisters and hide over there between the cupboard and the wall. Stay away from the windows." She moved to the table and picked up the rifle and shooting pouch.

Fear contorted James's face while he watched her movements. "Don't leave, Mama."

"I have to." Molly studied him, memorizing his features in case she was wrong about Red Moon and wouldn't see her oldest son again. Then turning, she strode out the door and waited until she heard him shoot the bolt behind her. *God be with me.*

Moonlight illuminated the path leading to the cowshed and the woods beyond. The night rustled and creaked and hooted. Were those the sounds of owls and other nocturnal creatures—or Indians, calling to each other as they gathered to attack?

Something crashed through the brush at the edge of the trees. Molly whirled, aiming the flintlock at the sound. Her hands felt clammy with fear. Gripping the stock, she squinted into the darkness. *Why didn't I tell Mr. Wolcott where I was going tonight? I've risked all of our lives.* Her finger trembled above the set trigger. She couldn't risk firing into the brush without seeing her target. What if it was Red Moon with Franklin?

But what if it wasn't?

After a long moment, she lowered the rifle and crept ahead a few paces. The dark woods stood like a wall in front of her when she drew close. *Is this a trap?* A vision of herself lying dead in the field and her children murdered flashed through her mind. Molly's steps faltered.

A few more yards and the forest would swallow her. She clutched the rifle and moved forward under dim and silent trees. On her left, a branch swayed. She swung the flintlock, pointing it at a misshapen hackberry.

Red Moon stepped into her field of vision. "You think to shoot me?"

Trembling, Molly lowered the rifle. "Where is my boy?"

Turning sideways, the Indian woman held out her hand and a lean youth wearing a breechcloth, leggings, and a fur cloak over his shoulders moved to her side. His hair hung down the back of his neck. He looked more Indian than white.

Molly stepped toward him, searching his shadowed face. Could this be the boy she'd lost? He was taller, thinner. He stood rigid next to Red Moon.

Cradling the rifle in the crook of her left arm, Molly reached for him. "Franklin?"

His composure cracked. "Mama!" In one bound, he slammed into her, wrapping his arms around her waist. The flintlock hit the ground.

She smelled grease and wood smoke in his hair, felt his ribs under her fingers. Franklin's body shook. "I lost you! I ran and ran, but you weren't there."

Eyes blinded by tears, Molly rocked her son in her arms. "It's all right now. I've got you." She swallowed a sob. "You're safe."

When she glanced up, Red Moon had vanished.

Molly crumpled to the ground, Franklin locked in her embrace. The enormity of what had happened engulfed her. She couldn't move, couldn't rise. *Franklin. Alive. Here. I was right all along.* Between sobs she managed to choke out a prayer. "Thank you . . . for bringing my son back." She cuddled Franklin close, smoothing his hair away from his forehead.

After several minutes, Molly drew a deep breath and tore her gaze from her son's face. Arrows of moonlight shot through the trees, carrying fear with them. *We mustn't stay here. The Fox people are searching for him.* She stood and drew Franklin to his feet.

"Come, Son. Let's go home."

❧

Molly pounded on the door. "James! It's me! Let me in." She clutched Franklin's arm, feeling him tremble beneath her fingers.

The bolt hammered back and James stood in the doorway. He stared at them. "Who—?" He gasped, then screamed his brother's name. He grabbed the younger boy, pulled him into the cabin and capered around him. "You're back! You're back!" He burst into tears against Franklin's shoulder.

Roused by the commotion, Luellen stumbled from bed and ran to her mother. Suddenly shy, she stared at the boy in Indian clothing who stood in their cabin.

Franklin bent down and tugged at her braids. "Lulie." Tears streaked his face, leaving tracks in the dirt on his cheeks. He walked to the fire and squatted on his haunches, staring into the flames. His shoulders heaved.

Molly dropped to her knees beside him and wrapped him in her arms. Lifting her head, she turned to James. "Take the lantern and go get Dr. Karl. He needs to be here."

In less than thirty minutes James returned, the doctor at his heels. "Molly? James said—" Karl took a step backward, staring. "It's true!" In three long strides he covered the distance between himself and Franklin. He enfolded the boy in his arms, then lifted him and whirled in a circle in front of the hearth. When he put Franklin down, Karl's eyes were wet.

Molly watched as he walked toward her, seeing him cross the great gulf that lay between them.

"Tell me," he said.

29

Karl sprinted the distance between Molly's cabin and the livery stable. *I don't care if it is past midnight. This can't wait.*

Once inside he lit a lantern hanging by the entrance, then hurried to the stall where his horse waited. Duchess raised her head and nickered as soon as she saw him. He untied the lead line and walked her to the area where the tack was stored.

"You're always ready to go, aren't you, girl?" Karl tied the lead to a post and quickly ran through the routine of grooming to be sure her coat was free of mud or dirt before he dropped the blanket and saddle on her back. Under the flickering light of the lantern, the star on her forehead gleamed white against her glossy black hide.

While he worked his mind remained on Franklin's stunning reappearance. *I held him in my arms and I still don't fully believe it.* The boy's face had narrowed, probably from not having enough to eat. His thin shoulders and prominent ribs bore that out. *But he's definitely the same boy.* Karl's hands shook as he threw the blanket over Duchess's back and smoothed it in place. *It's like seeing him come back from the dead.*

He pulled his saddle from a rack and swung it over the blanket.

A mental picture of Franklin standing beside Molly shone behind his eyes. His heart pounded at the thought of her going alone into the woods to meet Red Moon. *So brave. She could have been murdered—scalped. I'm glad I didn't know her plans. I'd have stopped her.* A smile twitched at the corner of his mouth. *She wouldn't have listened to you, Karl, and you know it.*

He mounted, then leaned over and blew out the lantern before guiding the mare into the moonlight. Beldon Grove lay sleeping, houses dark and quiet. Karl held Duchess to a walk as he traveled south along the main road toward Wolcotts' farm. The moon hung suspended in an indigo sky, casting an ashy light over the well-worn track. Karl wanted to race the two miles to Wolcotts', but he didn't dare. Shadows in the road could hide a low spot.

Hope Ben won't be angry at being awakened at this hour. He tapped Duchess's side to urge a faster gait. The track ahead looked clear of dark areas—he could risk more speed. Soon Wolcotts' tall barn came into sight, a black outline against the sky. Karl blinked and frowned. *My eyes must be playing tricks. Is there a light in the barn?* His heart thumped. *Fire!*

Abandoning caution, he nudged the mare to a trot, at the same time sniffing the air for traces of smoke. *Nothing. But the wind's blowing away from me.* He covered the remaining distance between road and farmhouse at a near gallop, then pulled up outside the barn doors.

Karl jumped off the horse, paused to tie her to the hitching rail, then sprinted toward the building. He didn't hear crackling. *Good. I got here in time to stomp it out.*

One of the barn doors creaked open. Light from inside trickled along the double barrels of a shotgun. "Who's out there?"

Karl froze, icy fear sluicing over him. Inside the barn, he heard what sounded like running feet. *I've interrupted horse thieves.* Sweat prickled his forehead. "Don't shoot. I'm unarmed."

He cursed himself for leaving his pistol behind when he left town.

The door swung wider. "Doc? That you?" Ben Wolcott stood silhouetted against the yellow glow from inside the barn.

Karl took a cautious step forward into the patch of light thrown onto the ground. He kept his hands out at his sides, palms up. "Ben? Why are you out here in the middle of the night?"

"I might ask you the same thing." Ben lowered the gun, then cast a quick glance behind him. The sounds of running feet had stopped.

"Is there someone in there with you?"

Ben stepped away from the door and motioned Karl to enter. "Nope. Just me."

"I thought I heard—"

"I said, just me." Ben placed the shotgun across the seat of his wagon, which stood hitched in the center of the barn. His team of chestnuts stamped and jingled their harnesses.

Then why's your wagon hitched? Karl glanced around the interior of the building, noting pieces of hay dangling from the ladder that led to the loft. He followed the trail with his eyes, but noticed nothing out of place.

Leaning against a wagon wheel, casually, as though it were broad daylight in the town square, Ben asked, "What's wrong, Doc?" He faced the loft, his eyes darting between Karl and the ladder.

"I couldn't wait till morning. Sorry to . . . interrupt."

"You're not interrupting anything. Go on."

Excitement seized Karl, and he moved next to Ben and put

his hand on the man's shoulder. "Franklin McGarvie is alive. He's with his mother right now."

Ben's face whitened. A long moment passed. "Alive? After all this time? How can he be?" His fingers closed around one of the spokes. "Are you sure?"

"Saw him myself, not an hour ago." Karl stopped and bowed his head. "It's a pure miracle." His hands were trembling again.

Ben led him to a bench near the door. "Sit. Tell me everything." His voice sounded as shaky as Karl felt.

"An Indian woman came to Molly last night—well, night before last, now. Told her she'd rescued Franklin from another tribe. She said she'd bring him tonight."

"Tonight," Ben murmured. "No wonder."

"What?"

"Never mind. Go on."

"Molly went out there alone after moonrise. Alone, Ben!"

Ben seemed preoccupied with his own thoughts. Above them, boards creaked in the loft and flakes of hay drifted between the openings. "What happened then?" His voice seemed unnaturally loud, like he wanted to drown out the sounds overhead.

Glancing upward, Karl saw nothing amiss. He took a deep breath and told Ben everything Molly had said about the encounter, ending with a description of Franklin. "I knew you'd want to hear as soon as possible, since we were both responsible for the boys that day."

"I can't thank you enough for coming." Ben walked out the door, shaking his head. "I'll wake Charity and tell her right now." He stopped beside Karl's horse. "D'you want to borrow a lantern for the ride back?"

"No need. Thanks."

As Karl rode away he had the distinct impression he'd been rushed off the property.

The air in Molly's cabin remained thick with steam, even though she'd had Franklin bathe over an hour earlier. Now he sat on a stool in front of the fire, dressed in a pair of James's outgrown britches and the new shirt she'd made for him in January. *Good thing I allowed extra room. He's grown so tall.* She circled her son, scissors snipping his damp black hair off to above his collar.

Franklin's feet, still shod in moccasins, wiggled back and forth. "Are you almost done, Mama? James is going to show me his arrowhead . . . collection." He smiled. "I can show him how to make them."

"Just another minute." Molly kissed the top of his head. It was all she could do not to pull him onto her lap and keep him in her arms all day.

When a knock sounded at the door, Luellen shot over to answer it without waiting for permission. "It's Mr. Wolcott."

He hurried into the room, holding his wife's hand. "Doc came out last night and told us. We came as soon as it was a decent hour."

Beyond the open door, early morning sunlight dappled the grass in front of the cabin.

"So this is Franklin." Charity Wolcott faced him and took his hands in hers. "You don't know what a miracle it is to have you here."

Franklin's face flushed. He pulled his hands away and looked at the floor.

"You're embarrassing him." Mr. Wolcott stood beside his wife. "D'you remember me, boy?"

"Yes sir. You drove the . . . buggy when we left home." Franklin chose his words carefully, like someone speaking an unfamiliar language.

"That's right!" Mr. Wolcott patted Franklin's head, but the boy jerked away from him.

Molly moved next to Ben. "He's not used to being touched kindly. Give him time."

Franklin jumped off the stool and headed toward James. "Let me see those points." The two boys settled on the edge of the bed, Luellen at their feet.

Charity whispered in Molly's ear. "We need to talk to you. Can you come outside for a moment?"

❧

Molly stood next to Wolcotts' buggy, waiting. Was it only yesterday that they had told her of Betsy's arrival? A cloud passed over the sun, and she shivered. *If only I could have seen her before she had to leave.* She looked at Mr. Wolcott. "Did you get Betsy safely to the next stop?"

"That's what we came to tell you. Betsy refused to go once she heard that Franklin is alive. She insisted on seeing both of you, even though it's dangerous for her to stay hidden here." Mr. Wolcott shifted his weight from foot to foot. "Thing is, I can't risk taking a child to our hiding place. You know how youngsters are. Can't keep a secret." His mouth tightened. "I'll take you right now, though. Charity will stay with your children."

Charity's eyes twinkled. "I'm looking forward to spending the morning playing with that baby, and getting acquainted with Franklin. I know he'll warm up to me, given time."

Molly looked from one to the other. She shook her head. "I will not leave Franklin today. Not even for a moment. How can you ask such a thing?"

"I thought you'd be happy for the chance to see Betsy after all."

Hot tears slid down Molly's cheeks. "Don't make me choose again. I won't go unless Franklin comes with me."

Mr. Wolcott and Charity exchanged a glance, then he nodded. "Go get him. I'll wait here."

❧

The buggy bowled along the road leading south to Wolcotts' farm. On the eastern horizon, heavy clouds obscured the sun. The overcast sky wore a peculiar yellow-gray tint.

Mr. Wolcott glanced up, appraising the approaching storm. "We should be under cover before it hits."

Molly drew Franklin closer and wrapped a buggy robe around the two of them. Her heart sang with joy at the thought of seeing her friend again.

Franklin stirred beside her. "Will Betsy remember me?"

"She asked for you special." Mr. Wolcott turned his head in Franklin's direction. "You've got to remember your promise, though. No one can ever know where I'm taking you and your mama."

Franklin lifted his chin. "I gave you my word."

For a moment, Molly saw Samuel in the expression on their son's face. She closed her eyes and drew a deep breath. Too much was happening all at once.

The tall barn beside Wolcotts' house loomed ahead. Beyond it a green row of willow trees outlined the creek bordering Matthew's property. Mr. Wolcott slowed the horses and turned them onto the track leading to his cabin. He guided the team past the red and white North Star quilt flapping on a line, then stopped the horses in front of the barn. After opening the wide barn doors, he drove inside.

Smells of hay and livestock greeted Molly's nose. A shaft of light shone under the closed doors at the far end of the building, transforming the dust raised by the horses' hooves into a column that swirled toward the rafters. Molly felt stirrings of apprehension. *It looks like a funnel cloud.* She clutched Franklin's hand. "Where is she?"

Mr. Wolcott helped her from the buggy. "Come with me."

Molly and Franklin walked across the hard-packed dirt floor, then followed him up a ladder into the hayloft. The wooden flooring creaked beneath their feet. Piles of sweet-smelling hay lay banked on each side of them.

Frowning, Molly stopped. "There's no one up here."

"She's here, all right." Grabbing a pitchfork, Mr. Wolcott pushed a mound of hay to one side, revealing a low door in the seemingly solid sidewall of the barn.

Taking another look at the wall, Molly realized the width of the loft didn't match the floor space below. Mr. Wolcott had built a room onto the side of his barn and used the hay in the loft to hide it.

He stepped in front of her and Franklin and tapped twice on the door. He paused, then tapped twice again. "It's me. I've brought Mrs. McGarvie . . . and Franklin."

The door flew open. Molly pushed past Mr. Wolcott and seized Betsy in a suffocating hug. In the process, Betsy dropped the quilt she had wrapped around her shoulders. Ignoring the shabby coverlet, the two women clung together, laughing and crying. Then Betsy pulled from Molly's embrace and grabbed Franklin.

This time he showed none of the aversion he had to Mr. Wolcott's touch. "Betsy, oh Betsy!" He broke into sobs. "I missed you so much."

"Best get inside," Mr. Wolcott said behind them.

Molly ducked through the entrance into the narrow room, which appeared to be ten or twelve feet long and maybe six feet wide. Openings near the roof allowed faint daylight to illuminate the space. A crate flanked by two wooden chairs stood near the doorway, and a pallet lay under the eaves at the back. Her mind registered Reuben's presence in the shadows, but her heart focused on Betsy.

Before entering the hiding place, Betsy gathered the quilt from the floor and brushed flakes of straw from its surface. She held it toward Molly. "Still got your mama's Sunflower quilt."

Red and indigo blurred through sudden tears. One corner was shredded, and some squares had worked loose, exposing the batting, but the memories remained intact. Molly stroked the diamond-shaped flower petals adorning alternate blocks. The glazed wool felt smooth beneath her fingers. She remembered the day she'd given it to Betsy. *So much has happened—seems like years, not months.*

Mr. Wolcott spoke from the loft area. "I'll return in about an hour. Wouldn't be prudent for you to be gone too long." With that he closed the door.

Molly heard the pitchfork scratch the hay back into place. She turned and studied her friend. "I thought I'd never see you again." She took both of the dark-skinned woman's hands in her own, holding the quilt between them. "You ran away from Marjolaine?"

"Yes'm. I come with Reuben." A smile painted Betsy's face with light.

Molly remembered him as one of Brody's slaves—the one who

brought fish to them after Samuel died. She moved to the pallet and knelt to get a closer look at the wounds Mr. Wolcott had mentioned.

When she reached for his shirt, Reuben enclosed her wrist in his calloused palm, moving her hand away from his back. "Leave it, Miz McGarvie. Miz Wolcott's been tending to me."

Sitting back on her heels, Molly looked from Reuben to Betsy. Her joy at the reunion turned to sadness, knowing Betsy hadn't come to Beldon Grove to stay with her. She was an escaping slave, headed for Canada.

While she watched, Betsy stroked Franklin's hair, then tipped his chin up so she could better see his face. "My little Franklin. I thought you was dead. It's like seeing a ghost." A tear slid down her cheek.

"Don't cry, Betsy." Franklin wrapped his arms around her and burrowed close. "I'm not dead at all."

Over the top of his head, Betsy grinned at Molly. "I see you're not. You stay close to home now, you mind that? I want you to grow up big like your papa."

A bolt of lightning flashed, momentarily brightening the dim room. Within seconds, the air shook with a crash of thunder. In spite of herself, Molly jumped.

Betsy met her eyes. "You always was scared of thunder."

"And you weren't." Molly stood, taking Betsy's hand. "Why'd you run away?"

"It just happened like." She kept Molly's hand pressed within her own, her free arm around Franklin. "At first I never did think of running away from Miz Marjolaine. But . . . me and Reuben want to be married." Betsy glanced at Rueben. "He's a mighty good man. But I couldn't marry him, long as we was both slaves."

She squeezed Molly's hand. Her eyes seemed to plead for

understanding. "Then came the night Mr. Brody beat him so bad. Right then and there we decided to run. I took the money I was saving to buy my freedom." She patted the drawstring waist of her dress. "It's tied under here."

Molly studied her friend, trying to understand. "How'd you get all the way to Illinois?"

"Running at night, every night."

"But, crossing the Mississippi? You can't swim."

"Mr. Otto. He brought us across."

Otto Cooper. So he's part of the Underground too.

Betsy continued. "Mr. Otto told us how to get to Quincy, and from there we come here." She smiled. "Remember Mr. Wolcott telling me about the red and white quilt on his clothesline? Well, sure enough, there it was."

Lightning flashed again. Molly squeezed Betsy's hand, waiting for the thunder. When it had passed, she told her, "I've been weaving for people here and saving the money. I hoped to have enough to buy you from Marjolaine, maybe by next year." Her voice gathered enthusiasm. "You could've stayed with me seven years, then we'd say you worked off your indenture and you'd be free."

Reuben stood, hunched with pain. He eased over to the two women and laid his work-scarred hands on Betsy's shoulders. "She be free now, Miz McGarvie."

Raising her hands to cover his, Betsy looked straight into Molly's eyes. "Mr. Wolcott is taking us to Industry tonight. We're going to keep moving until we get to Canada." She stood tall. Tears glistened on her cheeks. "Part of me'd be happy to stay with you. Lord knows, I miss the chil'ren. But, Miz Molly, don't you see? Whatever you call it, 'indenture' or anything else, I'm still not free." Reuben's arm encircled her waist and she leaned her head against his chest. "In Canada, we'd just be people, free people, like you."

Molly swallowed the lump in her throat. *How could I have been so blind? Wanting Betsy with me isn't freedom for her.* Strength left her, and she dropped to her knees in front of her friend. "Forgive me. I've been selfish beyond belief."

Betsy lifted her to her feet. "Nothing to forgive. You done the best you knew." She threw her arms around Molly, weeping. "Saying good-bye to you is the hardest thing I ever had to do."

Lightning flared. They waited for the thunderclap. Rain pounded the roof, sweetening the air.

"We don't have much time," Betsy said. "Tell me about the other chil'ren."

30

Early June 1839

Molly stood at the cabin door gazing north across unbroken prairie. Tall grass rippled as though stroked by an unseen hand. *Where are you, Betsy? Are you safe?* She rested her head against the frame. *Please let her be in Canada.*

Franklin staggered up to her, bent sideways from the weight of a filled pail of milk. With his hair cut and wearing new linsey-woolsey britches and a linen shirt, he was an older, leaner version of the boy who had disappeared. "See how much milk Flossie gave, Mama! You can put Luellen to work churning butter tomorrow."

"Let me worry about what Lulie's going to do. You just take care of your own self." Molly ruffled his straight black hair. Even though more than a month had passed since Franklin's return, she still had to resist the temptation to follow him around each minute so she'd know where he was. She squeezed his shoulder as they entered the cabin.

After dipping a pitcher of warm milk from the bucket, she poured the remainder into shallow earthenware pans to allow the cream to rise. "Suppertime. Go tell James and Lulie."

She looked out at the road, hoping Karl would stop by to eat with them.

⟳

Molly balanced Lily on her knee and fed the baby spoonfuls of barley farina simmered in milk. Lily's mouth opened like a baby bird's after each bite, eager for the next one.

"She seems to approve of her new diet."

Molly looked up at the sound of the familiar voice and drew a breath to calm the sudden fluttering in her chest. Karl leaned against the doorframe, sunset turning his blond hair to a crown of gold.

"She loves it."

"And how's my best patient doing?"

James grinned at the doctor, dropping his spoon into his bowl of crumbled cornbread floating in milk. The jagged red scar on his cheek moved when he smiled, pointing at his sightless left eye. "I hit the target with my slingshot every time today. I think I'm better with one eye than I was with two."

"Could be." Karl leaned over and placed his hand on James's forehead, examining the healed wound. "Looks good. When that scar fades, no one'll be able to tell anything happened to you." He patted James's back and settled himself next to Franklin, face creasing with pleasure as he studied the boy.

Molly watched him, knowing he shared her opinion that her son's return was nothing short of miraculous. Her gaze slid to Franklin. *Eating with his fingers again.* She stood, shifted Lily to one hip, and handed Franklin his spoon.

"Sorry, Mama. I forgot." He scooped a bite into his mouth.

Molly dropped a kiss onto the top of his head. Having him

home was such a joy that it was a challenge for her to be stern with him about anything.

She placed a bowl and spoon in front of Karl, pushing the pan of cornbread and pitcher of milk in his direction. Her sons scraped the last of the food from their bowls, hurrying outdoors to play before bedtime. Luellen stayed at the table, eating slowly and watching Karl with adoring brown eyes.

"She waits for you to come," Molly said. "You're her new favorite person."

Karl stroked the child's hair. "She's one of my favorites too—next to her mama, that is."

She felt herself redden. Still holding Lily, she filled a bowl for herself with her free hand.

The doctor studied Molly's face. "You look tired. Aren't you feeling well?"

"I worry about Betsy. What if they got caught?" She bit her lip. "It's almost as hard as losing Franklin, except Betsy has Reuben to help her."

"How long's it been?"

"Five weeks tomorrow."

"It could take months for a letter to arrive from so far away."

Molly sighed. "I don't want to wait months. I want to know now."

"She promised she'd write. Be patient." Karl's grin teased. "I know that's hard for you."

She smiled back. He knew her so well.

∽

The conversation with Karl reminded Molly of Amber and her missing son. Ever since Red Moon's appearance, Molly's heart had ached for the wrong that had been done to Landon. *Poor Amber.*

If only I hadn't been so quick to judge. She bit her lip. Karl was right—she often jumped to hasty conclusions. *He should know better than anyone.*

The next morning she hefted Lily onto her hip and, taking Luellen's hand, set out for her neighbor's house. *Maybe a visit will cheer her up.* A little over halfway there, Molly realized it had been a mistake to attempt to carry Lily such a distance.

"My land, you're getting heavy!"

Lily flashed her a smile decorated with four tiny teeth and grabbed at Molly's earlobe.

Huffing her way onto Amber's porch, Molly raised her hand to knock when the door opened.

"Molly!" Her neighbor beamed at her. "You look done in—let me have that baby."

Gratefully, Molly handed Lily over, then loosened the binding at the neckline of her dress and fanned herself. "She didn't seem that heavy when we left the house."

Amber sat, still holding Lily, and indicated the chair next to hers for Molly. "It's good to see you. It's quiet around here with Daniel and Ridley gone to Galena, and Landon—" She clapped a hand over her mouth. "Oh! I got something to tell you." She reached into the pocket of her apron and took out a folded piece of paper, its edges grimy. "Word from Landon!" she said, a lilt in her voice. "He's all right." She unfolded the letter.

"He's in St. Louis, readying to go up the Missouri with a fur company. Says they're going all the way to the Rocky Mountains." Amber paused and stared out the window for a moment. "So far away." She drew a deep breath. "Anyways, he says he'll send money home and he's sorry he ran off."

"You must be so relieved."

"You have no idea."

312

Oh yes, I do. She straightened. "Is there an address for that fur company?"

"Yes. Right here. Why?"

"I'd like to write Landon and tell him about the Indian woman coming and bringing Franklin. And that she found me by looking in my window."

Amber glanced at the letter and then back at Molly, a puzzled frown wrinkling her forehead. "Why would he want to know that?"

"I can't explain, but I'm sure he'll be happy to hear it. Perhaps he'll even come home."

"You get some strange notions." She passed the letter to Molly. "But you said you knew young Franklin was alive when no one else believed it. So maybe you'll be right about this too. Lord knows I want my son back."

Luellen walked around her mother and leaned against Amber's leg. Reaching down, she patted the child's sweaty head. "How's my little girl?"

"Looks like Lulie would rather be with you than me," Molly said, relieved to change the subject. "She's that way with Dr. Spengler too."

"Is the doc still coming around? Thought James was all healed up."

Molly's cheeks warmed. "He brings us the food people trade him for doctoring, and I cook it for him and us." She couldn't quite meet Amber's eyes. "That's all there is to it."

"Hmmm." Amber rubbed Luellen's back. "How do your boys get along with him?"

"They think the world of Karl . . . Dr. Spengler. He . . ." She searched for the right words. "He pays attention to them, like they were important."

313

"That's a good thing in a man." Amber nodded approval. "How's Franklin doing? Has he got over living with them Indians?"

"Pretty much. He still forgets and eats with his hands sometimes, and of course he's behind in his studies. James is helping him with his lessons."

"And the other pupils at school? Does he fit in?"

"The boys treat him like a hero." She smiled. "He's teaching them to make arrowheads."

Amber's questions about Karl stirred in Molly's mind while she walked home. The boys had become increasingly attached to him. She saw it in their eyes whenever he came through their door. Her heart lifted at the image of his face smiling at her and the children. *Like a husband and father.*

She stopped in the middle of the road. *Is that the way I see him? As a husband?* A pulse danced in her throat as she allowed her feelings for Karl to fill her thoughts. *I never dreamed I'd love anyone again. But I do.* Her arms tightened around Lily. *Karl.*

Luellen tugged at Molly's skirt. "Why are we standing here?"

Startled out of her reverie, she shifted Lily to one arm and took Luellen's hand. "I just discovered something important."

❦

Molly studied her sons sprawled asleep on the trundle bed, her heart swelling with joy at the sight of Franklin next to his big brother. *I'll never take my children for granted again.*

After straightening the blanket that covered the boys, she slipped outside to sit on a bench and watch stars emerge. Fireflies skipped through the air, their tiny lights flashing. She leaned against the wall of the cabin, her shoulders soaking up the last heat of the day from its logs. *It's been almost a year since Samuel died. I thought I couldn't go on, but here we are.* Molly shook her head, remembering how inept she'd felt when Betsy was first taken from her.

Then, after Franklin disappeared . . . She trembled at the memory of her frantic plans to find him. Try as she might, the task of earning enough money to buy Betsy had proved to be beyond her power. Molly cringed when she considered her selfishness. *I wanted Betsy to mind the other children so I could hunt for my son. I never once considered her needs.* Her cheeks burned with fresh shame. How gratifying now to imagine her childhood companion as a free woman safe on the other side of the Canadian border.

Molly stared at the evening star glimmering in the western sky. Somewhere up there was the One who brought Franklin home. Words from a favorite hymn came to her mind: *Nothing in my hand I bring, simply to thy cross I cling.* Her plans were nothing in God's sight. She'd never have dreamed of the way he would work to give her son back to her. *Matthew's right, God gives us light for each step, not the whole path at once.*

She heard Karl's footsteps before she saw him approaching through the dusk. *Thank goodness. I was afraid he wasn't coming.*

"Evening, Molly. How's Franklin today?"

"Wonderful. He's teasing Luellen like he'd never been gone." She slid over on the bench to make room for him to sit. "You're late this evening. We missed you."

"Had a difficult delivery out in the country." He flopped down next to her. "Young girl's first baby. No midwife, and the husband didn't fetch me 'til both of them were nearly dead."

Molly closed her eyes, remembering Karl's gentle hands helping with Lily's birth—a memory that now brought comfort rather than mortification. "What happened?"

Karl shook his head. "Couldn't save the baby. Maybe, if I'd had help . . ." He leaned forward, burying his face in his broad hands. "The husband was next to useless."

Her heart twisted at the sound of despair in his voice. It took all her effort not to pull him into a comforting embrace. "I'm so sorry."

They sat in silence for several moments, then Karl straightened and turned toward her. "On the way back to town I kept thinking about how you assisted me when James was hurt. You were so steady, so calm."

"Not inside, I wasn't."

"Doesn't matter about inside—good doctoring's about how you do on the outside." He took a breath and let it out with a whoosh. "Thing is, I think we'd make a good team."

Molly stared at him, astonished. "You want me to be your nurse?"

He slapped his hand against his knee. "Hang it, I'm making a botch of this! I'm asking you to marry me."

Her breath caught in her throat. His words so closely echoed her own earlier thoughts that she was speechless. Karl as her husband—a father to her children. *God's giving me light for my next step.*

Before she could respond, Karl said, "I've been drawn to you ever since I first laid eyes on you back in St. Lawrenceville. I just didn't know it then."

She scooted closer to him. "But, Karl, I didn't give you a kind word for months." Her voice teased.

He grinned at her. In the dim light she saw his eyes crinkle at the corners. "I like spunky women. Those little sweet ones bore me."

Molly laughed and laid her hand over his. "Well, I'll do all I can to keep that from happening."

Acknowledgments

For the past several years, I've been blessed to be part of a wonderful critique group. Each member has a particular strength, and together they have contributed greatly to this book. Bonnie Leon, Billy Cook, Diane Gardner, Sarah Schartz, Julia Ewert, and Meddie Sims—special thanks to each of you.

I owe an extra debt of gratitude to Bonnie Leon, a wonderful author, who has mentored me every step of the way on my journey to publication as a novelist. Bless you, Bonnie. You've helped me more than you'll ever know.

For the scenes about weaving and flax preparation, I'm indebted to Suzie Liles. She invited me to her home and taught me how to use a full-size loom, gave me samples of spun flax, answered endless questions, and later reviewed portions of the manuscript for accuracy. Thank you, Suzie! If there are any discrepancies in the book, they're my fault, not hers.

Thanks, too, to Lorraine Micke-Hayden, who with her husband participates in frontier reenactments. Lorraine showed me how pioneer women's dresses were constructed in the 1830s and explained the purpose of the drawstring system.

I've been privileged to have the wise counsel of my agent, Tamela Hancock-Murray, as well as the guidance and expertise of my editors, Vicki Crumpton and Barb Barnes, along with that of the entire team at Revell. Thank you all—it's been a joy.

My special thanks and love to my husband, Richard, who has supported and encouraged all my writing efforts. This book wouldn't have happened without him. I praise God for bringing us together.

Above all, I owe overwhelming gratitude to God the Father, through the work of the Holy Spirit, who gives me ideas and the ability to form those ideas into stories.

Ann Shorey has been writing for over fifteen years. She's been published in the Adams Media Cup of Comfort series, and had one of her stories included in *Chicken Soup for the Grandma's Soul*. Ann has also written articles for various local and regional publications. After completing a narrative family history in 1998, she realized she had uncovered a treasure trove of inspiration, and turned to fiction as a way to put that inspiration to good use.

Ann teaches classes on historical research, story arc, and other fiction fundamentals at regional conferences. She works in Sutherlin, Oregon, where she lives with her husband, Richard. *The Edge of Light* is her first novel.

Contact Ann through her website at www.annshorey.com.

Journey into the heart of the West with new historical fiction!

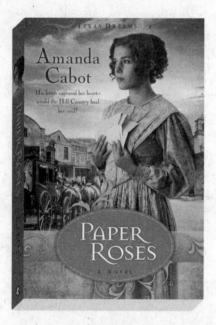

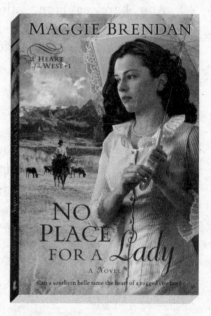

His letters captured her heart. Will the Texas Hill Country heal her soul? Be swept away by book one of the Texas Dreams series.

Can a Southern belle tame the heart of a rugged cowboy? Fall in love with the Colorado setting and the spunky heroine who wants to claim it as her own in book one of the Heart of the West series.

Revell
a division of Baker Publishing Group
www.RevellBooks.com

Available wherever books are sold